PRAISE FOR THE KITE SHOP MYSTERIES

"Emmy and her kite shop will blow you away!"
—Fran Stewart, author of the ScotShop Mysteries

"Clover Tate's well-crafted plot soars . . . Two thumbs up for *Blown Away*."
—Christine Husom, author of the
Snow Globe Shop Mysteries

"Readers will find themselves easily invested in Emmy and her kite shop . . . [A] well-rounded story sure to appeal to many different reading preferences."
—*RT Book Reviews*

"The author takes a unique approach with Emmy . . . Her growth and development, along with that of her fellow Rock Point neighbors, promise for even more entertaining mysteries in the future." —Kings River Life Magazine

"Delightfully charming . . . This was an entertaining read and I look forward to the next adventures with Emmy and her friends." —Dru's Book Musings

"*Blown Away* is a fun and delightfully cozy mystery that has me excited for more." —Marie's Cozy Corner

"[A] solid debut novel with many elements hitting a delightful chord . . . A fun read." —Mysteries and My Musings

Live and Let Fly

clover tate

BERKLEY PRIME CRIME
New York

BERKLEY PRIME CRIME
Published by Berkley
An imprint of Penguin Random House LLC
375 Hudson Street, New York, New York 10014

Copyright © 2017 by Penguin Random House LLC
Penguin Random House supports copyright. Copyright fuels creativity, encourages
diverse voices, promotes free speech, and creates a vibrant culture. Thank you for buying
an authorized edition of this book and for complying with copyright laws by not
reproducing, scanning, or distributing any part of it in any form without permission.
You are supporting writers and allowing Penguin Random House to continue to
publish books for every reader.

BERKLEY is a registered trademark and BERKLEY PRIME CRIME and the B colophon
are trademarks of Penguin Random House LLC.

ISBN: 9780425283554

First Edition: December 2017

Printed in the United States of America
1   3   5   7   9   10   8   6   4   2

Cover design by Sanny Chiu
Book design by Kristin del Rosario

For Angela M. Sanders.
I couldn't have written this without you.

acknowledgments

Thank you to my amazing editor, Katherine Pelz, and agent, John Talbot. Your professionalism, kindness, patience, and support are first-class.

I have the critique group of which other writers dream. Its members—Cindy Brown, Doug Levin, Dave Lewis, Ann Littlewood, and Marilyn McFarlane—deserve a gigantic thank-you for their flexibility, honesty, and insight. I'd also like to thank authors Lisa Alber, Charlotte Rains Dixon, Kate Dyer-Seeley, Christine Finlayson, Holly Franko, Kelly Garrett, and Debbie Guyol for all the writerly talk with which I've bent their ears, either in one-on-one conversations or in our Drink and Think get-togethers and Not the Usual Suspects group.

Finally, my biggest thank-you of all goes to readers. There's nothing so uplifting as knowing your stories entertain others and maybe even make them laugh or keep them in suspense. I am so, so grateful.

chapter one

"OW!" ONCE AGAIN, I'D STUCK MYSELF WITH A NEEDLE. I pressed my thumb to my mouth and tasted salty blood.

For two solid weeks, I'd spent every morning in the back room of my kite shop, Strings Attached, working on my entry for the kite festival. I intended it to be a masterpiece. It had to be. My livelihood depended on it.

While tourists bought their morning coffee over on Main Street and locals dug for razor clams at the beach a block away, I was settled in the kitchen-turned-workshop of the Victorian house that held my shop, stitching ribbon-thin slips of fabric into an appliquéd portrait of the town. On the left side of the kite, the sea rolled in on waves of green and blue with tiny whitecaps. A brown fishing boat with a slip of white mast pulled up its net. The town of Rock Point rose up on the right, from the docks to the small town center and up to the homes in Old Town. I'd even sewn in a tiny replica of Strings Attached, complete with windsocks blowing from the porch. Right now, I was piecing together a sunset.

At a sharp knock on the shop door, my fingers jolted again, this time sending the needle into my palm. Strings Attached wasn't scheduled to open for another half hour. With a growl of exasperation, I set aside my kite and stomped through the shop, which was rippling with a summer garden of kites.

I flung open the door. "I'm sorry. We're not—"

"Hi, Emmy."

My icy tone instantly melted, and I hugged my little sister, pushing one of her blond dreadlocks away. "Sunny! What are you doing here?"

She slid a backpack off her shoulders and set it on the porch. "I'm moving in with you."

I was so stupefied that I only stared as she passed through the shop to the workroom. "Aren't you supposed to be at college, getting ready for the semester?"

"Yes." She glanced at my kite, but didn't seem to find anything there that interested her. She filled the teakettle and set it on the stove.

"So, why are you here? You know I'm happy to see you, but this is unexpected."

"Do you have any coffee, or is it all tea? I had to get up while it was still dark to get to the bus."

"Sunny. Answer me."

When she turned, I saw that despite the confidence in her voice, her eyes were reddening and her lips trembled. "I can't go back. Emmy, I can't." She plopped into a kitchen chair.

I sat across from her. "What's wrong?" Although Sunny had given herself the nickname—her real name was Belinda, after my aunt—normally, it suited her. I'd always been the responsible sister, reading or drawing in my room, and she was the ebullient one. At the alternative grade school our parents had sent us to, Sunny had been chosen to lead the Maypole dance. When I had been a student there eight years earlier, I'd spent my days poring over Van Gogh lithographs in the library.

"Everything's wrong," she said. "I hate my major, for one thing."

"Feminist theater?"

"Fermentation and digestive health," she corrected. "Feminist theater was last year."

"Big deal. Everyone changes their major. Change yours."

Sunny erupted into tears just as the kettle started whistling. I leapt up to turn off the stove. "Honey. You're only a sophomore. Take some of your required classes while you figure it out. Everyone goes through this."

"You didn't."

True. I'd been set on being an artist since I cracked open my first box of Crayolas. I'd loved kites, too, ever since I flew my first one. Blending the two by designing kites had been only natural. "You can't compare yourself to anyone. Just give yourself time."

She sniffed and took a wavering breath. "That's why I'm moving in with you and Avery. I need time to think things over."

"You can stay for a few days, if you like. The term starts—when? A week?"

"No. I mean I want to stay here for good. Or at least for a few months."

I folded my arms over my chest. "You can't simply run away from your problems."

"You sound like Mom."

Sunny always did know how to shut me up. "You know what I mean. Besides, it's not just up to me. Avery has a say—it's her house, after all. And what about Mom and Dad? I can't believe they're letting you do this."

She stuck out her lower lip and looked away. "It's my life. Not theirs."

"You're joking." I sat across the table from her. "You haven't told them, have you?"

Once again, she didn't respond.

"Good grief, Sunny. They're paying your tuition, and you don't even tell them you don't plan on showing up for classes?"

She looked earnest. "They'll get a full refund as long as I cancel before the first week of class. If they invest that money, they can fund a few more years of their retirement."

Sunny? Giving Mom and Dad investment advice? "I can't keep a huge secret like this from them."

"I need you to. This is my only hope to figure out what I should do with my life. I need you to help me." Her eyes still glistened with tears. "Please?"

I swore under my breath. If my parents found out—my mother, especially—they'd never forgive me. My mother liked to recite the Three Musketeers' motto, "All for one, and one for all," when referring to our family. The reality was more like, "When I'm happy, we're all happy." Not that she didn't want the best for all of us, which she proved with constant phone calls, recipes for gluten-free casseroles, and quotes from Indian mystics. It's just that there wasn't a lot of room for other personalities when Mom was around.

"I get it," I said, "but this isn't something I can hide. I won't lie to them."

"You don't have to lie," Sunny said quickly. "Just don't volunteer it. Besides, I'll tell them. Eventually." She tilted her head a few degrees to the side, just as she did every time she needed to sway me.

"A few days, and that's all."

"You'll see," she said, her voice all efficiency. "I'll be a real help to you. I can work at the shop so you can make more kites."

She had a point. Normally Stella, a retired school-teacher and friend, worked on my days off, but she was spending a lot of time in her studio lately, getting ready for a show of her paintings. "I suppose so."

"Good." Sunny bolted to her feet, upending her mug and sending a wash of black tea toward my kite.

I grabbed the kite's elaborately appliquéd body, but I was too late. Dull brown soaked through its gem-toned panes.

Please, I thought. *Let this not be a sign of things to come.*

I DECIDED TO DELAY OPENING THE SHOP FOR A FEW hours. We walked the mile home, me pushing my bike and Sunny carrying her backpack.

It was a gorgeous August day, with a warm breeze perfect for flying kites. On our left, the blue ocean rushed to shore under an even bluer sky. Tourists would be streaming into town any time now, knocking around the antiques mall and checking into bed-and-breakfasts. Until a few years ago, Rock Point had been mostly a fishing town without much to recommend it to tourists. But lately, its fishermen's cabins had been snatched up by out-of-towners, and visitors had been coming to walk the beach to the lighthouse just north of Avery's house— my home now, too—or eat at the Tidal Basin, a popular gastropub.

"You really didn't tell Mom and Dad?" I asked Sunny. I still couldn't believe she'd simply skipped out on college.

"I couldn't."

We were silent a moment while a truck passed us on the mostly quiet road. It was Ace, the local plumber-slash-odd-jobs guy. I waved.

"You're going to have to tell them sometime," I said.

"I will. Just not yet."

Our path took us up Perkins Road, past fewer and fewer houses, then up the hill, into the woods.

Avery was on her way out when we arrived at the house. The sun illuminated her hair like a halo. She waved and smiled. "Sunny! What a surprise. Are your parents here, too?"

I looked at my sister. "You tell her."

"No Mom and Dad," she said. "Just me. Could I— uh—stay here?"

"Only for a few days," I added.

Avery followed us back into the house. "Of course. You can sleep on the sunporch."

The house had a sleeping porch on the second floor. Nights on the coast were cool enough that neither Avery nor I used it, but it was screened in and had a twin bed. With a change of sheets and a wool blanket, it would be fine for Sunny.

"That's perfect," Sunny said.

Avery exchanged glances with me. I lifted an eyebrow in what I hoped communicated, *I'll tell you about it later.*

"How's the kite coming?" Avery asked.

I thought about my kite soaking in the sink back at Strings Attached and silently groaned. "Hopefully all right. I'm almost done with the appliqués. There was a mishap—"

"I spilled tea on it. Was that an important kite?" Sunny said.

Bear, my family's Australian shepherd, who was on semipermanent loan to me, came bounding from upstairs, wagging his tail so hard that his whole hind end wiggled.

"Bear baby!" Sunny dropped her suitcase and bent to her knees to kiss the dog. "I missed you."

"Yeah, that kite is important," I said.

"Why?" She stood, a hand still on Bear's head.

"Because I'm counting on it to win the contest at the kite festival. If it does, the publicity will boost Internet sales over the winter. I need that income to make it past tourist season." Strings Attached had only been open since early this summer. I hadn't yet experienced a rainy winter, when the tourist trade—and kite flying—dropped off.

"I thought the shop was doing well," Sunny said.

"It's doing great. If it stayed warm and dry all year, we'd be eating filet mignon."

"I'm vegan," Sunny said.

"You know what I mean."

"It's a big deal," Avery told Sunny. "The honorary judge is a reality TV star who grew up in Rock Point. Jasmine Normand."

"From *Bag That Babe*," I added. Not that I'd ever seen the show.

"*Bag That Babe*? I know her. What does a dating safari show have to do with kites?" Sunny asked.

"Got me," Avery said. "She's our most famous resident. I guess that's enough. Why don't you come upstairs and we'll get you settled?" We followed Sunny up the stairs. "Dave told me that Jack has been obsessing over his kite."

I'd suspected as much. Our friend Dave was also a good friend of Jack Sullivan, the owner of Rock Point's other kite shop, Sullivan's Kites. Jack had been quiet about the contest. We'd dated a bit over the past few months, and while we'd shared a lot about our backgrounds, almost by unspoken agreement we hadn't talked about the competition.

Sunny didn't seem to be paying attention. "Do you own this house free and clear?"

"Sure. Why?" Avery said.

"Rock Point's tourist trade seems to be picking up.

Have you thought about turning this into a guesthouse? Could be a nice stream of passive income."

"But I live here," Avery said. "It's my family home."

"It's not like you'd have to sell it. Emmy could buy the building Strings Attached is in, and you two could live there, upstairs, and rent out this house. That would help both of your incomes."

Sunny must have noticed the "For Sale" sign in front of the shop. This was another source of worry for me. My landlord, embarrassed by a crime he was associated with last spring—a murder someone else had committed, but that he'd inspired—was retiring to Palm Springs and selling his property in town. I just hoped that whoever bought the building wouldn't jack up the rent.

"Thanks for the advice, Sunny, but I'm staying put," Avery said.

"Since when did you become an investment guru?" I asked my sister.

"Don't make fun of me," Sunny said. Bear jumped on the bed while Sunny gazed out the window toward the ocean. The screens let in the sound of the surf down the bluff. The sunsets would be magnificent from here.

At the thought of sky, my mind returned to the kite contest. "So, Jasmine Normand is in town, huh?"

"That's what Dave says. I haven't seen her yet," Avery said.

"Did you know her? Did she fly kites?" I still couldn't believe that a reality TV star was judging the contest. A lot rode on her say.

"Honestly, my main memories of her? Sleeping

through biology class, charming boys to do her homework, and always being teacher's pet without having to crack open a book." Avery shook her head. "She irritated everyone I knew. By the time graduation rolled around, we were all ready to kill her."

chapter two

I SPENT THE NEXT MORNING AT STRINGS ATTACHED, DAB-bing at my competition kite with soapy water between helping customers choose kites and replenish their lines. Thankfully, most of the tea Sunny had spilled on it had washed out.

Now it hung above the workroom sink. I was pinning my future on that kite. "Dry out, you hear? And don't let Sunny near you again," I told it. "I'll be back soon." The kite caught the early afternoon sun, glowing with an intricate palette of blues, greens, and oranges.

I closed the shop for lunch and trudged up the hill toward the older section of town. Rose, my accountant, lived up here and had set up her office in the detached garage behind her Queen Anne house.

Unlike the modest Victorian that housed Strings

Attached, Rose's house sprouted bay windows and turrets. Delphiniums bloomed up the garden bed lining the driveway. Rose couldn't be much older than I, but she'd already bought a house and established her business. I knocked on the double Dutch door before entering, even though I could see Rose's head through the window as she bent over a stack of papers.

"You're exactly on time," Rose said. "Have a seat." She pointed to the chair across from her. The garage might share property with a 120-year-old house, but her office furnishings were crisp and new. "I've got the expenses for your taxes tallied."

I brushed the seat of my pants before I sat. "Is it bad?"

"It's good and it's bad. Strings Attached did well this summer. You made an impressive income, considering that you've only been in business three months."

"But . . ." I said, waiting for the rest.

"But that means you'll have a hefty quarterly tax bill." She pointed to a number on a form for the IRS.

I sank into my chair. "Oh." I had the money, but without strong Internet sales, it would leave me only enough savings to make it through the fall. Barely.

Rose looked sympathetic. "I know. Starting your own business is rough." I opened my mouth to speak, but she continued. "You wouldn't have it any other way, right?"

Despite the shock that my tax bill had left, I laughed. "I feel like my life is finally on track. I'm doing what I'm meant to do. Should I write you a check now?" I asked.

"You can wait until September." She tucked the IRS slip into an envelope and handed it to me. "You're going to need a monthly net income of at least two-thirds of what you're making now to survive the winter."

"Could I claim a sister who appeared out of the blue as a deduction?" It was a lame attempt at a joke, but I had to say something to counter the anxiety about money stirring in my gut.

Rose laughed. Her laugh was as pure and orderly as her office. "A liability maybe. Not a deduction. But if it helps, I know what you mean."

"I'm sorry to be unloading. I bet accountants hear as many rants as bartenders."

"Or shrinks. True." She capped her pen and set it aside. "What's up with your sister?"

"She showed up, suitcase in hand, yesterday morning. She announced that she's quitting college, and she's moving in with me."

"There's a coincidence. My sister showed up this morning, too. Moving in with me would just about kill her, though. No hot tub, for one thing. Nothing like she has in Hollywood. She wouldn't even stay the night at my house. Instead, she rented that fancy new place on the bluff just north of town."

I knew the house. It was all designer angles and windows, and the first few months after it was built, locals slowed to stare as they drove by. "Hopefully she's not as klutzy as my sister, Sunny—" I stopped. "Jasmine Normand's your sister, isn't she? The *Bag That Babe* contestant judging the kite contest."

Rose grimaced. "That's her."

"Wow." Now here was an argument for nurture over nature. Rose was about as far from a TV star as you could get. She was pretty, sure, but didn't look like she'd spend money on lipstick unless it was a tax-deductible business expense, and I suspected her wispy bangs had happened in the bathroom with a pair of manicure scissors.

"I get that a lot."

"I'm sorry," I said. "I guess I have kite festival on the brain, and for me your sister is a big deal because of it. I haven't seen the TV show."

As Rose was wont to do, she skipped my comment on celebrity and went right to the financial part of my statement. "I'm not going to lie, Emmy. Four out of five new businesses fail within two years. I know tourism is growing in Rock Point, but is it growing fast enough to keep Strings Attached alive? I mean, we already have one kite shop."

Sullivan's Kites. Jack's place. "I know."

"Without savings to tide you over, you have to come up with a model to survive the whole year, including the rainy months when people aren't stopping by the shop on vacation."

"I know," I repeated, my voice quieter this time.

"I sound harsh, and I'm sorry. I just want you to succeed." She pushed herself away from her desk and clasped her hands across her lap. "Have you thought about what you're going to do in October, when the town goes back to the locals?"

My heart had sunk to somewhere below my belly button. "Strings Attached is the most important thing I've accomplished. I love it so much." I stopped and bit my lip. Rose didn't want to hear about passion. "My plan is to get by on Internet sales. I'm entering the most gorgeous kite I've ever designed into the kite festival. If I win, kite flyers all up and down the coast will check me out online. It's the publicity I need."

Rose listened, her gaze intent. "It might work. I'm not sure how you can make it otherwise. But . . ."

I waited for her to finish. She tidied her papers instead. "But what?" I urged.

She tossed her pen on a file folder of receipts. "With Jasmine as judge?"

"What do you mean?"

"I probably shouldn't say anything," Rose said.

I slid to the edge of my chair. "You have to, now. Why isn't Jasmine a good judge?"

"She doesn't take anything seriously—not her work, her relationships, nothing. A kite contest?" Rose shook her head. "Good luck."

STILL RATTLED BY THE MONEY TALK EARLIER, I CLOSED the store for the day and I walked up to the Brew House, Avery's café. Located a block off Rock Point's main drag, it attracted more residents than tourists. It also served up an excellent tuna melt. Pure comfort food. I'd take one home for dinner, plus something for Sunny.

As I crossed Main Street, dodging a family complete with a stroller and dog, I thought about Rose's warning. I knew that winning the kite contest was important, but I'd never thought about it in such black-and-white terms. True, most new businesses failed. Somehow I must have thought that the force of my will to succeed would be enough. What if Rose was right, and Jasmine wouldn't know a worthy kite when she saw one?

The front door to the large arts and crafts bungalow that housed the Brew House was propped open to the warm marine breeze. The faint sounds of Miles Davis's piano and the espresso machine's hiss reached me on the porch. The café was busy tonight. Trudy, the manager, was pulling shots of espresso and steaming milk at a practiced hustle. Avery waved at me with one hand and smiled as she deposited a bowl of soup on Marcus Salek's table with the other.

Marcus was one of the town cranks who wasn't exactly happy with Rock Point's transformation from fishing village to tourist destination, and he considered Strings Attached part of the problem. "Who's going to buy all those kites?" he'd asked me once when we were both in line at the supermarket. "Tourists, that's who. You'd do better to take your business to Seaside."

Today, though, Marcus wasn't paying attention to me, or even his soup. He was looking across the room at a gorgeous woman, but it wasn't admiration on his blond-bearded face. It was disgust. And it wasn't just Marcus checking her out, it was everyone.

The woman's figure nailed the line between fit and curvy, and her face might have graced cameo pendants. Honey-colored hair fluffed to her shoulders, and when I said honey, I didn't mean that it was light brown. I meant that it glowed golden, as if it were lit from within. Across from her sat a man with his back to me and another woman with short, white-blond hair.

Then I realized the obvious. This was Jasmine Normand, the *Bag That Babe* star and judge of the kite contest. Tearing my gaze away, I made my way to the counter at the café's rear.

"Tuna melt, please," I told Trudy, then turned again for a quick peek at the judge, now with her back to me. "I need something else, too. Do you have anything vegan?" I asked, thinking of Sunny.

"We have veggie burgers."

"Are they gluten-free?"

"I don't think so. Let me look at the package."

Jasmine Normand leaned across the table and laid her hand on the man's forearm. "I bet your kites fly like rockets," she said.

The man across from her was Jack Sullivan. My Jack. I straightened. He was looking at Jasmine Normand like he was a starving puppy and she was a rib eye steak.

"You'll find out soon," Jack said.

"*You'll find out soon*," I mouthed with annoyance. My hands flew to my hips.

"Maybe you could show me your shop? Give me a hint of what to expect?" Her hand moved closer to his elbow.

Jack and I might have only gone out a handful of times over the past few months, but people in town had started to consider us a couple, and I found that when one of us was invited somewhere, the other usually was, too. Right now, though, Jack didn't even register my presence.

"The veggie burger has wheat. What about soup?" Trudy said.

"What?" I didn't even turn toward her. *Jack, that two-timer.*

"Today's soup is tomato basil. No gluten, no dairy."

In two steps I was at Jack and Jasmine Normand's table. "Don't you think this is a conflict of interest?" I said.

Now Jack snapped out of his trance. He pulled his arm away from Jasmine's hand. "Hello, Emmy." He looked to the short-haired woman next to him first. "This is Caitlin Ruder. Caitlin, meet Emmy Adler." He returned his attention to Jasmine. "Have you met Jasmine Normand yet? We went to high school together for a semester."

"And studied what? Heavy petting?" Wait. Did that really come out of my mouth?

"Your sandwich, Emmy," Avery said.

"Don't let 'em get away with it, Adler," Marcus Salek yelled from across the room. "I saw him pay for her soy latte."

"What are you talking about?" Jack said.

"This contest matters to me. I will not let you mess it up."

"Emmy—" Jack started.

"Shut up."

"You tell him," Marcus said.

"You shut up, too," I yelled back at Marcus.

"What's got into you?" Jack said.

"You can't sleep your way to a blue ribbon, Jack. My kite is ten times better than anything you could rig up." I fastened both Jasmine and Jack with meaningful looks. "If it's a fair contest, that is."

Everyone in the room was watching, mouths agape, except for Marcus, whose head bobbed in a silent chuckle. The Miles Davis album had ended, and the record player's stylus bumped against the record's center. At the table next to Marcus, a man coughed. He was tall and tanned and looked as if he should be lounging on a veranda in Antigua, not in a tiny Oregon beach town. I had barely registered his startling presence when Jack drew my attention back.

"Why don't you join us?" Jack asked, his tone calm. "Have a seat."

As my father would have said, my ire was up, but it was quickly being replaced by a self-conscious shame. "You." I ignored Jack and jabbed a finger toward Jasmine. "Play fair, or you'll be very, very sorry."

I spun on my heels and, chin up, marched toward the door. I was on the street before I realized I'd forgotten my sandwich.

chapter three

IT WAS NO GOOD. I WASN'T GOING TO BE ABLE TO SLEEP. I looked at my alarm clock and fell back into bed, my head hitting the pillow. Almost three in the morning.

Forget it. I slipped out of bed and shrugged on a sweat-shirt. I was going for a walk.

The house was quiet, but for the slight groans of its joists as it settled in the cool night. Normally, I'd take Bear with me, but Sunny had kidnapped him. He was likely snoring away at the foot of her bed.

I pulled on a pair of tennis shoes and took the big flashlight by the back porch door. Easing the door closed behind me, I walked into the damp dark and descended the stairs to the beach.

It was a clear night. The tide was in. The stars were thick as clotted cream, and without even trying, I caught a shooting star streaking by before it vanished.

Man, how I'd muffed the day. I still winced over promising Sunny that I'd hide her from Mom and Dad. That was stupid. If they found out, I'd never hear the end of it.

Then there was Strings Attached. I needed to win the kite contest, and I was sure my kite was beautiful enough to nab first place. The publicity would draw buyers to my website. Then I had to go and threaten the lead judge.

"Stupid," I couldn't help saying aloud. The surf grumbled in sympathy.

I'd ticked off Jack, too. I remembered his adoring gaze at Jasmine. Had he ever looked at me that way? I slowed as I walked from sea-packed sand to the looser, dry sand near the bluff. The cool scent of salt and earth blew around me. Sometimes when we'd hang out I'd catch Jack studying me when he thought I wasn't looking. He'd always have a vague smile, as if looking at me had stirred up a memory of something happy, a little bit funny, maybe. But I don't recall him drooling.

I'd been the one to slow things between us. I'd barely lived in Rock Point for three months, and Strings Attached was only just getting started. It felt too soon to get involved with anyone, even a great guy like Jack. I wanted to be a little more established first, steady on my own two feet.

What a scene I'd made at the Brew House, though. I shook my head. I'd never blown my top like that over a guy before. Sure, some of it had to do with worry about Strings Attached and Marcus's egging me on, but it was inexcusable. Plus, I hadn't stuck around long enough for

Jack to say anything in his own defense. I would definitely apologize to him tomorrow, as humiliating as it would be.

I'd made it about half a mile down the beach. Time to turn back. Maybe I'd worn myself out enough to finally sleep.

Up on the bluffs to my left, houses appeared here and there, mostly vacation homes. They were dark. Or empty. Except for the farthest one, which had two lights on: one downstairs and one upstairs, on opposite sides of the house.

Normally, I'd assume someone couldn't sleep, like me, and was looking for comfort in warm milk or late-night TV. But this was the house Rose had said her sister, Jasmine Normand, was renting.

I walked a little closer. As with all the homes on the bluff, including Avery's, stairs were roughly cut into the earth, leading from the beach to the house. From where I stood, the houses were low enough that I could make out someone—Jasmine?—bending over the sink in the kitchen. I clicked off my flashlight and held my breath, but no one could see me on the beach. The upstairs bedroom darkened all at once, and the figure turned toward me. It wasn't Jasmine at all. It was a man.

Uncomfortable, and not wanting to be caught gawking at Jasmine Normand's house, I turned for home.

"ARE YOU SURE YOU CAN HANDLE THE STORE, SUNNY?" I hiked my purse to my shoulder, but I hesitated to leave.

"Of course," Sunny said. "How hard can it be? I used

to work at the co-op, remember? I know how to run a credit card machine."

"Kites aren't exactly kombucha and millet."

"I've flown kites all my life, too, you know. Go run your errand. Things will be just fine."

"Maybe it can wait—"

"Get out of here." Sunny turned toward the workshop door, her blond dreadlocks whirling behind her.

Well, I wouldn't be gone long. I walked the few blocks to Sullivan's Kites and, taking a deep breath, pushed open the front door. Jack's shop had been in Rock Point since his grandfather opened it just after World War II, inside the mechanic's shop he also ran. After a few years, the kite business overtook the automobile repair business, and old man Sullivan, as we used to call him, moved the shop to the former five and dime on Main Street. The shop had kept its no-nonsense interior of racks of kites interspersed with the occasional sun-faded kite poster. Jack also sold games to help him through the winter.

The store had a special place in my heart since it was where my parents had bought me my first kite, a red diamond. I'd had no idea Jack existed then, since he lived in Salem with his parents. His dad was old man Sullivan's son.

Seeing me, Jack tossed a piece of fabric over the kite he was working on. His competition kite. Had to be. "Hi," he said uncertainly.

I bit my lip and released it. "I've come to apologize. I'm sorry I was such a blockhead yesterday. I had no right to talk to you like that."

"You were really upset." To my surprise, he sounded more curious than angry.

"I lost it. I haven't let loose like that since"—I pondered this a second—"since I don't know when. It's inexcusable. I was tormented all night thinking about it."

He smiled, right up through those pale gray eyes. All at once, I relaxed. "You're forgiven," he said. "Besides, it was cute, seeing you jealous."

"I wasn't jealous, I just wanted to make sure I got a fair shot at the kite contest."

"Jasmine and I got to talking when I was in line behind her at the Brew House. Her credit card was declined, so I bought her latte for her."

"You don't have to explain," I said, grateful, of course, that he'd explained anyway.

"I might have looked a little starstruck." He laid his forearms on the counter and leaned forward. "Although I didn't expect you to blow up like that."

"I'd just been at Rose's talking taxes, and my sister showed up in town unexpectedly, and I was out of sorts. I took it out on you. That wasn't right." Feeling shy, I smiled, and he did, too. Heat crept over my face. "Anyway, I won't do it again. Unless you really deserve it," I amended.

He laughed. "Life's too short to be upset."

"Thank you." I leaned forward, too. Voices on the sidewalk drew near, and then passed. "What's that under the fabric?"

From the glance I'd had of Jack's kite, I knew mine would outclass his in looks. Jack didn't make many kites from scratch. His shop's kites came in kits. But Jack had gone to engineering school, and he knew a fast kite from one that would take a nosedive. He didn't need to win the contest. His selection of games, on top of what he saved over the summer, kept him solvent. I, on the other hand, had to keep my kite sales going.

"You know what it is, and I'm not going to show it to you." He double-checked that his kite was hidden. "Hey," he said, his voice low.

"What?" I was all too aware that our heads were only a foot or so apart.

He fidgeted with a piece of line on the counter. I played it cool, but my pulse had gone from waltz to rumba.

"You want to go for a hike this week?"

"Maybe the day after tomorrow?" My voice might have been a little breathy.

Just then, the front door flew open with enough force to ricochet off the wall, knocking a display kite to the ground. Both Jack and I swiveled to face the front.

Darlene, the head of Rock Point's chamber of commerce—such as it was—stood, gasping, holding the door frame. "I can't believe it."

"Are you all right?" In a second, I was at Darlene's side and so was Jack. He led her to a chair.

"What's wrong?" Jack asked.

"I had to come tell you." Darlene plopped into the chair and put a hand to her chest. "I don't know what we're going to do."

"Do you need some water?" I asked, and looked at Jack.

He turned, presumably to head to the sink in the rear, but Darlene grabbed his arm. "Stay." She was beginning to regain her breath.

"What's wrong, Darlene?" I crouched next to her.

"It's Jasmine. Jasmine Normand. She's dead."

chapter four

"JASMINE NORMAND WAS KILLED?" I SAID. I'D HEARD THE words, they'd come out of my mouth, yet it was incomprehensible. I rose and clutched the back of her chair. "I can't believe it."

"No one said anything about murder." Darlene examined me. "What makes you think someone killed her?"

"I guess it was the first thing that came to my mind. She looked fine yesterday. She's really dead?"

"But you said 'killed.'"

I had. I didn't know why. "Maybe it was all the excitement. The worst came to mind."

"This kind of is the worst," Jack said.

Darlene clutched her purse. "I'll take that water now, please." When he returned, cup in hand, she took a gulp, then continued. "Jasmine's friend Caitlin found her this morning in bed."

"Caitlin," I said. The name sounded familiar, but I couldn't place it.

"You met her yesterday at the Brew House," Jack said. "Jasmine's friend with the short hair."

Darlene took another long sip of water. "Ace said Deputy Goff said Caitlin said she'd knocked on Jasmine's door, but she didn't get up. I guess Jasmine sleeps in sometimes, so she wasn't overly worried at first. Jasmine's husband, some guy named Kyle—"

"Kyle Connell," Jack said. "Used to play for the Colts, but he was sidelined by an injury. Word is he's aiming to be a sports announcer."

"Yeah, well, Kyle had been trying to get in touch with Jasmine, but she wouldn't pick up. So he called Caitlin to wake her up. Caitlin went into the room and found her. Dead." Satisfied she'd got out her story, Darlene fell back into the chair and handed the half-empty water glass to Jack.

Jasmine Normand dead. Unbelievable. "How?" I asked and rose from beside Darlene's chair. I remembered the lights at Jasmine's beach house before dawn, and the man at the window. But it couldn't have been Jasmine's husband, since he'd called for her this morning. Anxiety fluttered in my stomach.

"Don't know," Darlene said. "The sheriff is over there right now."

"Poor Rose," I said.

"Yep," Darlene said. "She's a good kid. This can't be easy."

We all stared out the Sullivan's Kites front window for a moment. How strange life was. One day you're on top of the world, lauded in your hometown, getting your lattes paid for by handsome guys like Jack, and the next day you don't wake up.

Jack and I glanced at each other. I think we both had the same thought, but he said it first. "Are you going to cancel the kite festival?"

Darlene stood and sighed. "I don't see how we can, although it feels heartless to hold it now. The festival committee is meeting this afternoon to talk it over."

I was still in a daze. "You'll let us know?"

"Naturally." She straightened her suit jacket. "I guess I'll stop by the gas station and the post office, make sure the word gets around."

After Darlene left, Jack turned to me. "Amazing." He shook his head. "At least there's still more than a week and a half until the festival. Plenty of time to find a judge."

"If the festival is still on. No kite festival, no kite buyers." No chance for my kite to earn a ribbon.

"I wonder how it happened? Jasmine's death, that is," Jack said.

"She looked healthy yesterday," I said, remembering the scene at the Brew House with a twinge of embarrassment.

We settled our plans for a hike the day after next, but we both seemed to have our minds somewhere else.

Jasmine was dead, and there was possibly no kite contest. My shop's future was on shaky ground. Sunny was camping out on the sleeping porch.

Needless to say, I was in a distracted mood when I returned to Strings Attached.

"Anything happen while I was away?" I asked Sunny. I expected her to say "no," after which I'd tell her about Jasmine.

Instead, she stared at me like a nun caught at the slot machines. "Um."

"What?"

"I was only making tea. I didn't see it there."

"See what?" I stepped closer. "Sunny, what did you do?"

She lifted her hand from behind the counter. In it was my competition kite, with a hole the size of a fist burnt right through the middle.

I SNATCHED THE KITE FROM MY SISTER'S GRIP AND EXAMined it. It was ruined, no doubt about it. No amount of patch appliqué would be able to cover the massive burnt hole with its blackened edges right through my meticulously stitched depiction of Rock Point's old marina. I held the kite to my face and looked through the hole to Sunny's red, swollen eyes.

All that work, all those hours for nothing. For a moment, I teetered between the desire to burst into tears and the urge to yell. I took a steadying breath. Then I tossed the kite to the side.

"Don't cry. It's not a big deal. The kite festival might be canceled, anyway." What the heck. Like Jack said, life was too short. Maybe I'd learned something from losing my temper yesterday.

Sunny dabbed her eyes with a tissue and sniffed. "What?"

"Jasmine Normand, the contest judge, died last night."

"Jasmine, from *Bag That Babe*?" Her eyes were wide now, the kite forgotten.

"They found her in bed." I remembered blurting out that she was murdered. Was it Jasmine's bedroom that had the lights on? I needed to talk to Sheriff Koppen.

"What happened?" Sunny came around the corner, as if the counter would somehow slow the news from getting to her.

"I don't know. I was talking to Jack when the president of the chamber of commerce ran in and told us. Listen, are you up to watching the shop for another hour?"

"Do you still trust me?" She reverently lifted the destroyed kite and leaned it against the wall. "Honestly, I was making tea, and I guess I forgot to turn off the burner, and then the kite must have fallen—"

"I know it was an accident." Frustration rose as I looked at my kite's carcass. I breathed deeply. "You get a second chance. I have to see the sheriff."

I left Sunny standing in a daze.

The sheriff's office was in a tiny storefront next to Martino's Pizza on Main Street and had the garlicky aroma to match. I pushed open its door and came face-to-face with Deputy Sheriff Goff. Damn.

"Can I help you?" she said, looking as practical and annoyed as ever. Just because I'd called her out on her rendezvous with her boyfriend down at the dock a few months ago, and just because she'd probably received a formal reprimand for not disclosing a relationship with a homicide suspect, was no reason for her to get snippy.

"I have some information for the sheriff."

She practically growled as she picked up a pen. "What?"

"I need to tell the sheriff. It has to do with Jasmine Normand's death."

"The sheriff's not here. I'm an officer of the law. I'm fully capable of passing along your message to him."

I bit my lip. It's not that I didn't trust her with the facts—I was sure she'd do her job—it's more like I didn't trust her with the implications for me. "Do you know when he'll be back?"

"When who'll be back?" came the sheriff's voice from behind me. Sheriff Koppen was stern and dark—his mother had been Clatsop Indian—but not imposing.

"Oh, good," I said. "I wanted to talk to you about Jasmine Normand."

"I had a few questions for you about Jasmine Normand, too." His placid expression told me nothing.

"What a coincidence . . ." My voice trailed off.

"I understand you had an altercation with Ms. Normand yesterday at the Brew House."

Deputy Goff watched both of us, her gaze first on the sheriff, then on me.

The sheriff cleared his throat. "Come on back. Deputy Goff has work to do." He led me to his tiny office at the rear of the space. The smell of garlic was even more intense here, tinged with oregano. Martino's multilayered sauce was the key to its success. The sheriff must know every layer intimately by now. He pointed to a beat-up chair on the other side of his desk. "We'll get to the conversation at the Brew House in a minute. First, what did you want to tell me?"

I told him how I had been out on a walk, and how I'd seen lights on in rooms on the opposite sides of Jasmine's house. I also told him about the man's figure I'd seen leaning over the sink.

Koppen's features could have been carved in marble for all the interest he betrayed. "You were alone?"

"Yes."

"What were you doing out at that time of the morning?"

"I couldn't sleep. A lot's been going on. I thought a walk might help. Sometimes I do that."

Sheriff Koppen's stare pinned me like a butterfly to a specimen book. "And you got into it with Ms. Normand at the Brew House yesterday."

Did everyone know everyone's business in this town? "I might have, well, had a few words."

"We have witnesses, you know. I want to hear it in your words."

"Look. I just wanted you to know what I saw in case it helps you pinpoint times," I said. "I don't see what the discussion at the Brew House has to do with Jasmine's death."

"I'll make that determination." He steepled his fingers. "Start with when you got to the café."

I'd come here to give the sheriff information, and now I was the one being grilled. "Fine." To put off talking about the brouhaha I'd stirred up, I spent a bit longer than necessary recounting my desire for a tuna melt. The sheriff waited patiently. "And then I saw Jasmine Normand. I didn't know who she was right away."

"And?"

Lord, this was embarrassing. "She was talking to Jack, and I gathered that they were flirting." I smoothed my hair to hide my embarrassment. "I told Jack to lay off and told Jasmine she'd better be a fair judge of kites," I added as quickly as I could.

If the sheriff was amused or shocked, I couldn't tell by his expression. "Anything else?"

"No. Well, Marcus Salek was cheering me on from his table."

"Marcus, eh?"

At last, I saw a glimmer of reaction. "Sure. You know how he is. Anyway, I'm not sure why my story matters." When Koppen didn't reply, I added, "I mean, her death was an accident, right?"

"The medical examiner will make that determination, but as far as we can tell, it was health related." The sheriff examined a finger.

"Health related," I repeated.

"Yes. Apparently."

Koppen wasn't sure. I could tell by his tone of voice. "Apparently" was about as extreme an expression of doubt as he'd share. "Is there any reason it wouldn't be?" I asked.

"Show me again exactly what you saw," he said and ripped a sheet of paper from a lined pad. "Draw a map."

I pulled the paper toward me and took the pen. Pen and paper felt good in my hands, although the sheriff's pen was a scratchy felt-tip number. I capped it and pulled a soft pencil from my bag. I always kept a sketchpad and pencil with me for kite ideas.

"I was standing here." I marked an X on the thin strip of beach I'd drawn between the high tide and the bluff. I quickly sketched two stories of the beach house, complete with deck, and filled in squares for the windows where I'd seen light. I tapped the pencil on the upstairs window to the left. "This light was on here at first, then it went out. Here, this lower one"—I tapped the lower, right-hand window—"stayed on the whole time. Maybe it's the kitchen?" I glanced at Koppen, but he was still examining my drawing. "I saw a man. He looked out toward me."

"A man, you say."

"I think so."

"How long did you stand there?"

"Not more than a minute or two."

The sheriff sat back. "You were standing far away. Are you sure it was a man?"

I closed my eyes and recalled the height and broad shoulders. Could it have been a tall woman? "Now that I'm trying to remember exactly, it isn't as clear. But my first thought was that it was a man. Now, on second thought . . ."

A metallic clang out back told me that someone was taking trash to the Dumpster behind Martino's. The sheriff didn't seem to notice the noise.

I tried again. "You seem to think maybe Jasmine didn't die of natural causes."

"She was diabetic. The medical examiner will say for sure, but she might have taken too much insulin."

"By mistake?" Depression was a mysterious illness, but Jasmine didn't seem particularly down when I saw her. I doubted it was suicide.

"Don't know." The sheriff stood. I wasn't going to get any more information out of him. "The media are descending on Rock Point," he said, seemingly as an afterthought.

"Already?"

"Deputy Goff spent her lunch hour chasing one reporter out. She said he wouldn't give up. He had some pointed questions." He gestured toward a business card.

I read the card upside down, one of my specialties. "The *National Bloodhound*." The *Bloodhound* was mostly known for celebrity exposés and diet schemes.

"He asked about you, in particular."

"Me?" My jaw dropped. The thought that a reporter for a tabloid as huge as the *Bloodhound* was interested in me boggled my mind.

He nodded. "Knew you by name."

"What? What did he want to know?"

The sheriff led me to the hall and shut his office door behind us. "He wouldn't say, but I'd imagine it's about your scene at the Brew House."

"Oh." My throat tightened.

"You'd better watch yourself. It would be easy for someone to jump to conclusions."

chapter five

AVERY STOOD IN THE KITCHEN WITH THE PANTRY DOOR open. "We can make spaghetti for dinner. Do you eat meat, Sunny?"

"No," I said.

"Yes," my sister said at the same time.

"Since when do you eat meat?" I asked her. "I thought you told me you were vegan."

"How come you think you know everything about me?" She turned to Avery. "I eat meat, but only ethically raised. No hormones or antibiotics."

"Fine. I have some beef from a ranch up the road. Let's have spaghetti and meatballs. A good old-fashioned dinner." Avery pulled a few vegetables from the refrigerator and set them next to a can of tomatoes on the counter.

"What did you do this afternoon after you left the

shop?" I said. Once I'd returned from seeing Sheriff
Koppen, I'd spent the rest of the afternoon convincing
myself that the reporter from the *National Bloodhound*
had moved on and forgotten about me. Surely some
celebrity's affair with the nanny or a botched face-lift
would kick me off his radar.

Avery knew I wasn't talking to her. Her afternoon
had undoubtedly been filled with the Brew House and
probably a visit from Dave. Dave was ostensibly Avery's
good friend, but was clearly crazy about her. She ignored
us and chopped onions.

"I went for a walk along the cliff by the lighthouse,"
Sunny started. "In that park—"

"Clatsop Cliffs State Park." The park was just north
of Avery's house and curved gently toward Rock Point
with a view of town from the cliff. It was a lovely walk,
but it was useless for flying kites since wind-twisted
pines covered its top and the beach below was all rocks.
Locals called the rocky area under the cliffs the Devil's
Playpen for the fishing boats that had been dashed upon
its boulders before the lighthouse went in.

"Yeah. It gave me time to think."

"Did you find yourself?" I asked.

"Don't make fun of me," Sunny said.

"Stop squabbling, you two." Avery scooped a handful of onions into a sauté pan. "Honestly, you'd think
you were sisters or something. Anyway, I heard a few
things down at the café today."

"Do tell. You want a beer?" I asked Sunny. She was
just barely twenty-one, and I hoped she'd say no. She
satisfied me by shaking her head.

"First, the kite festival is on," Avery said. "Darlene came in and said that Caitlin Ruder, Jasmine Normand's friend—"

"And co-star on *Bag That Babe*," Sunny added. "Although she did get knocked out fairly early. I think it was her conniving. Even the hunter noticed it."

"You watch reality TV and eat meat?" I asked.

"Get used to it," Sunny said.

"Yeah, well, Caitlin's going to be the judge," Avery said. "Darlene asked me to tell you."

Relief. I tried to remember Caitlin, but my attention at the Brew House had been focused on Jasmine and Jack. I vaguely remembered another Barbie-like blond, maybe slightly taller than Jasmine and with shorter hair. "That's good news." I shot a glance at my sister. "I think I can salvage the frame from my old competition kite, although I'll have to redo the pattern." Sunny turned away. I felt bad. She hadn't meant to destroy the kite. She never *meant* to destroy things, but that didn't limit the carnage. Over the years, her clumsiness had cost me a butterfly collection, a Popsicle-stick model of Notre Dame, and a Girl Scout uniform, among other things. "I needed to make a few improvements, anyway. The kite will be even better now."

Sunny looked at me gratefully. "What happens at this festival?"

"Lots of stuff," Avery said. "It's an all-day event."

Bear trotted to Avery and lay down, his furry back to her heels. She was getting skilled at cooking with forty pounds of pooch under her feet.

"First there's a parade," I said. "Stella's"—my friend

and part-time employee—"Corvette's going to be in it this year. Then everyone goes down to the beach. There's a contest for the biggest kite and one for the funniest kite. Then there's simply 'best kite.' That's the one I need to win."

"I have more news," Avery said as she stripped oregano leaves from their stalks.

"What else?" I asked.

Sunny crouched behind Bear on the kitchen floor to scratch his ears. Avery might be good at cooking around a dog, but I wondered how she'd do with a college sophomore down there, too.

"Jasmine's husband arrived in town. I made him an iced coffee."

"Poor guy. He must be in bad shape," I said.

"It was hard to tell. He's one of those muscular dudes who doesn't seem to get very emotional."

"I feel awful for Rose," I said. "Jasmine's sister," I added for Sunny's benefit, "and my accountant."

Just then, my phone broke into "Mamma Mia." My first instinct was that Sunny should hide, but I stopped myself. There was no way Mom could see all the way from Portland. I answered the phone.

"Emmy," Mom said, "I'm worried about your sister."

I turned away from Sunny. Maybe if I couldn't see her, Mom wouldn't know she was there. "Why's that?"

"She's being strangely evasive. And the last time I talked to her, she told me about an article she'd read in the *Wall Street Journal*. A businessman's paper! Imagine that."

"Not everyone restricts their reading to *Mother Jones*

and *Croning Monthly*," I said. "Besides, she's getting ready for the term. She's probably too busy to talk." With my free hand, I crossed my fingers. "She's finding herself." Okay, those last words faltered a bit. I peeked back at my sister.

She stared at me in fascination.

"It's a mother's instinct. I just wanted to see if you knew anything."

"Not a thing, Mom," I lied.

"What's this I hear on the radio about a reality TV star dying in Rock Point?"

Mom and Dad didn't watch TV. In fact, their old Prius (which was currently in my possession) had a bumper sticker that commanded "Kill Your Television," right next to the one that said "Bowl Naked." At last, someone who didn't know *Bag That Babe*. "She was the kite festival judge. Now one of the other contestants is taking over. Caitlin is her name."

"Caitlin?" Mom said. "Really? My friend Judith thinks she shouldn't have been kicked off *Bag That Babe* so early, but I never liked her attitude."

"Mom! Don't tell me you've seen the show."

"What? You know I don't watch TV. I heard about it at the croning circle, that's all. We can't talk about hot flashes all the time, you know." A hand muffled the phone, but my mother's voice was still clear. "Honey, watch that. I put the sprouts on the windowsill." Then, hand removed, "Sorry. Your father is refilling the bird feeder and he's making a mess."

"So Jasmine Normand's death is on the news?" I asked. Marcus Salek, the town crank who'd egged me on at the Brew House, wasn't going to be happy about that. With the media in town, he'd have to double up on his blood pressure meds. I remembered the sheriff's warning to me, too, and gripped the phone more tightly.

"Public radio did a short clip. Poor girl."

"Are you still coming down for the kite festival?"

"Definitely," Mom said. "I'm thinking we might detour by the college on the way back and see how Sunny's getting on."

Sunny was still watching me. I raised an eyebrow to her in warning. "Well, thanks for the call." Almost as soon as I'd hung up, Sunny's phone rang from inside her tote across the room. "God Save the Queen." That'd be Mom.

"Hi, Mom," Sunny said. "The weather's great. Blue skies." A pause. "Oh, right. I mean, it's overcast. Maybe a quick summer rain. No, I'm fine. Perfectly fine."

chapter six

WITH TREPIDATION, I WALKED TO THE BREW HOUSE THE next day at lunch. It was time to wipe the ugly scene with Jasmine from Rock Point's memory with friendly, dignified behavior. Besides, I never did get that tuna melt.

Donning a calm smile, I raised my chin and strode across the café to the back counter. Diana Ross serenaded my arrival from the record player with the theme from *Mahogany*. "I'd like a tuna melt, please," I told Trudy, and laid a five and a one on the counter before stuffing another dollar bill into the tip jar.

I turned to face the room, to show the lunchtime regulars that the old levelheaded Emmy was back. My smile dropped with my jaw. The café was busy, sure, but not with regulars. Suited professionals, one with a movie camera hoisted on his shoulder, filled the room.

"Emmy," Avery whispered from behind me. "They're here about Jasmine. You'd better watch out. I saw Jeanette giving them an earful this morning. One of them asked me about you, but I refused to tell them where to find you."

Jeanette, Rock Point's postmistress, was the town's locus for information. She knew everyone's business, but good luck if you wanted to hear it. She was willing to dish, all right, but you'd better have information to offer that was at least as good as what you came for. She might have cracked for a few insider movie-star tips, though, and this crowd looked more like the nighttime entertainment network than the *New York Times*.

"Can't you make them go away?" I pleaded.

"Maybe they won't recognize you. Besides, business is great. I'm already out of scones."

A sleek-haired brunette with glossy coral lips approached me. At her shoulder, a bearded man wielded a camera. "Ms. Adler?"

"What?" I knew my eyes darted side to side. I probably looked like I'd just stolen a car and this reporter was the police. I gripped the edge of the counter behind me and tried to channel poise.

"I recognize you from your charming shop."

This was a lie. She'd never been in Strings Attached, and we both knew it.

She smiled a confidential smile that made the rest of the room melt away—almost. The camera was now leveled at my face. "I'm Meredith Sedillo with Presto Entertainment. Such an awful tragedy about Jasmine

Normand. I understand you shared words with her during her last day alive."

Think, Emmy, think. I cleared my throat. "Jasmine was here to judge the kite festival. I own Strings Attached and make beautiful kites by hand. Come see me down by the waterfront, or find my kites online at—"

"You fought with her, am I right?" the reporter said, her mouth tightening.

"You can't fight the beauty of my wonderful kites," I said. My voice had jumped to soprano territory, but I was sticking to my script.

"I understand you accused Ms. Normand of making moves on your boyfriend." The honey had evaporated from her tone.

"A beautiful kite like those from Strings Attached makes moves in the sky that will thrill your heart." My own heart was pounding. I had no future in marketing talk, that was for sure.

"Come on," the reporter said to the cameraman. She threw a disgusted look over her shoulder.

Trudy tapped my arm and handed me a tuna melt. Keeping a wide smile pasted across my face, I took the sandwich to the table the reporter had just abandoned. Another reporter, this one a man with teeth as white as Chiclets, took a seat at my table before asking, "May I?"

"Strings Attached," I said and spelled out its website.

He chuckled. "I admire your spunk."

I narrowed my eyes. I detested the word "spunk." Who did he think I was, Tinker Bell? "I'm eating lunch."

"And in such a wonderful town, too. Perhaps you'd

like to share a few words with the nation about Jasmine Normand?" He nodded to a cameraman at the table behind him. The man lifted the camera to his shoulder.

I'd had enough. I put down my knife. "Leave me alone. You're not going to get anything out of me. Let me eat in peace."

"I know you don't—" the man started.

"Didn't you hear the girl?" a voice bellowed. "Get the hell away from her. In fact, get out of Rock Point altogether." Marcus Salek stood at my side, hands on hips. Where I'd merely been intensely irritated, Marcus was mad enough that spittle clung to the side of his mouth. He wiped it with the back of his hand. "Out!"

The man looked at his partner with the camera. They stood. Before he left, he smiled at me. "I hope we'll meet again, Ms. Adler."

"Out. All of you. Go dig up your trash somewhere else." Marcus opened the Brew House's front door and gestured down the porch to the street.

Surprisingly, they listened. One by one, strangers in city clothes filed from the café, leaving coffee cups and half-eaten muffins behind.

"Are you all right?" Marcus asked me, his voice now gentle.

I looked up in surprise and gratitude. He'd never shown me this kind of care before. In fact, I'd suspected he barely tolerated me, since I'd brought Strings Attached to town. "Yes. Thank you."

"Damned muckrakers," he said. All at once, his shaggy brows and unkempt beard looked adorable, not bedraggled. With better grooming, he might actually be good-looking. Maybe he wasn't so bad, after all.

"Thank you," I repeated.

"I'd best be getting on," he said. "The Brew House makes a great tuna melt."

"Agreed." I'd been looking forward to this sandwich for two days now.

He scooped up half of my tuna melt and wrapped it in a napkin.

"Marcus! That's my sandwich."

"Not as good cold, but it'll do." I watched him carry it out of the café.

Shoot. At least I had half a sandwich left. Two bites in, a stranger approached my table. I was wary, but he couldn't have been a reporter. Not with the pudgy frame that lifted his pants to his ankles and the row of crooked bottom teeth that showed as he smiled. A fine layer of makeup covered acne scars.

"I admire the deft way you handled those sharks." The man's voice was silver-smooth, at odds with his schlumpy appearance.

"Thank you." To show I was finished with him, I returned my attention to my sandwich.

"Nicky Byrd." He slid his card across the table. "Nicholas Byrd III, *National Bloodhound*," it read. In the corner was the tabloid's logo, a jowly hound holding a magnifying glass.

"Nicky Byrd the Third?" I said.

"What about it?"

"Look, I'm just trying to get lunch. You heard me. I'm not going to tell you anything. You can leave now."

I bent to my sandwich and studiously ignored him. The moment of enjoying the tuna melt was over, though. My mouthful tasted like cardboard.

"What a lovely town. I'm reveling in Rock Point's beguiling assets. Its residents are charming and colorful, and the crystalline air scented with salt and balsam fir refreshes me. I'd love to learn more about it."

Since when did Charles Dickens write for tabloids? He scratched his nose. He could have used a manicure. I returned my attention to my sandwich. Maybe I could freeze him out.

"Into this idyllic atmosphere comes Jasmine Normand, born of this small town, but milled in Hollywood. Alas, you can't go home again." He tapped the table. "That's Thomas Mann."

"I know," I said, not removing my gaze from my plate.

"And she tragically dies in the arms of Morpheus."

My sandwich was almost done. All this fast chewing had really dried out my throat. "Sad," I choked out.

"Unless there is more to the story."

A few locals had wandered into the café, and the usual friendly chatter had arisen again around me. Trudy had changed the record, and Joni Mitchell sang to us about clouds getting in her way.

Now the reporter had my attention. "Like what?"

"Those hacks from the TV stations, they want a quick quote, and they're gone. They'll run some stock footage of Jasmine, try to wring a few tears from the story, and they'll move on. They're not real journalists."

"You implied that Jasmine might not have died of natural causes," I said. "What makes you think that?"

"Why don't you tell me what you know, and we'll figure it out together? I might be able to supply a few missing pieces."

The reporter's oily tone left me feeling in need of a shower. "Forget it. I have nothing to say. Good-bye." I grabbed my plate and made for the tub where customers left their dirty dishes.

Nicky Byrd rose and dramatically slipped on a pair of sunglasses that would have looked cool on Roy Orbison but only served to accent this guy's nerdiness. "Very well. We'll be meeting again."

THAT EVENING, STELLA WAS AT HER DOOR WHEN I ARrived to visit, looking as elegant yet down-to-earth as ever in a European-cut linen tunic and leggings. She glowed. "I got tickets to the Lovepipers concert next week."

"That's fantastic. Are they at the casino?" If my arms hadn't been full of kite-making supplies, I'd have hugged her. The Lovepipers were a sunshine pop group Stella had adored during high school in the 1970s. Whenever I came in the shop after Stella had been working, it was their music she'd been playing.

"Yep. Oldies tour to Spirit Mountain. I was on the phone all morning. I'm sure they're sold out by now." She pointed toward my supplies. "Do you need help carrying that up?"

"No, I've got it." I'd struggled from the car with a bag of nylon scraps in one hand and the salvaged kite frame in the other.

Stella met me at the foot of the stairs, anyway, and took the bag. Once I was in Stella's home, I felt my tension roll away. My sister, the kite contest, the reporters— all the drama evaporated. From the view over Rock Point to the ocean, where the sun would set in a few hours, to Stella's paintings and waxed oak floors, I always felt at home here. After her husband's death, Stella had retired from teaching middle school and settled in Rock Point to take up a long-delayed career of painting. Now her canvases of landscapes hung in galleries up and down the West Coast.

"Why don't you set up at the dining room table?" she asked.

"If you don't mind, I'll spread out here." Stella's living room centered on a low, large round table in front of the fireplace. Around the table sat mismatched chairs, each from a different era, like a tribal meeting of bohemian artists. I spread my pattern over the table and placed the frame on top. The first step was to cover the frame completely in Tyvek.

"Are you doing the same pattern as the first kite? The landscape of Rock Point?" Stella set a glass of chilled pinot gris next to me. Her white cat, Madame Lucy, one eye blue, one amber, stared from the pink 1950s armchair across the table.

"Yes, but since I have to redo it, I'm going to tweak it a bit and add more detail on the bluffs. Plus, I thought I'd make the horizon a sunrise this time." Like the wrecked kite, the background would be blue. I laid the nylon over the table and pressed it flat with my palms.

"I'm glad the kite festival is still happening, at least. Jasmine Normand, dead. In my mind, she'll always be snoozing through an episode of *Bag That Babe*."

My jaw dropped. "Not you, too? Am I the only person who didn't watch that show?"

"Well, she was a local girl, remember." Stella smiled with a touch of guilt. "I have the season saved, if you're interested."

For the first time, I noticed the television discreetly pushed into the corner. "Maybe just a sample, if you don't mind."

I sometimes watched movies while I sewed kites. Most kites I made with the sewing machine, but the delicate bits of appliqué on this kite required careful hand-piecing. Each color—say, for a sliver of rising sun—I'd stitch to the background fabric with careful, even stitches. Once it was on, I'd flip the kite over and cut away the background under the appliquéd patch so that the kite was one sheer layer, not two.

"Just some highlights, then," Stella said. She pulled the television over on its wheeled stand. "The show's premise is that the bachelor is a safari hunter, and his potential dates are all—"

"Animals," I finished. "Oh, Stella. Really? People watch this show?"

She pressed her lips together. "So, the women all stay in a jungle-themed mansion on a few acres."

"With a pool, so they can lounge in their swimsuits, am I right?"

"Please don't interrupt," Stella said in her schoolmarm voice. "When the bachelor comes over, he hangs out with them, then they scatter over the property. He hunts down the babe he wants and points his gun at her—"

"Stop! This is awful."

"And a little flag comes out that says, 'Bagged.' Then he goes on a date with her."

I had to set down the needle I was threading to groan. "And people watch this garbage." Remembering that Stella had said she'd seen the season, I added, "I'm sure there's lots of suspense."

"Just watch." Stella took the remote control to the chair next to Madame Lucy, who jumped into her lap. "I'll cue up the show where the hunter first chooses Jasmine."

The television erupted into sinister music with a dance beat. Stella turned down the volume a few notches. Behind the opening titles, a bevy of bikini-clad women ran from the pool like a thicket of quail chased from a bush. The camera focused on a buff man in a safari suit, complete with pith helmet.

"I can't believe it," I said.

Stella shot me a warning look. "Hush."

Slung across the bachelor's shoulders was a gun. "Stay tuned as we watch Chad *Bag That Babe*!"

"Okay, here's the good part," Stella said.

Credits over, the show opened on a dorm-style bedroom strewn with sleeping women. An older woman in a military outfit entered the scene ringing a bell. "Who's she?" I asked.

"The game warden."

"Everyone up! Out of bed!" the game warden said. "Chad will be here any minute."

With squeals, the women leapt from their bunks and hurried offstage, presumably to dress. I thought I recognized Caitlin in the mix, although except for hair color, the women looked pretty much the same: nice figures, even features, fruit-toned manicures.

One figure remained in bed. The game warden slapped the woman's rump through the blanket. "Up!" she said.

The figure rolled over. Jasmine. "What?"

"Chad's on his way. You've got to get up and into the wild. Here's your outfit." The game warden tossed a tiger-striped garment on the bed.

Stella paused the television. "Later they discovered that Jasmine was diabetic. That's why she slept so much." She pressed "play" again.

Jasmine stumbled toward a rear exit. The camera flashed to the other women, now freshly coiffed and lipsticked, scattering in the garden. A moment later, clad in a tiger-striped minidress, her hair still mussed, Jasmine came through the door, yawning.

Just then, Mr. Pith Helmet, Chad—or whatever he was called—burst in the bedroom door. Chad and Jasmine stared at each other, each surprised to find the other one. Chad lifted his rifle and shot. "Bang," he added. A pink flag reading "Bagged" slid out the rifle's muzzle.

"This is too much," I said.

Stella clicked the television off. "So, they go on a date. Chad lets her stay around for future safaris."

"And eventually she wins. Then what? Do they have

to get married?" I knew Jasmine already had a husband, but I remembered his name as Kyle.

"No. They won cash and a free trip to a safari in Botswana. Jasmine got a leg up on her acting career, and Chad ended up hosting a fishing show, I think."

I fitted a piece of orange nylon onto the blue background and anchored it with a few stitches. "This kite is going to take forever." I threaded green into the needle. "What about Caitlin? How was she on the show?"

"You know how every reality TV show has the character you love to hate?" Stella looked at me for confirmation, but I couldn't say yes or no, since I hadn't watched any. "Well, they do. And Caitlin was it. I'm surprised she and Jasmine were such close friends. But you know what they say, 'Keep your friends close'—"

"—And your enemies closer," I finished. "Interesting." I snipped a piece of pine-hued nylon to the shape of the trees on Clatsop Cliffs. "Why didn't people like her?"

"She lied. A lot. Really, when she said something, it was best to assume the opposite."

"Like what?"

"Well, she'd tell Chad that Jasmine was trash-talking him, for instance, when she wasn't. Or she'd dump a margarita on one of the other girls' dresses and say it was an accident."

"Sheriff Koppen didn't seem completely satisfied with the idea that Jasmine's death was an accident, but he wouldn't tell me more than that." I tied off the thread. "You said Jasmine just discovered she was diabetic. She died of an insulin overdose. Maybe, since she was new to taking it, she miscalculated."

"Could be." Stella sipped her wine and leaned back. Madame Lucy's purr resonated from all the way across the table. "I heard you and Jasmine went at it at the Brew House."

"'Went at it' is kind of strong."

Stella waited.

"It's embarrassing."

"And?" she said.

"I was more angry at Jack, really. I know it's stupid," I added quickly. Unlike with the sheriff, talking with Stella was easy. She'd been my confidant from nearly the first day we'd met.

"Not stupid. Tell me."

"I saw Jack all gaga over Jasmine, and I was jealous. Plus, I'd just come from Rose, who had reminded me how many new businesses fail and how I had to have a better plan for getting Strings Attached through the winter. Then I go to the Brew House, and Jack is making eyes at the festival's judge. I lost it."

Stella looked at me, then at my empty glass. "You want another one?"

"No, I'm good, thanks."

She nudged Madame Lucy aside and went to the refrigerator for the bottle, anyway, and added a splash to my glass. "You might need it."

I looked up from my stitching and caught her gaze. "Oh, come on," I said. "You don't think I had anything to do with Jasmine's death?"

"Of course I don't," she said. "But others might."

"The sheriff asked a few questions, but he didn't lock me up. Sure, that *National Bloodhound* reporter made a few insinuations, but that's what they do, see murder in an unfortunate accident."

Stella sighed. "It's like we're our own wacky reality TV show."

chapter seven

THE NEXT AFTERNOON WAS MY DATE WITH JACK, SO I'D reluctantly agreed to let Sunny watch the shop for the two hours it remained open that day. Jack and I had planned to meet at the parking lot at Clatsop Cliffs for a leisurely walk. August was the rare time of year that wasn't rainy on the Oregon coast, and it would have been a shame to pass such a glorious afternoon indoors.

Thinking of Jasmine and Caitlin's California glamour, I'd carefully combed my wavy hair and even put on some lip stain. Mom had always praised my skin's rosy glow, saying it was the result of good gallbladder function, and Avery liked to call me Snow White for my dark hair and pale skin, but I'd never be a beauty queen.

Jack pulled up in his old Jeep and smiled as he leapt

from the driver's side. "I thought I was on time, but you beat me."

"It's such a nice day, I left a few minutes early."

We both leaned against the hood of my Prius and looked toward the ocean, where waves left ridges of white that flattened as they came closer in to lap the sand below. At the horizon, the sea was a slightly richer blue than the sky.

"Ready to walk?" Jack said.

"Let's go."

Within a few yards of the trailhead, the trail plunged into woods, trees muffling the whooshing surf. Here and there between the wind-stunted pines, the ocean appeared. As the trail climbed the cliffs, it delved more deeply into the trees and the rich scent of dried pine needles and loam surrounded us.

"How're your preparations for the kite contest coming?" Jack asked, a bit too smugly, I thought.

"Fine." After my start on the kite at Stella's, and a few hours more work this morning, I was feeling good about it. "And yours?"

"Great, actually."

And there conversation flagged. Normally, Jack and I talked for hours, running through old television shows, our favorite rides at an amusement park, why we liked cilantro or not—you name it. But we'd never been head-to-head in a contest before.

Jack probably had no idea how important winning the contest was to me. He knew I was competitive, but I'd never talked to him about Strings Attached's finances. His grandfather had bought the building Sullivan's Kites was in long ago, so Jack didn't face the same financial pressure.

He wanted to win the contest, too, no doubt about it. My guess was that it had more to do with his ego than any desire for publicity and sales. He'd always admired how my kites looked, but sometimes he couldn't help pointing out that they weren't built for fast maneuvers. I didn't care. My kites were beautiful and flew just fine. For the contest, I hadn't fooled around with an innovative shape—rather I was counting on its artistic appeal and reliable airmanship to win. I rubbed my fingertips, raw from stitching, against my thumb.

We came to a clearing in the trees. I decided to change the subject. "I heard Jasmine Normand's husband is in town, but I haven't seen him."

"Kyle Connell. He stopped by Dave's shop to rent a kayak while I was there. Said he wanted to be alone for a while. Seems like a nice guy. It can't be easy for him to be here," Jack said.

"No. His wife's hometown, and now a funeral. I wonder if it will be a public ceremony?" More cameras, more reporters like Nicky Byrd, I thought. More ugliness.

"I'm sure they'll do something private. I know I would." Jack seemed lost in his thoughts. Abruptly, conversation took another turn. "Have you seen a stranger around?"

"Besides the reporters?"

"A tall guy, nicely dressed, really tan."

I remembered him. He'd been at the Brew House the afternoon I picked a fight with Jack and Jasmine. Maybe

I wouldn't mention that. "Yes. I have, in fact. You've seen him, too?"

"He stopped by the store yesterday. Took his time looking at my stock, but he didn't buy anything."

"Must be an investor. Or a visitor." In the past few years, the town had changed so much. "Do you know why Marcus Salek is so anti-tourist?"

"No. I guess I figured it was because he was from a family of fishermen." That would make sense. Thanks to stiffer environmental rules and competition from overseas, fewer independent fishermen were able to make a living these days.

We'd come to the top of the trail, just above Devil's Playpen. Some civic group had placed a bench in the clearing years ago, and time had eroded the cliff and weathered the bench's wood until it was a rickety seat only five or six feet from the edge. It was stable enough for two careful adults to sit on, though.

"I love this view," I said, taking a seat. The wind blew hair across my eyes. I brushed it out of the way.

Jack sat next to me, a palm's width away. He leaned back, squinting against the sun, his elbows resting on the bench's back. "There's town." He looked down the beach. "It doesn't look like much from here."

Down the beach, Rock Point was a collection of tiny buildings hugging a bay, with two docks and a strip of toast-colored sand.

"So much drama down there," I said, thinking of Jasmine and the reporters I'd seen the day before. "You'd never know it from up here." I made out a red kite bobbing in the air just off the new docks.

Jack saw the kite, too. "I think that's one of mine. I sold it to a couple of boys this morning. Their mother bought them only one to share."

He'd had to raise his voice. The surf was louder here as it crashed against the jagged boulders of Devil's Playpen. I thought for a moment of the dozens of ships that had met their end on the rocks below before the lighthouse behind us went in.

"Sunny's been coming here almost every day for walks," I said.

"Your sister."

"Yes." Wind tugged at my hair. "I'm surprised you two haven't met yet. You should come by the house."

Jack smiled. I think he actually did want to meet Sunny. It warmed me and set off a warning bell at the same time. "I'd like that," he said.

I jolted my gaze away from Jack's mesmerizing eyes and toward the surf. *Bag That Babe* made dating seem so easy. I wasn't ready to have a serious relationship in my life, not yet. But Jack was getting harder to resist.

"Emmy," Jack said. He placed a hand, warm and firm, over mine on the bench. His lips widened into a lopsided grin.

The alarm in my head rang full-on now. *Abandon ship! Abandon ship!* it screamed. Yet I couldn't pull myself away.

Just then, my phone rang, playing "Strangers in the Night," my tone for an unknown caller. "Let it ring," I said.

Jack's grin faded as the phone continued to ring. Suddenly, I despised that song. Why couldn't I have programmed in something more romantic?

"You'd better answer it," Jack said.

With a mixture of disappointment and relief, I pulled the phone from my bag and glanced at its screen. It was the sheriff.

chapter eight

I SHIVERED IN THE COLD NIGHT. PER SHERIFF KOPPEN'S instructions, I was on the beach again, in the dead of night, staring up at Jasmine's house. The sky was perhaps a bit cloudier, and the wind rustled the beach grass with a bit more vigor, but I was there, in the same spot I'd been three nights earlier. When Jasmine died.

I yawned.

"Is this what you saw?" Sheriff Koppen asked. When he'd called that afternoon, he'd told me he wanted to reconstruct the night Jasmine died. He wouldn't say why. I passed the evening mulling it over. He clearly had some reason to suspect the death wasn't an accident, but he wasn't sure of it himself. Yet, who would want to murder Jasmine Normand? I tried to nap after dinner to prepare myself for the long night, but instead of sleeping,

I made a mess of my bedding by twisting and turning while going over that night in my head.

At last it was three in the morning. Feeling a lot sleepier than I had three nights earlier, I left the house and walked up the beach, just as I had that night. Only, this time, the sheriff was waiting for me below Jasmine's beach house.

"Well, you weren't here," I said in reply to his question.

"I know that. But the house. Is this how everything looked? We need to make sure it's right."

As I'd instructed, the light in an upstairs bedroom had been turned on, and a woman's shadow moved against the filmy curtain. A light also burned in the kitchen, and another figure stood over the sink. I gave it another look.

"Yeah, that seems right." Despite my exhaustion, anxiety thrummed within me. "Why is this so important?"

"Never mind that. What about the kitchen?" The sheriff seemed to be checking the moon, the tide, even feeling the breeze.

I straightened. "The guy inside." Remembering how he'd looked down at me that night, a chill ran through me. "Do you think he saw me?"

"I doubt it." The sheriff talked into his radio, listened, then lowered it again. "Birk says he can't see us at all."

My muscles slackened with relief. Why I should be so relieved, I wasn't sure. "Why are we here?" I asked again.

Sheriff Koppen faced me. His black hair was pulled into a short ponytail that melted into the night. "Look again at the officer in the kitchen. Does he look about the right size?"

The sheriff hadn't answered me. He obviously suspected that something about Jasmine's death wasn't right. I knew I wouldn't get anywhere by badgering him, so I followed his instructions. "That guy's too small."

The sheriff glanced to the house, then back at me. "Are you sure?"

"The guy I saw was bigger. Not fatter, just bigger." I squinted. "At least, I think so."

The sheriff moved closer. "Emmy, I want you to be sure. You're the only eyewitness we have. Are you certain he wasn't about that size? Take your time."

He sure was harping on this one detail. I looked to the kitchen again. The man leaned against what I assumed was the kitchen counter, but after the sheriff said a few words into the radio, the man stood upright again.

"The moon is a little more full, and this is the right time of night—at least, the tide is about where it was when I came the other night." I squinted. "No, he's too small."

He let out a long breath. "Come up."

The sheriff and I walked up the stairs set into the bluff to the deck and wiped the sand off our shoes. The sheriff pulled open the sliding doors.

What a house. Maybe I'd become used to Avery's charming bohemian home—okay, it was slightly rundown, but I wouldn't trade it for anything—but this place was immaculate. A sectional sofa rimmed the room, and a fluffy white rug lay under a glass table. A chair made of leather and chrome tubing sat across from the sofa. My first thought was that the owner didn't have a dog. Or children.

"Is that all, Nick?" the officer in the kitchen asked the sheriff.

"No. Wait a bit."

"Can I come down?" came a voice from upstairs. Caitlin Ruder.

"Yes," the sheriff said.

"Finally." Caitlin, pulling her bathrobe closed, descended the stairs. She halted when she saw me. "Why are you here?"

I glanced at the sheriff before replying. "By chance, I was taking a walk down the beach the night Jasmine died."

Her expression changed subtly, as if she were doing split-second calculations, before it lapsed back into sullenness. "I don't see why you weren't in bed, like a normal person."

"Is that your bedroom upstairs?"

"No," she said.

The sheriff raised an eyebrow. "You said it was."

"I said I was sleeping there. That doesn't mean it's my bedroom."

I remembered Stella's observation that Caitlin had been known for bending the truth on *Bag That Babe*.

Sheriff Koppen placed a hand on his hip. "Answer me clearly. The night Jasmine died, were you sleeping in the upstairs bedroom?"

"Sleeping?"

"It was three in the morning. You've already told me

that as far as you knew, only you and Jasmine were in the house. What else would you be doing?"

Now it was starting to come together. There was an intruder, a man. He wasn't a guest.

Caitlin seemed to lose interest. She dropped onto the sectional sofa, laying an arm along its edge. "Fine. I had the downstairs bedroom. Why shouldn't I move upstairs once Jasmine left? It has the better view."

I stared at her. She had taken her dead friend's bedroom and didn't see anything wrong with it. The sheriff had apparently had enough, too, because he went into the adjoining kitchen and motioned to the man standing near the sink.

"Sir?" the man said.

The sheriff turned to me. "Still think it was a larger man?"

"I'm not sure anymore. I think so, but I could be wrong," I said. All this second-guessing was messing with my memory.

The man raised an eyebrow. "But I'm exactly Marcus's size," he said.

"Marcus Salek?" I said.

"Birk, you can go home now." The sheriff glared at his retreating back.

"You're talking about Marcus Salek," I said.

"It's nothing," he said to me.

"What do you mean, nothing? You were grilling me down on the beach. You thought the man could have been Marcus?"

"What man?" Caitlin said from the living room. I'd forgotten she was there.

The sheriff sighed. "Emmy said she saw a man in the kitchen the night Jasmine died."

"There was no man here," Caitlin said. "Are you implying I'm having an affair with that village weirdo?"

"He's not a weirdo," I couldn't help saying, even though a part of me agreed. "He's passionate. That's all."

The sheriff ignored us. He stared at the sink, then out the window above it, then turned back toward us.

"Why Salek?" I asked.

The sheriff drummed his fingers on the counter. "A neighbor reported seeing his car up the street."

"He could have been checking his crab pots," I said. "A lot of the locals do that at night."

"Hmm," the sheriff said, but he didn't sound convinced. "Jasmine's rental car's tires were slashed, too."

I straightened. "The same night?"

"So what?" Caitlin said. "That kind of stuff happens all the time in L.A. Not a big deal."

He didn't reply.

"Well, what does Marcus say? I assume you asked him," I said.

The sheriff shifted on his feet. "Can't find him. He's not home, and no one's seen him in town."

"Maybe he's on vacation or something. I saw him at the Brew House yesterday—or I guess it would be the day before yesterday now," I said, noting the early hour.

"That's the last anyone's seen of him."

Caitlin fidgeted with her robe's belt. "Anyway, there wasn't anyone here."

I grew uncomfortable. Either Caitlin was lying, or someone had broken in. Or, Caitlin was asleep and didn't know Jasmine had a visitor. The sheriff clearly suspected the visitor was Marcus.

But for the ocean's constant murmur, the house was quiet. All up and down the beach through Rock Point, residents were sleeping. It was even too early for the fishermen to be up. Mrs. Jurgenson, suffering from one of her regular bouts of insomnia, might be watching the shopping channel, or the Bensons might be tending their baby, but otherwise we were possibly the only people awake in town.

Caitlin yawned without covering her mouth and examined a fingernail.

"Jasmine's death wasn't an accident, was it?" I said.

The sheriff had also been lost in thought. He pulled his attention back to me. "I don't know."

Caitlin, again in full yawn, instantly snapped her mouth shut. Her eyes widened. "What do you mean? Just because there was some guy lurking around here? Like I said, this happens in L.A. all the time." The sheriff's silence seemed to be too much for her. "She took too much insulin, right? Maybe she saw creepy Marcus through the window and it freaked her out and she didn't pay attention to her dose."

Caitlin ambled to the refrigerator and pulled out a bottle of expensive French sparkling water and set it on the counter. With one hand still holding the fridge open, she lifted a second small glass bottle from inside the door and without warning tossed it toward the sheriff's chest. He caught it and set it on the table without even looking at it. "There's your culprit," she said. "Isn't that what the medical examiner said?"

I picked it up. It was about the size of a pill bottle and cold in my hand. Its blue label told me it was insulin. My mind whirled back to the night Jasmine died. Had I overestimated the size of the man in the kitchen? Or maybe it hadn't been a man at all. I squeezed my eyes shut, then opened them. Was I missing something?

"So she did die of an insulin overdose?"

"Appears so," the sheriff said.

"Maybe Caitlin's right. Why are you sure it wasn't an accident?" I asked.

I'd never seen the sheriff so out of sorts. Usually he was disconcertingly calm. Something had wormed its way under his skin. He took a step closer. "Jasmine got in touch with me the day before she died," he said. He looked toward the sea, still black, although dawn was close now. "Said she'd been threatened. Said she'd been warned to leave town."

I gasped. No wonder he had his doubts. "Someone threatened her," I repeated. "Did they leave a note?"

"That's what she said, although she didn't show it to me."

"Did you—?"

"Yes," he cut in, "we searched the house and can't find it."

So, Jasmine might have accidentally overdosed. But it also might have been something more serious. Sheriff Koppen clearly didn't like the odds.

"Jasmine wasn't exactly a rocket scientist," Caitlin said all of a sudden. "She'd only known she had to do insulin for about a year."

"What do you mean?"

Caitlin looked at me as if I were firing on too few pistons. "She probably messed up. That's all. Maybe she forgot that she already shot up."

The sheriff rubbed his eyes. I realized that I'd seen him as a sort of superhero whose energy never flagged. He had a family. It was getting on to four in the morning. Naturally, he'd be tired.

"Thanks, Emmy, Caitlin," he said. "Why don't you get to bed? I'll be in touch."

I hesitated to leave. The sheriff clearly wasn't satisfied, but what could I do?

Caitlin had only to go upstairs, but I had a long trek home. He walked me to the back deck. "You want a ride?"

"So it was an obvious overdose," I said, ignoring him. "If Jasmine was murdered, the killer had to know she was diabetic."

Sheriff Koppen nodded. "True."

"He either knew where she kept her insulin, or he brought his own."

"And next you're going to ask if we've checked her garbage and sharps container for a different brand of syringe or insulin."

I nodded. So much for my brilliant deductions.

"We did check, and everything was consistent. The insulin and syringes were the same."

"What about doses? Could you tell if there were more bottles used than there should have been?"

The sheriff glanced toward the upstairs bedroom. The window was closed, but he lowered his voice anyway. "It doesn't work that way. Diabetics don't always take the same dose. It depends on what they've eaten, what their insulin levels are."

"Oh." I turned toward the ocean. Before long, the sun would bleed pink on the eastern sky. The fishermen who still worked the ocean would rise and unlatch their boats in the damp dark, hoping for a thick enough catch to see themselves through winter. I knew how that felt.

"So, would you like a lift home?"

I considered it, but shook my head. "I'll walk. It will do me good."

"You're sure?"

"Yes. Thanks."

"I suppose it's all right." The sheriff's voice trailed off.

I knew what he was thinking. I would be safe. Even if Jasmine's death wasn't an accident, it wasn't random, either. She had been targeted.

I clicked on my flashlight and started down the steps to the beach. The sheriff thought Jasmine had been murdered, but he couldn't prove it. Tonight he'd been looking for something to solidify his theory. He suspected Marcus might have killed her, but he couldn't find him. The thought made my head spin.

Down the stairs I went. With each step I felt that much more removed from reality. On each side of the steps, rocks and grass took over the bluff. I passed my flashlight right and then left. The light flashed on something in the rocks. Something glass. I returned the flashlight to that spot and held it. Something was there. Something shiny.

I looked up to the house. Its lights flickered off, one by one. "Stop!" I yelled.

"What?" the sheriff's voice came from the deck.

I stepped off the stairs toward the glimmering object my flashlight had caught. "I found something." But maybe I hadn't. Maybe it was just a piece of trash the beach house's prior residents had left. In my gut, I knew it wasn't.

In a moment, the sheriff was at my side. "What?"

"That." I pointed toward what my flashlight had caught.

Sheriff Koppen rolled a latex glove over his hand and reached for the object. I was strangely gratified—he'd taken me seriously. He picked up a small bottle. "Insulin," he said.

If it hadn't been dark out, and my flashlight hadn't caught the glass, I never would have seen the bottle. Whoever wanted to get rid of it must have thrown it from the house, thinking it would disappear forever.

He showed me the bottle, and I knew. This one had a gray label. The label on the one in the house was blue.

"Jasmine Normand didn't use this brand."

This was proof. Jasmine Normand had been murdered.

chapter nine

ONCE AGAIN, I WAS TOO WIRED TO SLEEP. THIS TIME IT
wasn't worry over Jack, it was the knowledge that a
murderer was loose in Rock Point. I had to get my kite
finished for the festival, so after a few unproductive
hours in bed, I went to the shop. Stella was an early
riser, so as I stitched slips of fabric to the kite, I kept an
eye on the clock until it was a decent hour to call. Then
I begged Stella to join me.

"It was murder. Jasmine's death, that is. Not an accident at all," I told Stella as soon as she arrived, my
kite set aside.

"Someone killed Jasmine Normand," Stella said,
maybe to make it more real.

I knew how she felt. I'd been telling myself the same
thing all morning. I filled her in on the night's reenactment.

Considering that she'd been practically yanked from bed by my call, Stella had the easy, natural beauty she always did: long gray hair pulled into a chignon, a linen shift chosen for the afternoon's heat with a worn cashmere cardigan to ward off the morning's chill, and a necklace with an abstract silver pendant dangling mid-chest.

"The sheriff seemed to think that Marcus had something to do with it. Remember how I told you I'd seen a man in the house?" I wrinkled my brow.

"Yes?"

"The sheriff had someone stand inside and pretend to be him. He specifically chose someone about Marcus's size."

"Do you mind if I make some tea?" Stella rose to help herself. She'd worked at Strings Attached off and on over the summer, and was as at home in the workshop as I was.

"Please do."

"I wonder where the sherriff got the idea that Marcus would hurt anyone. I admit he can be abrasive, but he's not violent."

"He sounds violent, though. You should have heard him at the Brew House." I sighed and pulled over the kite's limp body. It wasn't going to sew itself. "Do you have any idea why he's so hell-bent against tourists coming to Rock Point?"

"I don't know much about him, really. I know he grew up here. His family were fishermen. He married and moved away for several years. When he returned, he was alone and had enough money not to need to work."

"His anger is too intense, though. More than if he'd simply objected to traffic and a fudge shop on Main Street," I said.

"Yes." Stella fidgeted with her pendant. "But you told the sheriff it couldn't have been Marcus."

Down went the kite again. "I did. I think he might suspect me."

Stella sat across from me. "What are you talking about? You mean because you and Jasmine had it out at the Brew House?"

"And because I was on the beach that night."

"But you told him you were on the beach. If you were a murderer, you wouldn't be blabbing about hanging around the murder scene in the middle of the night." The kettle whistled, and Stella rose to turn off the stove.

"Unless I was a crafty murderer. Think about it. Say I had killed Jasmine. If I were really smart, I'd tell the sheriff that I was there that night because I couldn't sleep. That way, if someone saw me, I'm in the clear. Plus, I could tell him I saw someone else at the beach house, like a man standing in the kitchen window, and throw the suspicion away from me."

"I see what you mean," Stella said.

Reluctantly, I pulled the kite back over and picked up a needle. "Of course, presumably I wouldn't have been stupid enough to tell him that the double for Marcus he posted inside wasn't the man I saw." I let that sink in a moment. "And then there's the reporter from the *National Bloodhound*."

"The what?"

"A reporter from the *National Bloodhound* cornered me at the Brew House the day before yesterday. He asked Sheriff Koppen about me, too."

"No one knew Jasmine's death was murder until this morning, though," Stella pointed out. "So the reporter couldn't suspect you."

"He made insinuations."

"He was just trying to stir up trouble. Anyway, he's probably left town by now with the rest of them."

That may have been true. I hadn't seen him, and the sheriff hadn't mentioned him last night. "I hope you're right."

Stella lifted the tea ball from the pot and poured herself a mug of tea. "Listen. Are you positive you saw a man at the beach house?"

"Yes." I bit my lip. "Or maybe not. Now I'm not sure. I would have sworn that I did, until last night."

"It was dark," Stella offered.

I nodded.

"You were tired."

"Exhausted," I agreed. "Worried, too."

Worried about Sunny. She was probably up by now, hopefully taking Bear on a walk at the cliffs. She needed to get her act together.

"Then again, if you did see someone, that person might be the murderer."

"True." This was not a new path of inquiry for me.

"Are you sure it was a man?" Stella asked. "Could it have been a woman, maybe?"

"Possibly. The sheriff and I already covered this ground."

"And the light was on in the upstairs bedroom?"

"Yes. Caitlin's moved up there now, but it had been Jasmine's bedroom. At least, that's what she said."

Stella stared at me. "You aren't helping. You don't seem sure about anything."

Once again, I pushed the kite aside. At this rate, it would never get done. "When it was just an accident, things seemed clearer. Now that it's murder, well, more is at stake." I dropped my arms from the table and leaned back. "People really think I'd kill someone to win a kite contest?"

Winning the contest was a big deal to me, it was true. The future of Strings Attached depended on my winter sales. But I couldn't very well operate a kite shop from the state pen.

Stella rose, and the schoolteacher in her came out full force. "What we need is a plan. We need to know more about Jasmine's life. Her friendship with Caitlin, her marriage, her relationship with her sister."

I watched in admiration. I wished I had a blackboard for her to write on.

Stella poked a finger into the air. "We also need to know what Marcus has been up to. Sheriff Koppen is no dummy. If he had reason to suspect Marcus, then something was going on."

"Do you really think we'll learn anything that the sheriff can't figure out?"

"You found that insulin vial, right? If it wasn't for

you, Jasmine's death might have ended up ruled an accident. The sheriff is not infallible."

I worried at a piece of fabric. "Say we do poke around a bit. How are we going to find anything out?"

She folded her arms over her chest. "We start at information central. The post office."

chapter ten

I WALKED INTO THE POST OFFICE WITH MORE CONFIDENCE than I felt. The lobby of Rock Point's post office was no bigger than a small bedroom. Once a customer walked in the door, he or she faced a narrow counter. Post office boxes—maybe fifty of them—were stacked to the right, positioned so that the postmistress could fill their contents from her throne behind the counter.

And it *was* a throne. Jeanette was the queen. She looked at me with narrowed eyes.

"May I help you?" she said.

"Jeanette." I put on my most cheerful voice. "How are you? I bet you get thirsty back there. Maybe I can bring you a coffee?"

I could tell from the look on her face that Jeanette wasn't having any of it. This was not going to be easy. Everyone knew that Jeanette had her finger on Rock

Point's pulse. You couldn't get a package from your pharmacy or a letter from your grandmother without Jeanette silently noting it. If you were behind on your electric bill or a subscriber to *Cat Fancy*, she knew. If you ordered piano music or wore a size 12 wide shoe, she knew that, too. And she remembered. Honestly, why the CIA didn't hire her right away, I had no idea.

"I find I'm amply lubricated, thank you. Perhaps you'd like a book of stamps?"

"Ha-ha-ha," I choked out. "Sure. Stamps would be great."

She shot me a calculating look and said, "What type of stamps? We have flowers, flags, and"—she raised an eyebrow with meaning—"movie stars."

"Movie stars would be great." I cast her what I hoped was a significant glance and angled my way to the counter. "Such a shame about Jasmine Normand."

"Indeed." She made a show of sorting through a few pages of stamps.

"Her untimely death. So young. So beautiful." Okay, I was putting it on. I watched Jeanette's expression. Would she take the bait?

"Tsk tsk. Such a shame," she repeated.

This wasn't working. It was time to throw something in the kitty. "Have you seen my sister around? I don't know what I'll do about her."

Jeanette stopped sorting the stamps for a split second, then pulled a sheet of Katharine Hepburn stamps from the stack. "You don't say?"

"She ran off from college and insisted on coming to live with me while she figures herself out. Of course, it's all top secret. No one can know. If our parents found out, we'd be toast."

We locked gazes. I had her interest, but barely. Sunny wasn't going to provide the currency I needed.

"Hmm," she said. "Have you seen this?" She lifted a copy of the *National Bloodhound*. I reached for it, but she drew it back.

I kept my eyes on the *Bloodhound*. "If only my sister had some of the drive Jasmine did," I said. "That would make all the difference." Naturally, I wouldn't trade Sunny for Jasmine even if Jasmine came with one-hundred-dollar bills taped to her.

"Ten fifty for the stamps," Jeanette said.

"Is there something in the *National Bloodhound* I should see?"

"I don't know what you're talking about. Now, do you want the stamps, or not?"

Okay. She knew something, but wasn't ready to give it up. Fine. "The sheriff is very concerned about her accident." I kept my eyes trained on Jeanette's. "Very concerned. He told me." I drew out a sigh. "I shouldn't say anything more."

Now I was getting somewhere. Jeanette turned to face me full-on. She lowered her voice. "Just the day before yesterday—the afternoon Jasmine Normand died—she sent a fat packet. Nearly eight ounces. Overnighted. You know how much that costs?" She looked both ways, although we were alone in the post office. "She sent it to Los Angeles. It might have been to a movie producer."

A movie producer. So, Jasmine was up for a role

somewhere. But what did that have to do with her death?

"I supposed she wouldn't be getting mail here," I said.

"No. Rose gets all Jasmine's mail. Mostly bills."

"Bills?" Why would Jasmine have her bills sent to Rock Point? Surely she had a whole team in Los Angeles to deal with things like that.

"I think I know what a bill looks like after all these years." Jeanette waited expectantly for a juicy tidbit in return for hers.

"I think"—I leaned closer—"Sheriff Koppen suspects it wasn't an accident at all. It was murder."

Jeanette swallowed a cry and drew back. "Murder?"

Shoot. I'd dropped my payload too soon. I could have collected more. Rookie move. I tried again. "How is Marcus Salek these days? Anything new with him?"

"Marcus? What? Oh, he got a package from a tool company, but—murder? Really?" Her face had blanched, and she didn't seem to be able to keep up with her breath.

"Are you all right?" I asked.

"I just—I just need to sit down. Someone killed her?" she repeated.

"I don't know if I'd go that far." I'd overdone it. "Maybe he was just concerned because she's so young and all."

"Wait." She sat up straight. "How do you know this?"

"Well . . ."

Jeanette's gaze pinned me like steel shanks.

"Well," I tried again, "when we did the reenactment—"

"Sheriff Koppen wanted a reenactment?"

This was getting out of control. I backed away toward the door. "Come to think of it, I have plenty of stamps."

"But why were you part of a reenactment?" she said.

She waved the *National Bloodhound*. "Take this. Come back. Did I tell you about the Wilson twins?"

I grabbed the tabloid and made for the door. Safely down the street, I leaned against the ice cream shop and opened it. Jeanette had thoughtfully folded down a corner, presumably to add more stock to her coffers of gossip. "A Byrd Told Me," the column read. I squinted at the photo of the columnist. It looked more like Cary Grant than the Nicky Byrd I remembered. I took a deep breath and read.

Dreamy reality star Jasmine Normand's premature demise has whipped an ill wind through the coastal town of Rock Point, Oregon, her hometown, where the hunk-bait was visiting to judge a kite contest. A snitch reports that the day the starlet died, a local kite shop owner pitched a hissy fit when the pretty prize made a play for her boyfriend. Could Jasmine Normand's death be more than an accident?

AS I FLIPPED STRINGS ATTACHED'S SIGN TO "OPEN" AND flipped on the lights, I let the column from the *Bloodhound* sink in. I'd been called out as a possible murderer in mini-mart newsstands across the nation. *Whoa.* This was not in my business plan.

I ruminated over what I'd learned from the postmistress. Jasmine had mailed a package to Los Angeles, then was murdered that night. Maybe something in that package pointed to a motive.

Or maybe the man I'd seen had simply been a burglar.

Every once in a while a rash of burglaries hit the vacation homes now just starting to be built north of town. But what burglar keeps a vial of insulin in his pocket?

I was pondering these thoughts when the front door's bell dinged to announce a customer. I put on my best customer face, then let it droop when I saw Sunny. "It's you," I said.

"I'm thrilled to see you, too." The wind off the ocean had pinkened Sunny's cheeks, and her dreadlocks were pulled back and tied with a scarf. Bear burst in behind her and did his usual trot around the store, sniffing the corners to see if there was anything new. He disappeared into the workshop, and I heard him lapping from the water dish I kept filled for him.

"Been out on the cliffs again?" I asked. Sunny wasn't acting like she'd heard about that awful tabloid article, and I didn't want to tell her.

"Yep. I love it there. I can really think. It's like Mother Nature whispers in my ears."

Bear emerged from the workshop and nuzzled my hand. I gave him a thorough scratching between his ears and under his chin. Man, how I loved that dog. Even if all of Rock Point turned against me thanks to the *National Bloodhound*, at least I'd have Bear.

"Want some coffee?" I asked Sunny. I'd brought coffee beans in from home after Sunny's complaint that first day, and now I was glad for it. "I was just going to make a pot. I'm still worn out from last night."

"Let me do it," Sunny said and pushed behind me to the workshop. "What's this?" She picked up my copy of the *Bloodhound* and flipped to the turned-down page.

"Don't read that." I tried to snatch the tabloid away, but was too late.

"It's talking about you, Emmy." Openmouthed, she stared at me.

As she set down the tabloid, the shop's front door chimed. The slender, dark man I'd seen earlier in the week at the Brew House stood just inside. Most of Rock Point's visitors were families from up and down the coast or those who had driven the few hours over from Portland. They were generally well-fed, smiling, and clothed in sportswear. I counted on them for sales of simple sports kites and diamond kites or maybe a more whimsical kite with a flower pattern or woven tail. With these customers, I had the satisfaction of seeing children break into wide grins and jump around in place as they anticipated the fun they were going to have down at the beach.

I'd just recently started attracting kite aficionados who searched out one-of-a-kind, handmade kites. Kite enthusiasts of that sort often had a more bohemian look about them, sporting interesting jewelry and handmade-looking clothing. I could also spot them by the way they touched a kite's edge and hefted it for its featherweight feel. I looked forward to these customers. We could talk kites all day—artistic subtleties, kites they'd known, the entries at the international kite festival in Cervia, Italy.

This customer was neither type. Nor did he look like a member of the media. He simply came off as expensive and vaguely international, as if he'd spent his years tanning, buying knife-pleated linen trousers, and sampling high-end rum.

"May I help you?" I asked.

"Yes. I understand you make kites, not just sell them."

I detected a hint of an accent in his voice, but I couldn't make out where it was from. "I do. What sort of kite are you interested in?"

I was making my way to my premier kites, hung above the dangerous toddler level, when I heard a crash come from the kitchen. The customer and I turned toward the door.

"Sorry," Sunny said from beyond the door. "Nothing serious. I'll clean it up."

My competition kite was back there. Sunny knew I'd flay her alive if she touched it, but all the same it made me nervous.

I turned back toward my kites and pulled one down I'd patterned after photos of Monet's garden. The kite had a basic diamond design, but I'd loosened its edges and deepened its center to boost its flight-worthiness, then adorned the border with rose-petal-shaped snippets of chiffon-weight nylon. The kite's center showcased a handful of bright yellow daffodils surrounded by the ridged petals of mauve poppies. It had been a challenge to keep the weight from holding the kite down, but the prototype's test flight on the beach had drawn lots of *ooh*s and *ahh*s.

"I'm interested in all sorts of kites. May I?" The customer reached out long brown fingers to touch a petal.

I handed him the kite. "I call this one 'Oregon Giverny.'"

The man's gaze darted through the shop, even as he appeared to be absorbed in the kite. What did he really want? He surely wasn't thinking about flying kites on the beach. Not in those polished leather loafers. He flipped the price tag and didn't even flinch. A good sign. The kite had taken me hours to sew and was priced accordingly.

Another crash came from the workshop, this time accompanied by Bear's howling, interspersed with quick yips. I whipped my head toward the workshop door.

The customer must have heard me gasp. "Perhaps I will return later. You are busy at the moment."

Shoot. "Don't go," I said. At the same time, all hell was breaking loose at the back of the house.

The customer already had a hand on the doorknob. "Until later, then."

As he left, the door to the kitchen opened slowly. At least the barking and crashing had stopped. Still, from the look on Sunny's face, I dreaded what she was going to say.

She said nothing. Instead, she raised a hand above the counter. In it were the shreds of my competition kite.

chapter eleven

"I DIDN'T MEAN IT," SUNNY MOANED. "I JUST WANTED TO look, and—"

I snatched the nylon ribbons from her hand. Destroyed. There was no salvaging this kite. My blood began to boil. "Do you know how long it took me to put this kite together? There's only a week until the festival."

"I was just looking at it, then the kettle whistled, and I guess I must have dropped the kite, but it got stuck on the bench, then—"

"Hush!" I couldn't hear any more of this. My hands were already cramped up from hand-stitching the panes on the now-wrecked kite. The thought of another eight hours cutting the pieces and laying them out, then days stitching them together, oh-so-carefully cutting away the backs . . . I couldn't bear it.

The dog seemed to notice my distress and leaned against my leg.

"Maybe I could watch the shop for a while, and you can start on your new kite. Which I'll never ever touch. Ever," Sunny said in a small voice.

I silently counted to ten before speaking. "Okay. I know you can't help it. You take care of customers. I'm going for a walk." It was either that, or push Sunny into oncoming traffic. "Come on, Bear."

We paused on the sidewalk below the shop. A cool breeze blew off the ocean. I thought of my kite and groaned. I had to walk off some of this frustration. I could head up to the cliffs and look at Devil's Playpen, but remembering sitting there with Jack the day before, I felt self-conscious and decided against it. Jack's kite was probably finished and waiting safely in a closet somewhere.

Rock Point was built on a narrow shelf. To the west lay the Pacific Ocean, sometimes soothing and sometimes thundering with surf. To the east, a gentle hill rose to the graceful Victorian homes of Old Town. Just above the hill, into the woods, wound Highway 101. I decided to head up. It would do me good to work up a lather. Only when I was calm would I face Sunny again.

Bear paused at my feet, waiting to see what direction I took, then trotted a few steps ahead as we walked up to Rock Point's main drag.

"Look at the doggie!" A grade-school-aged boy pointed an ice-cream-stained finger at Bear, who, with a dignified look, ignored him. This summer had brought more tourists than I ever remembered from our family vacations in Rock Point over the years.

"That's nice. Come on, Dylan."

We dodged another family with a caravan of strollers and waited to cross the street. A teenaged couple waited next to us.

"Where did Jasmine Normand die?" the girl asked.

"Don't know," her boyfriend said.

"Let's go," I said to Bear. I was starting to feel a touch of Marcus's resentment for tourists.

Marcus. If I remembered right, he lived in one of the older, smaller homes just south of Old Town. Maybe Sheriff Koppen had been in touch with him by now. With a shudder, I thought about Jasmine's slashed tires, and the threat she'd reported.

I led Bear a few blocks past Main Street, then turned right. After a quarter hour's walk, leaving the tourists far behind, we were on a quiet street with a gravel shoulder. It was strange how most towns, no matter how touristy, held pockets that the outside world never touched. I bet even Paris had neighborhoods the Eiffel Tower keychain sellers called home, neighborhoods that didn't show up on the tourist maps. These few blocks of modest homes were Rock Point's.

Marcus's truck was parked in the driveway of a mint green house with a tangle of pink roses beside the door. I paused in front of the house. Mail stuffed the box by the front door. The living room curtains were pulled nearly shut, but the flicker of a television showed between them. I crept closer and peered inside. No one sat in the recliner facing it. I glanced behind me, then flipped through the mail. I could tell from the advertising circulars that there were at least two days of mail here. Jeanette would have a fit and start citing federal code if she knew what I was up to.

The street was calm. It was too far away, even, for the ocean's muffled roar, a sound that had become a constant in my life. Each of the little houses was closed up, its owner at work. The homes were too small and run-down to draw out-of-towners to spend the night—yet. Drawing a deep breath, I rapped on the door. No one responded.

I had turned toward the street when a thought occurred to me. Marcus's truck was in the driveway, and his TV was on. But no one was home. What if—I swallowed hard—What if Marcus was inside, but not able to answer the door? Maybe he had been at Jasmine's that night. Maybe he'd seen something he shouldn't have, and—my heart skipped a beat—the murderer followed him home.

Back up the driveway I went and, fear be damned, I knocked on the front door. No response. I called Bear and circled the house to the back door, where an overgrown lawn edged a cement patio, bare except for a rusted grill. I knocked again, and, again, no response.

It was so quiet here, so eerily quiet. If Marcus were inside, maybe—I forced myself to think the word—maybe dead, I needed to know. Grasping the doorknob through the bottom of my T-shirt, I tried the handle. It turned.

My breath came in short puffs. I stopped and drew a long breath and, for focus, held it five counts before releasing it, as Mom had taught me to do after her meditation retreat a few years ago. Then I went inside.

The back door led into Marcus's kitchen. Its counters were clear, and an empty coffee cup and cereal bowl sat in the sink, attracting ants. The TV droned from the other room. Taking steady, even steps, I forced myself to round the corner to the living room. "Marcus?" I said.

No one responded. His empty recliner faced the television, a coffee table next to it. On top of the television was a framed photo of a younger Marcus in a tuxedo with his arm around a smiling, freckled bride. Judging from the style of the bride's dress, the photo was only ten years old or so. Marcus was probably in his midforties now—younger than I'd assumed by his looks. I glanced through the crack in the living room's curtains. The street was still empty.

As I turned back toward the room, a flash of movement caught the corner of my eye, and I backed into the wall. Pulse throbbing, I waited. The house was completely still, completely quiet. A minute passed, then two. It had been nothing. Just nervousness.

I forced myself to pass through the living room to a small hall with three doors off it, each door ajar. To the right, at the front of the house, was a guest room with a tidily made bed and little else.

The middle door had to be the bathroom. I pushed it open. Nothing here but the usual. The mug that would have held toothbrushes was empty.

The last door must be Marcus's bedroom. Bear had gone before me and nosed the door open. Here, too, the bed was made with military precision. Again using my T-shirt to cover my hand, I pulled open a few dresser drawers and saw a gap where underwear and socks might have been. In another drawer, next to a partially full box of bullets, was a black box meant to hold a handgun. I raised its lid. Empty. I closed the drawer and caught my breath.

Marcus had left town. He didn't want anyone to know it. And he was armed.

Just then, I heard gravel crunch outside, as if a car were slowly driving up the street, close enough to be on the shoulder. "Bear," I whispered and drew him to me. He seemed to sense my hammering heart and rested his head against my chest. "Good boy."

The car crawled by. After a moment, when its engine's low murmur had disappeared, I crept to the front window and, staying well to the side, glanced out to catch the back of the sheriff's car. He was clearly on the lookout for Marcus. He wasn't going to find him here.

chapter twelve

"WHAT'S WRONG?" AVERY STEPPED ONTO THE PORCH from the kitchen. She'd lost the round of rock, paper, scissors and had just finished the dinner dishes. "Are you worried about the kite contest?"

Sunny and I were watching the sunset. I had a pile of multicolored nylon in my lap. My fingers were cramping from basting the pieces together. I had to admit, though, that this time—attempt number three—the kite's construction was going faster, and I'd improved the design to bring more light to its edges.

"Yes," I said. I didn't see any reason to go into it more than that. Both Avery and Sunny knew the score.

"I'm sorry," Sunny said again. She turned her giant brown eyes toward me, just as she'd been doing since she was a toddler and had laid my Barbie under Dad's VW Bus's tires. I think my parents were actually happy about that, since they didn't approve of Barbies, but I was inconsolable. This time, as then, Sunny truly was upset.

"You couldn't help it," I mumbled.

"Maybe I could visit Sullivan's Kites and spy on Jack's kite for you. You know, make sure yours is better."

Or maybe you could just "accidentally" destroy it, I thought. "That's okay. Like I said, you couldn't help it. This kite will be even better than the last one."

Avery watched us. "Is it strange to compete against Jack? I mean, both of you can't win."

"Nope," I said quickly. Of course it was strange, but it helped that our styles were so different. Thanks to his engineering background, he built aerodynamic kites that swooped and darted and steadily climbed. But my kites were beautiful. People saw Jack's kites in flight and gasped. When they saw mine, they relaxed and smiled. I'd be thrilled for Jack if he won, but that wasn't going to happen as long as I could help it.

"If you're worried about money, maybe I can help," Sunny said.

"How?" I asked, grateful for the change in the conversation's direction. "You don't even have a job."

At Sunny's look of anguish, I felt awful. She'd had her own challenges lately. It couldn't have been easy for her to gather the courage to quit college and run off. My mother's idea of her beloved "rebel" daughter focused on her dreadlocks, self-designed major, and involvement in the campus Endangered Species League. It took courage for Sunny to reject that.

"I'm sorry. I'm cranky and taking it out on you." I reached out to affectionately tug one of her dreadlocks.

She pulled away and smiled. "Like I was telling you," Sunny said, "you should buy the building Strings Attached is in. With the tourist economy here picking up, land values are only going to rise. You could rent out the upstairs as a vacation apartment, if you wanted. I bet the view is great. Or, you could even live there." Sunny pulled out her phone and switched to the calculator app. "How much is the shop's rent?"

"Sunny." My heart warmed at the earnestness in her voice. "You're so sweet. Don't worry about me. Let's think about you."

"Yeah, it's great having you here," Avery added. "But you probably don't want to stay forever."

Bear responded to the warmth in Avery's voice by jumping into the wicker chair next to her and cramming his body along hers. Meanwhile, the horizon was tossing off another of its jaw-dropping shows as tangerine light spilled above the darkening blue ocean. Avery lit a candle on the little coffee table between us.

"Have you thought at all about what you want to do?" I said. "So fermentation isn't for you. It's not too late to find another major. Mom and Dad would spring for an extra year."

Sunny stared at the ocean a moment. "I don't want to go back to that college. I think . . ."

Avery and I traded glances. "Think what?" Avery prodded gently.

Sunny shifted in her seat. "Well, today I was out on

the cliffs, and I got a sign." She turned to look at me, then Avery. "Of what I should do with my life."

Uh-oh. "What kind of sign?"

"I know this is going to sound crazy—"

"What kind of sign?" I repeated with a little more urgency.

"I saw '401k' written in rocks."

"What?" Avery and I said simultaneously. Bear jumped down from Avery's chair and curled up on his bed.

"Maybe it wasn't super clear like that, but the '0' and the '1' were easy to see." Excitement had crept into her voice. "The '1' was a stick," she added.

"401k? What does the universe want you to do? Retire?" I said.

"Study finance, right?" Avery asked. When Sunny smiled, Avery added, "Sunny found my insurance file yesterday and had a few recommendations for cutting costs and changing up my coverage."

"A higher deductible would save you quite a bit in the long run," Sunny said. "Maybe *you'd* be interested in buying Emmy's building."

"I've got enough to shore up around this house," Avery said. Her family's house was sturdy and long on charm, but any house in the Pacific Northwest's climate was perpetually in need of new windowsills or repointed masonry. I knew Avery was saving up to have the creaky porch rebuilt.

"Finance, huh? Mom and Dad will crucify you." My father was a retired environmental attorney, and Mom spent her time mixing herbal remedies for members of her croning circle. There was a hundred-to-one chance that Mom knew more things to do with quinoa than the entire staff of the Food Network.

"I know." Sunny's lower lip trembled. "I can't help it if I'm good with numbers. I just happen to have a knack for it. And it's fun. It doesn't mean I have to be a slumlord or hide money in the Seychelles or anything."

"Does Evergreen College have business classes so you can get a taste of it?" Avery, ever practical, asked.

Sunny raised her eyebrows in a "what do you think?" expression. Evergreen was known for its progressive approach to education. Its Latin motto translated to "Let It All Hang Out."

"Oh," Avery said.

"Avery has a good point," I said. "If you could get some firsthand experience with finance, you could see if you truly do like it, or if you're just handy with numbers." I sat straighter. "Rose."

"What do flowers have to do with anything?"

"No, Rose Normand," I said. "She's my CPA, and she knows about planning for retirement and that kind of thing. I bet she'd do an informational interview with you. She's not a big-time banker or anything—"

"I don't want to work for some giant corporation." She wrinkled her nose. "Cubicles. Ugh."

"Rose has her own business. Her office is in her garage."

"Really?" Sunny's tone was cautious, but I could tell she was interested.

"She's doing my taxes and giving me some financial direction for the shop. She works with a lot of the businesses in town."

Now Sunny faced me full-on. "Do you really think she'd talk to me?"

I hadn't seen her so excited since she'd come to Rock Point. At last, I was fulfilling my big sister role and helping her out. Even if Mom and Dad still didn't know.

"I'll tell you what. I'll ask first thing tomorrow morning, before I open Strings Attached."

"I'll work at the shop for you, if you want," Sunny said. She was practically bouncing in her seat.

By now, stars were beginning to salt the night sky. I pulled a blanket over my lap. No matter how warm the day might be, nights were chilly here.

If Sunny took over Strings Attached tomorrow, I could not only visit Rose, but put in a few hours on my competition kite, too. Plus, maybe drop in on Darlene and see if she knew anything about Marcus.

"Thanks, Sunny. I'll take you up on that." I yawned. It had been a very long day. And who knew what tomorrow held?

chapter thirteen

THE NEXT MORNING, AS PROMISED, I SET OFF TO SEE Rose. Not only did I plan to ask her if she'd talk to Sunny about financial planning, I wanted to offer my condolences about Jasmine. I hadn't seen Rose since her sister's death. And now the situation had become more gruesome with the death being a murder. Avery had given me a bag of pastries from the Brew House to take along.

As I'd expected, Rose was in her office behind her house. She didn't seem like the type to shut herself in the house and mope. She'd power through her grief by immersing herself in work.

I leaned my bicycle against the old garage's wall, ruffling loose a handful of rose petals in the process. Through the door's window, I saw Rose flipping through a stack of papers. I knocked.

Rose lifted her head. She didn't smile, but her expression did soften when she saw me. "Come in. Why don't you leave the door open? It's going to be another warm day."

"Rose, I was so sorry to hear about Jasmine. You must feel awful. I brought you these." I set the pastries on her desk.

She peeked inside the bag but didn't take one. "That's so thoughtful, thank you." She pushed the bag away. "I suppose you heard it was murder?"

My heart throbbed in sympathy. "Awful."

"I still can't believe it." She shook her head. "Murder." She whispered the word. "It must have been some crazy fan, and that's what I told the sheriff. I'd wanted Jasmine to stay with me—I have plenty of room—but she insisted on renting the beach house."

"I guess she wanted her own space." It was an odd choice. Rose wouldn't see her sister that often, and her two-story house looked to hold at least three bedrooms.

"Jasmine said Caitlin didn't want to stay here." The scorn on Rose's face was impossible to miss. "And, of course, Jasmine liked her modern conveniences."

"Sounds complicated."

"Everything with Jasmine was complicated." She cast a glance toward the stack of papers. "I took care of her finances, and, well . . ."

I wasn't sure how to respond to this. Jeanette at the post office had said Jasmine was on the receiving end of a number of bills. Did she have money trouble? If Jasmine wasn't flush with cash, it would remove greed as a motive for her murder. Unless she had an insurance policy that paid out.

"I hope you don't blame yourself for her death just because she didn't stay with you," I said. "If someone was determined to kill her, they would have done it even if she were here with you."

Rose let out a long breath. "I know. I was in Portland that night, anyway. I've been going over that night again and again, wondering if there was anything I could have done . . ." She stared through the open door a moment, then drew her attention back to me. "I suppose you brought your tax documents?"

"No, actually, I came to ask a favor." I wondered if it was too soon. Perhaps I shouldn't have suggested this to Sunny.

"What can I do for you?" Rose's energy was a little lower than normal, but she was calm. Maybe a distraction was the best balm for her grief.

"It's about my sister, Sunny. She's interested in finance—personal finance, especially—and I wondered if she could talk with you a bit."

"Sunny, the girl with the dreadlocks? Finance?"

"I was surprised, too. She's taking time off from college to figure out what she really wants to do, and right now it's business."

"She could have chosen a worse path. She'll always have work if she can keep books."

"She seems to have a good brain for this sort of thing, too. She already has a scheme for me to buy the building Strings Attached is in."

"Not a bad idea." Her voice gathered strength. This sounded more like the Rose I knew. "You could take the deduction for the shop, then rent out the upstairs as a bed-and-breakfast."

"Sunny suggested that Avery and I live up there and rent out Avery's house."

"Even better. The Cook house would earn you a nice income, at least in the summer." Rose nodded. "Yes. Tell Sunny I'd love to talk with her. Have her drop by tomorrow morning. I'll be here sorting out my sister's estate."

The thought of Rose working alone to untangle her murdered sister's finances was almost unbearably sad. Whatever happened in my life, I had Sunny and Avery, at least. "Maybe Sunny can help."

Rose sighed. "I doubt it. Not this mess."

"An entertainer's estate probably has lots of complications. Movie contracts, that sort of thing," I said, remembering my conversation with Jeanette the day before.

A movement in my peripheral vision startled me. A tall man with broad shoulders filled the doorway. He was lean, but all muscle. If it weren't for his blue jeans and T-shirt, he might have materialized from an ancient Roman gladiator fight. "Jasmine just signed a movie contract, in fact," he said.

"Oh." The word came out of my mouth as a whoosh without sound behind it. "I'm sorry. I didn't know you were there."

"Emmy, have you met Jasmine's husband, Kyle?" Rose said. "Kyle, this is Emmy Adler. She owns a kite shop in town. I do her taxes."

"Kyle Connell. Pleased to meet you."

His hand dwarfed mine. Jack had mentioned he'd been a pro football player, and it showed in his physique. He had something else, too—charisma. With his hand over mine, he looked into my eyes, and I, with my messy hair and haphazard wardrobe, actually felt like the freaking *Venus de Milo*.

"Pleased to meet you, too," I squeaked. "Sorry for your loss."

He released my hand and stood upright again. "There was only one Jasmine."

Rose's glance darted from me to Kyle, and I caught a flash of a grimace. She'd likely become immune to Kyle's charm a while back, not that she seemed the type to succumb to it in the first place.

"I hope Rock Point is treating you well," I said. I'd found my voice again. "Where are you staying?"

"Here, with me," Rose said.

"Through the funeral. I couldn't stay at the beach house," he said. He clearly was more sensitive about it than Caitlin was.

"No. Of course not." An uncomfortable moment of silence passed between me, the movie star's husband, and the accountant. "Will you be here for the kite festival?"

"That's Saturday, right?" he asked. His gaze was icy blue. Jack had said Kyle would probably end up a sportscaster since an injury kept him out of football. If his patter was as good as his looks, he had a long career ahead of him.

"Yes. The parade's in the morning. My friend Stella's

1967 Corvette will be in it." Now I was blabbering. I was beginning to understand Jack's momentary infatuation with Jasmine. "The kite contest is right after that."

"If all goes as scheduled, the funeral home will be ready for us by then," Rose said. "We're going to have a private ceremony."

"Of course. And again, I'm so, so sorry." When neither Kyle nor Jasmine replied, I added, "I guess I'd better be moving on. Thank you, Rose, for agreeing to talk to Sunny."

"I'm looking forward to it."

"And, both of you, let me know if there's anything I can do to help. You must have a lot to deal with now." I moved toward the door and had to pass through Kyle's charisma zone to leave. I nearly swooned.

I pulled my bicycle away from the wall and walked it down the driveway. Man, that Kyle was something. Was that how Clark Gable bewitched the moviegoers of the 1940s? I couldn't help stealing a backward glance.

There he was, tall and broad-shouldered, leaning against the doorjamb and talking to Rose.

I shivered.

Tall. Broad-shouldered. Just like the man I'd seen the night Jasmine was killed.

AS I WALKED DOWN THE HILL TOWARD ROCK POINT'S center and Strings Attached, I drew my mind back to the night Jasmine was murdered. Could it have possibly been Kyle in the beach house? Each time I formed the picture in my brain, it seemed to get murkier. They always say that the victim's partner is the surest suspect in a murder case. But why would he kill Jasmine? Well, it wouldn't hurt to drop in on the sheriff and let him know.

On Main Street, tourists continued to trawl through the shops, candied apples or ice cream in hand. I passed Martino's Pizza and opened the unassuming door to the sheriff's office.

"Can I help you?" Deputy Goff said.

Shoot. Not her. "Is the sheriff in?"

"Why?" She sounded about as happy to see me as I was to see her.

The door pushed open behind me. A woman decked out in shades of pink came in, a somberly dressed man trailing her. She lifted a pair of pink sunglasses up to her head. "I lost my dog."

"Look, is Sheriff Koppen here or not?" I asked.

The tourist muscled me away from the counter. "He's a parti poodle, white. He has tags, but he slipped right out of his collar."

"Just a moment, miss," Deputy Goff said. "No, Emmy, Nick is out. You can tell me anything you'd tell him."

"Never mind," I said.

The second I moved away from the counter, the woman seemed to expand to its width. She waved her arms and spouted the dog's description, from his frosted pink toenails to his brown eyes. The man stood stolidly at the back wall, hands behind his back like a general store Indian statue.

I left. Just outside the sheriff's office, a small white

poodle sat, waiting patiently and watching people walk
by. Through the glass door, I motioned to the man and
pointed to the dog. He nodded once. I heard the door
open behind me as I continued down Main Street.

I really needed to get back to Strings Attached to
work on my kite—and see if Sunny had burnt the place
down—but the chamber of commerce was just across
the street. If Darlene was in, she might be able to tell
me something about Marcus. Right now, he was the
sheriff's number one suspect. Both Marcus and Darlene
had been born and raised here. I needed to know more
about Marcus's background. Maybe it would provide a
clue to where he was now.

Rock Point's chamber of commerce was too small to
have its own storefront. Peggy, the owner of Old Timey
Antiques, let Darlene use the old storage room at the
back as an office, which doubled as the headquarters
for Darlene's real estate business. I waved at Peggy and
made my way past a rocking chair, a shelf of Mason
jars, and a display of Depression-era glassware.

Darlene was putting down the phone when I arrived.
For being in the back of an antiques store, her office was
about as modern as you could get. She'd laid down white,
plush carpeting and had a steel desk with an ergonom-
ically correct black mesh chair. A standing chrome lamp
and matching desk light filled the space with pure white
light. You'd never have known that a year ago this room
held mops and broken chairs.

"Emmy. Come in. Did you come to see if I've had
any bites on your building?"

Fresh anxiety brewed in my gut. I'd forgotten all

about the fact that Darlene was handling the sale of the building that held Strings Attached. "Have you?"

"I've had some nibbles, but Frank's insisting on a high price right now." She leaned forward. "I think he'd lower it if you were interested in buying."

"I wish I could. No bank would write me a mortgage as things stand now."

"You'll do fine, honey." She set her phone on a stack of papers. "Then you must be here about Jasmine. Did you hear? It wasn't an accident at all."

"I heard," I told her.

Darlene heaved a sigh. "Have a seat. Apparently, Marcus is the sheriff's number one suspect. The thing is, he's disappeared."

I lowered myself to a white-upholstered side chair. "I heard that, too."

She seemed disappointed. Unlike Jeanette, she actually enjoyed spreading news. "I forgot that your roommate owns the Brew House. You're probably pretty plugged in."

"I do get good coffee at home," I said. "But there's a lot I don't know. For instance, about Marcus. What's his story?"

"He's a strange one."

I waited a moment before prompting her. "In what way?"

"He grew up here"—she looked up to make sure I knew that fact—"moved away, got married, then came back to Rock Point, a bachelor again, about five years ago. In those years, something changed."

"In what way?"

She leaned back and crossed her legs. "Well, he was a regular guy before. Polite, hardworking—you know, regular. When he moved back, he'd turned sour. He wouldn't talk to anyone, and if he did, it was to complain about how awful the town had become." She looked like she wanted to say something, but shook her head instead.

"What?" I prompted.

"Marcus was single when he came back. I thought I might fix him up with my sister, Jill. When I suggested it to him, you'd have thought the house was burning down, he was so worked up."

That sounded like the Marcus I knew. "What happened to his wife?"

"I'm not sure. I guess I figured she'd had enough of his attitude and divorced him."

I pondered this. It made sense. But it didn't explain why he'd left town, unless he truly did have something to do with Jasmine's death. I played with the sharp edge of my armrest.

"You're thinking about Jasmine, aren't you?" Darlene asked.

"I am. I'm also wondering where Marcus might have gone."

"You and the sheriff both." Darlene picked lint off her skirt. She took her position as president of the chamber of commerce seriously and always wore suits. "He used to live in Bedlow Bay. Maybe he has friends there. Or maybe he's camping in the woods somewhere around here."

"If he's innocent, he'd be smart to come back to town."

"We plan to say a few words about Jasmine at the

festival. Honor her." Darlene looked into the distance, as if she were imagining herself on the dais. "Rock Point's most prominent citizen. Murdered, right here." She lowered her voice. "Shut the door."

Curious, I pulled the old storage room's door closed behind me. The smell of paint and Darlene's rosy perfume intensified.

"The media is here. A fellow from the *National Bloodhound*. He called not ten minutes before you came."

My stomach dropped. "Did he talk like a radio DJ? I mean, if the DJ were Alistair Cooke?"

Darlene waved the issue of the *National Bloodhound* with me in it. "Nicky Byrd himself. I saw you got a mention in his column."

I groaned. "Did he say he was still in town?"

She nodded. "He'll be by later."

I dropped my head to my hands. "No. I can't believe he's still here."

"Why are you complaining? You're lucky."

"Lucky? How many moms are going to take their kids into a kite shop whose owner is practically called a murderer in a national publication?"

"As a PR professional, I'm telling you that all publicity is good publicity," Darlene said.

"PR professional" might have been pushing it. She'd been in charge of marketing at her father's hardware store until he retired and sold the business. Her grandest scheme had been the "wrench of the month" club. Junk drawers across Rock Point were filled with wrenches that Darlene had bought in bulk for a song. The problem was that they fit Chinese bolt sizes, not American.

"All the same, I'd rather not have anything to do with him."

"I would. This is Rock Point's big chance to be in the country's eye."

I had to hand it to Darlene. She knew how to make lemons into lemonade. "The *Bloodhound* isn't known for its puff pieces. He'll make Rock Point sound as seedy as he can." I wasn't here to talk about tabloids. "Listen, do you happen to know why Marcus is so dead-set against tourists?"

"I don't know. His family were fishermen. Maybe he's simply sad to see the old way of life disappearing."

"It seems to be more than that."

Darlene scrunched her lips together. "Maybe he just needs a hobby in his retirement—"

"And being a curmudgeon is his hobby?" I thought about the threatening note, the slashed tires that the sheriff clearly suspected were Marcus's work. "And isn't he a bit too young for retirement?"

"Every town has someone like him. But you raise a good point. As chair of Rock Point's chamber of commerce, I should engage him. Figure out how to give him a role somehow."

Good luck with that, I thought. I rose. "I suppose I'd better get back to my store."

Darlene stood with me and opened the door. "Do you want to take the *Bloodhound* with you for your scrapbook?"

I grimaced. "No, thanks."

"I knew that approaching Jasmine to judge the contest was the perfect choice. Even in her death, she keeps giving." Darlene put the copy of the *Bloodhound* on her bookshelf. "Maybe even giving more. The chamber of commerce is going to send a huge wreath to her funeral."

I couldn't help but turn to her. "You almost sound like you're happy about her death."

Her tone was breezy. "Happy? No. Not at all."

True, she had seemed shocked when she rushed into Sullivan's Kites to tell Jack and me about the death. But it was the threat to the kite festival that shook her, not Jasmine's demise. "Rose is taking it pretty hard."

Now the humanity returned to Darlene's face. "I take it back. Poor girl. Maybe not all publicity is good."

chapter fourteen

A FEW MINUTES LATER, I WAS CLIMBING THE STAIRS TO Strings Attached. "Any business this morning?" I asked Sunny.

"Yeah, we sold two diamond kites and some line. You had two visitors, too."

"Visitors?" I wasn't expecting anyone. Sunny knew Stella, so it wouldn't have been her, or Sunny would have said so. "People who stopped by to ask about the building?" I was still nervous about that.

"Nope. What did Rose say? Will she talk to me about her business?" Sunny's face lit up.

"Sure. Who came to see me?"

"When can I see Rose?" Sunny said.

"Just a minute, Sunny. I'll tell you, but would you let me know first who came by?"

She rolled her eyes. "All right, all right. Just after

the store opened, a fancy-looking guy with a nice tan stopped in."

The man with the accent who was interested in my kites. "Did he look like he'd stepped off a vintage cigar box?"

"Yep. That's him. He came in and asked for you, and when I told him you were out for the morning, he left. Who is he?"

"I don't know," I said. "He didn't leave a card, did he?" What did he want? He seemed so out of place in Rock Point. "Who else came by?"

"Another man, totally different. He was tall, stringy hair. But he was super charming, almost like a television interviewer, and he talked like he was reading a Victorian novel. He did leave a card." She reached next to the cash register for a crisp business card with a familiar red and yellow logo.

I didn't need to look at it, but I did anyway. "*National Bloodhound.* Nicholas Byrd III." I set the card on the counter. "Did he say what he wanted?"

"Just that he needed to talk to you."

I swore under my breath. He obviously knew by now that Jasmine had been murdered. "I don't want to talk to Nicky Byrd."

"The Third," Sunny added.

"You know how those tabloids are. I don't trust him."

"Don't worry. I'll keep my mouth shut."

"That's all, then?" I asked. I'd been away for less than two hours, but I had to admit that I was a little wary putting Sunny in charge of the shop.

"Yep. That's about it." Sunny's face looked innocent.

Maybe too innocent. "What? Why are you looking at me like that?"

My kite. I only had parts of it basted together at this point, but I'd left it on the table in the workshop. I was headed to the kitchen door to check on it when a customer came in. At Sunny's gasp, I spun around to see who it was.

"Caitlin Ruder," Sunny said and ran around the front of the counter. "I heard you were in town, but I never thought I'd get to meet you. I loved you in *Bag That Babe.*"

Caitlin was dressed as if she were lounging on the Riviera. Sunglasses obscured half her face, a pink-and-orange silk scarf was wrapped in her hair, and she was Amazon-tall in espadrilles with a three-inch wedge. I was surprised that Sunny recognized her at all, until I remembered that this was likely a look she sported for a good part of her TV season.

Caitlin slipped off the sunglasses and let her gaze sweep the room. "So, this is your shop, huh? Cute."

"Thank you," I said uncertainly.

"Can I help you find a kite?" Sunny asked.

"Aren't you sweet?" Caitlin said, now the grande dame. "No, I just had to get out of the house. I'm bored out of my skull."

"Some people fly kites for entertainment," I pointed out.

Caitlin looked at me as if I'd asked her to stick her head in the toilet.

"You could walk along Clatsop Cliffs. The view is spectacular," Sunny said. "It's a great place to think."

"I can think on the deck," she said. She tapped a toe

as she turned to take in the rows of kites fluttering above the old fireplaces and the packaged kites nearer the counter. "What do I have to do to get a drink in this town?"

"The Tidal Basin doesn't open until five," Sunny said. "It's a nice place. You might like it there."

"The Rock Point Tavern's open now," I said. She'd detest its ancient indoor-outdoor carpeting, decaying sailor decor, and the owner's aged mutt, who slept behind the bar and beat a hasty exit when the health inspector dropped by. The tavern's owner liked to brag that he hadn't had to break up a fight in almost eight years. I wished I could see Caitlin trying to order some chichi Hollywood cocktail there.

"Forget it. I really don't drink, anyway."

"You drank all the time on *Bag That Babe*," Sunny said promptly.

"I mean drink in a tavern."

More lies, I thought. "Are you staying in Rock Point through the kite festival?" The festival was this coming Saturday, less than a week away. If Caitlin was bored now, she'd be comatose by the time she judged the contest.

"Yeah. Jasmine and I came as a sort of retreat. You know, get the city off our minds, regroup. Now it's just me."

"I'm sorry," came to my lips, but Caitlin didn't look particularly grief-stricken.

She slipped on the sunglasses again. "I suppose I'll walk a bit, then go home. Study my script."

"For a movie?" Sunny asked.

I couldn't see Caitlin's eyes through the dark lenses,

but her lips widened into a smile. "A terrific role. Perfect for me."

"What is it?" Sunny said.

"Not public yet. You'll know soon enough," she said. She ran a hand over her flat stomach. "Maybe I'll do some core exercises this afternoon."

Sunny followed Caitlin to the door. "Come back anytime," she yelled as Caitlin descended the steps and disappeared up the street. Sunny turned to me. "Have you thought about putting up autographed photos of stars who come to Strings Attached? Wouldn't that be great?"

I didn't even bother to respond to that suggestion. Then I remembered: my kite. I ran behind the counter and threw open the kitchen door. My kite lay over the table, just as I'd left it that morning.

"It's okay," I said.

"Of course it is. I don't know why you're so worried." Sunny turned her back on me and let the door swing shut.

AFTER MAKING SUNNY PROMISE TO TELL ME IF THE TAN Man, as I was beginning to think of him, came in, and to deny I was there if Nicky Byrd dropped by, I stepped through to the workshop to make some progress on my kite. Soon, tourists and kite fans from all over would be filling Rock Point's bed-and-breakfasts and even driving in from hotels in Cannon Beach and Newport. Caitlin Ruder might find Rock Point hard to bear for more than a few days, but the town had no problem attracting visitors.

I pulled my kite toward me and examined it with a fresh perspective. Yes, it would be a beautiful kite. Even in its raw state, the jewel-toned view of Rock Point, with the ocean to the left and forest to the right, drew in the eye. It could hang in the shop, and customers would stare at it, picking out landmarks and admiring—if I said so myself—the clever rendering of the flowered border down Main Street, or the boats anchored in the marina.

These details were fine, like a painting. In the shop, they'd sing. I straightened. Up close. In the shop. But on the beach? Maybe I was going about this all the wrong way. The kite festival would draw hundreds of people to the beach. My kite would get lost in the cacophony of shape and color.

I couldn't believe I hadn't thought of it sooner. I folded up the kite and set it to the side. Maybe I'd finish it someday and display it from Strings Attached's front porch. But now I understood that this kite was too precious. I needed a kite with drama. I wanted something that could wow from afar—sort of a Jasmine Normand of kites. Sure, it meant starting from scratch, but it was the only way. An appliquéd kite took days and days to perfect. A larger, simpler kite, on the other hand, was manageable in the week I had left before the festival. *Yes.* I'd do it. `

I went to the drafting table and pulled out a large sheet of graph paper. What would this new kite be? I began loosely sketching the elements of the coastal landscape. A sunfish. A large sunfish with fins that would ripple in the wind. No, the colors would be too garish.

What about a whale, a whale nearly as large as the real thing, with ribbons streaming from its spout? That didn't feel right, either. The key was to design a shape that would not only harness the wind, but would use it to animate the kite, to bring it motion.

As I sketched, I thought about Strings Attached. I was so lucky to create and sell kites. And live on the ocean, especially this stretch of Oregon's coast, with the rugged rocks jutting from the surf, and the balsam scent of the forest so close. Any evening I could watch the sunset from Avery's house on the bluff, surrounded by conifers. Any morning I could ride my bicycle into town and feel the salty air on my face. This had been my dream, and I was living it.

I didn't want to fail. I didn't want to have to return to Portland and camp out with my parents until I found another job at a chain outdoor store while I figured out my future.

Rose's warning about new businesses failing came back to me, laying a foundation of anxiety. Then, of course, Jasmine's murder. Someone had threatened Jasmine, then slashed her tires, then killed her. My anxiety mounted. I lifted my pencil from the sketch pad. Why would someone slash the tires of a person he intended to kill? It didn't make sense. Dead people don't drive. Yet the murder couldn't be a last-minute crime of passion, unless the murderer had surprised Jasmine while she was taking her dose of insulin, then forced more on her. But the different brand? No. This had been premeditated.

I began to sketch again, letting my pencil swoop and

shade almost on its own. Nicky Byrd's column came back to me. "An ill wind" blew through Rock Point, he'd said.

Sunny's voice cut the silence. "Why aren't you sewing?" she asked from the door. She picked up the basted-together kite and smoothed it on the table.

"I'm trying a whole different kite. No more appliqué. Something with drama."

Sunny looked confused for a moment, but she knew better than to question me on this. "All right. Well, I'm closing up the shop for the day. Are you coming home for dinner?"

The light through the old kitchen's windows had changed, slanted more from the west. Hours had passed, and I hadn't even noticed. "No. I'd better work."

"Don't be too late," Sunny said. "Make sure you lock the door after me."

I followed her through the shop. She'd already taken down the windsocks I hung from the front porch each morning and had flipped the sign to "Closed." I bolted the door behind her.

When I returned to the drafting table, my latest sketch surprised me. It was a cloud, with eyes narrowed and puffed cheeks, blowing wind. Nicky Byrd's ill wind. But maybe also the winds of change.

chapter fifteen

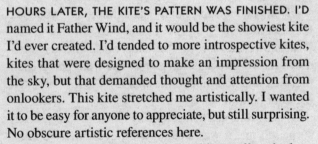

HOURS LATER, THE KITE'S PATTERN WAS FINISHED. I'D named it Father Wind, and it would be the showiest kite I'd ever created. I'd tended to more introspective kites, kites that were designed to make an impression from the sky, but that demanded thought and attention from onlookers. This kite stretched me artistically. I wanted it to be easy for anyone to appreciate, but still surprising. No obscure artistic references here.

Another benefit was that it would actually take less time to sew than my fiddly appliqué kite. I might even be able to put together a quick prototype to make sure it would lift and fill.

As I'd scaled my pattern to a fresh sheet of graph paper, I'd been giving thought to Sheriff Koppen's suspicions of Marcus. The only way to know if Marcus had killed Jasmine was to figure out where he was when she

was killed. The sheriff and deputy would have inter-
viewed Marcus's neighbors—and Marcus himself, if
they got to him—to determine his alibi and prove, or
disprove, it.

I pushed myself away from the drafting table and
stretched my back. Night had fallen, and the streets had
quieted. A thought occurred to me. I might have sources
the sheriff didn't. I made a plan.

Half an hour later, a garlicky Martino's pizza in hand,
I was at the old dock. Clouds like furling smoke raked
the stars, and the chilly ocean lapped at the dock's bar-
nacled posts. The pizza box warmed my arms, but the
night chilled the rest of me.

Unlike the new dock's pleasure craft, most of the old
dock's residents were working fishing boats and the
boats of a few of Rock Point's older families, like Avery's. One of the boats, though, belonged to Ace the
plumber. Ace was known to skip out on his "old lady"
several nights a week to hang out in his man cave here
at the old dock and drink cheap beer. I figured I had
about a fifty-fifty chance of finding him.

Luck was with me. Light spilled from his boat's narrow windows. I stepped onto the deck and avoided a
thick coil of rope. I rapped on the cabin door.

"Who's there?" Definitely Ace.

"It's Emmy Adler. And a pizza," I added for good
measure.

In seconds, he was at the door. "Come to visit, eh?
Entrez."

According to Stella, Ace hadn't grown up in Rock
Point, but he'd lived here since the late 1960s, when he'd

migrated from Ken Kesey's Merry Band of Pranksters. He'd kept his long hair, although it had thinned and grayed. He'd spent the intervening decades collecting a parade of tattoos up his arms and peeking out his T-shirt's collar. And that was only what I could see. Besides fixing toilets and installing water heaters throughout Rock Point, Ace made a few bucks driving the tow truck out of Lenny's filling station and doing other odd jobs as the spirit moved him.

"I couldn't resist the extra garlic pizza," I said. "I hope you don't mind."

"Mind? That's my favorite. Come on down. Yin, let the lady take a seat." He shooed a tabby cat away. Yang, Yin's sister, lounged on the narrow bed at the cabin's rear. "What can I do for you? Is it about that reality TV contestant's murder?"

I'd been made. "How did you know?"

"You wouldn't be showing up here with one of Martino's finest without wanting something from me. And after that tidbit I read in the *Bloodhound*—"

"You keep up with that?"

"I work in a lot of bathrooms, darlin'. And most of them have some kind of reading material handy." Yin had leapt to his lap, and Ace absently stroked the cat between the ears. "Beer?"

I eyed the cans in an ice bucket at his feet. "No, thanks."

He set diner-style white crockery plates in front of us and pulled a slice from the box, neatly detaching its cheese from the rest of the pie. "What do you want to know?"

"Well, it's Marcus Salek. What do you know about him?"

If my mentioning Marcus surprised Ace, he didn't show it. "Nice European-style kitchen sink, but a crappy faucet. Doesn't do the sink justice. Those plastic ball bearing washers can't stand up to regular use."

While he went on about the state of Marcus's water heater, I devoured a slice of pizza and wiped my greasy fingers on a paper napkin. "What about his background? I mean, aside from his plumbing fixtures?"

"Why Marcus?" For the first time, Ace looked serious. "Because he's disappeared? Didn't even take his car?"

I left the crust on my plate. "You know, then."

"Lots of people do. I admit it's unusual."

I couldn't tell him about the sheriff's suspicions. "He hates the whole idea of the kite festival," I said instead. "Loathes tourists. It's enough to make me wonder."

"He does have a bad temper. But murder? I don't see it."

"No one seems to know anything about him, except that he grew up here, moved away, then came back."

"He married a lovely woman. Naomi. I met her once around the holidays when he was back in Rock Point." He stopped petting the cat, and the cat went to join his littermate on the bed. "You still hanging out with that foxy lady?"

"Stella?" I'd first met Ace in the spring, when Stella and I had followed someone to the docks.

He got a faraway look in his eyes. "She's a class act."

I didn't want Ace to get distracted. "What happened to Marcus's wife?"

"Huh? Oh. Don't know."

"Divorce?"

"Could be. They seemed real happy, though. I asked him about her once, and he wouldn't say. I got the impression that she might have died."

If the wife was dead, it raised even more questions. "But when he came back to Rock Point, it was definitely alone."

"Yep. Set himself up in his little house and spends a bunch of time wandering around town, making trouble. What that man needs is a job." He reached into the bucket and pulled out a can. "You sure you don't want a beer?"

"Positive. Thanks." I decided to try a different approach. "How's the tow truck business going?"

"Great, ever since we got her a new alternator. Last week she broke down on the way to Lincoln City, and I had to call a tow truck, of all things. Imagine that. A tow truck towing a tow truck. Humiliating."

"I can imagine."

"Yep. It had to be Kenny out of Cannon Beach to come get me, too. That know-it-all. Thinks because he has a newer rig that he's somehow superior. Give me an old one any day. Well, an old one with a good alternator, that is."

For all his dropout, ex-hippie ways, there was something comforting about listening to Ace. His friendly voice, the purring cats, and the boat's cradling motion almost made me forget the dark dock above and the murder half a mile up the road.

"I heard someone slashed the tires on Jasmine Normand's car, and you towed it away."

"Now we're getting back to business, aren't we?" He

slid a third slice of pizza to his plate. "I towed it all the way back to the rental car agency in Portland. Then I had to rush back and install a dishwasher."

"The tires were definitely slashed? I mean, it couldn't have been an accident?"

"No, ma'am. No accident. Someone had taken a hunting knife, or something with a fat blade like that, and dug into both front tires. That car wasn't going anywhere."

"Do you have to be very strong to do that?"

"You do, in fact. Those tires are made to stay in one piece." He set his can on the tiny table between us and stood. "Here. Follow me. Yang, you stay in."

We stepped out onto the deck and made our way around the coiled rope again, to the boat's rear. The breeze stirred a chill down my arms, and I shrugged on the cardigan I'd taken off below. The fishermen were in for the night and the tourists at home. After the constant noise of the surf out at Avery's, the bay's calm water was almost disconcertingly quiet. Ace put his foot on a tire that was sitting on the boat's deck.

"You take this here tire." Ace pulled a knife from his belt and handed it to me. "Give it a try."

"Don't you need the tire?"

"Nah. It's sitting here until I get it out to the dump. Go ahead. The blade's good and sharp. Try to slash it."

I wasn't used to holding a hunting knife. Its wooden handle was smooth from years of use, and its blade widened, then came to a sharp point. It flashed in the mercury-vapor light from the dock.

"All right." I braced my legs and jabbed the knife at the tire. The knife's tip caught the rubber, but the tire merely depressed. I tried again, this time using both hands.

"Careful there," Ace said. "Of course, a tire on a car would be easier, since the air would offer some resistance. But you see that it takes some strength."

I handed back the knife. Chances were good that it wasn't a woman who slashed Jasmine's tires and, presumably, killed her. "Thank you. I'd better be getting home."

"Anytime. You want the rest of the pizza?"

"No, you keep it."

"You'll be competing in the festival this weekend, I take it?"

"Definitely. I'm hoping to finish my kite tomorrow." Tomorrow. When I'd find out what happened to Marcus's wife.

chapter sixteen

THE NEXT MORNING, I PLASTERED ON A CONFIDENT SMILE and strode into the coffee-scented Brew House and ordered a latte. Avery filled my cup from the vacuum pot while Charlie Parker's saxophone wailed from the record player. "Nice to see you here," she said as she handed me a large mug.

"Got to get back on the horse and all that," I said.

"No yelling at patrons or reporters, okay?"

I actually stuck out my tongue at her.

Under my arm was my laptop. I'd wanted to shut myself in the workshop at Strings Attached, but I had to show Rock Point that I wasn't afraid of the *Bloodhound*'s article. I had nothing to do with Jasmine's death. By avoiding attention, I'd only stir up more gossip. I doctored my latte with sugar and found a small table in the corner.

Only then did I dare to take in the room. Jeanette had filled her "Postal Workers Send You" mug and was on her way out the door. I forced a smile and nodded hello toward her. There. Let her spread the news that I was secure and happy. Rose sat across the room, where Jack and her sister had shared coffee just days before. She was spreading cream cheese on a bagel. Probably getting ready for a day with her ledgers.

And there were no reporters to avoid. Perfect.

I fired up the laptop. I didn't know if Naomi had taken her husband's last name, so I searched for "Naomi Marcus Salek obituary," and right away got a hit. Naomi Salek of Bedlow Bay died about five years ago, leaving her husband, Marcus Salek, and a list of relatives I didn't know. She was thirty-two years old. No cause of death was reported. Bedlow Bay was too small to have its own newspaper, so the obituary was part of a generic online service. I searched for "Naomi Salek" in the *News Guard*, nearby Lincoln City's paper, but came up dry. In fact, I couldn't find anything from the newspaper older than a year or two.

I wasn't going to get what I needed online. It was going to have to be done in person. I pulled out my phone. "Sunny? Could you watch the store today?"

"Today?"

"Right. Today."

"I was just about to leave with Bear for a walk along the cliffs."

"Please. The cliffs will still be there tomorrow."

"Why?"

I knew Sunny wasn't asking because she wanted to

challenge me. She was curious. I lowered my voice so no one in the café could hear me. "It's about Marcus Salek. I need to drive to Lincoln City, maybe Newport, too."

"You'll tell me everything when you get back?"

"Definitely."

After another minute talking about timing and a stern warning not to get within five feet of my kite, I hung up and punched in Stella's phone number. She was game for the trip. Within half an hour, we were in her Corvette and headed south.

Stella was a good driver, even if she tended to hover above the speed limit. She cracked the windows to let cool marine air rustle our hair. To our right, the sun sparkled on the waves. To our left, as we left Rock Point, the houses along the highway disappeared, and deep green forest took over. I knew we'd dip through farmland and tiny fishing villages, with the big, wide ocean always just around a corner or over a hill.

After I'd recounted what I'd found online about Naomi Salek, Stella asked, "So, do we go all the way to Newport to the courthouse first for the death certificate? Or do you want to stop at Lincoln City on the way?"

"Let's stop at Lincoln City. The *News Guard* might have what we need."

During the next hour and a half—Lincoln City was usually described as two hours south of Rock Point, but not for Stella—we talked about my new kite design and about Stella's upcoming art show in Portland. The Corvette had an old cassette tape player that the car's previous owner had installed in the 1980s, and we listened to a Lovepipers album. Stella sang along.

I told her about my evening with Ace, too. "He has a thing for you, Stella. He called you a 'foxy lady.'"

She laughed. "I don't know how his wife puts up with him."

At last we were driving into Lincoln City. Old park-at-your-door motels in pink and weathered green dotted the highway, and billboards advertising the aquarium in Newport and gambling at Spirit Mountain Casino rose over the road. The *News Guard*'s offices were in a small old building in a residential neighborhood, with a satellite dish in the shrubbery outside.

"I hope someone is here," I said. It didn't have the hive-of-activity look of a TV-show newsroom, that was for sure. No cars were parked outside, and the dark film over the glass front door made it hard to see if there were lights on. "Maybe I should have called before we drove all the way down here."

I pushed the *News Guard*'s front door open, sounding a chime. Stella followed me into a small lobby that was cordoned off from the rest of the office by a waist-high counter. A pink-haired woman not much older than Sunny came out from the back. She wore a full-skirted vintage dress and had a nose ring.

"Can I help you?" she asked. I caught the glint of a tongue piercing as she spoke.

"We'd like to look through your archives, if you have them. For something about the death of a Bedlow Bay woman."

"How far back?"

"Five years." I handed her the notes I'd taken with the date of Naomi Salek's obituary.

The woman's hands dropped to her sides. "Oh no."

"No archives that far back?" Stella asked.

"There are, it's just that they're in the basement, and it flooded last year. I mean, we can check. The last couple of years, we put those online. But these . . ." Her tone of voice said, *fat chance*.

I glanced at Stella, my heart already sinking. "We drove down from Rock Point. We should at least give them a look."

The woman sighed. "All right. Follow me." She lifted the counter to let us through, then led the way past the reception area to a back room with a copy machine, a couple of sickly plants, and an elderly man at a computer. "Junior," she said, "I'm taking these ladies to the archives."

He looked up, clearly surprised we were there. Maybe his hearing wasn't very good. "Great. I'll be finished with the story on Taft High by the time you come up."

The woman opened another door—one I'd have assumed went to a broom closet—and flipped on a light. Even before we entered, I smelled the mildew. The woman descended a wooden staircase and flipped another bank of switches, illuminating half a dozen rows of metal shelves holding banker's boxes.

"The boxes are labeled by date. Let's see." She walked up one row, running her index finger across the cardboard as she went. "If you're lucky, this date will be on an upper shelf."

"What happened?" Stella asked. "I wouldn't think it would flood this far inland."

"The gutters backed up during a rainstorm a couple

of years ago. It's just Junior and me here most days, and we don't get around to things like gutter cleaning very often. Ah, here it is." She pulled a box from a lower shelf—but not the lowest—and set it on a table by the stairs.

We stood around her as she pried off the lid. "The date I gave you was for the obituary. If there was anything about her death, it probably would have been in the papers the week before," I said.

Folded newspapers made a tidy stack in the box, like shirts in an upscale haberdasher's. The woman reached in to pull one from the box, but it stuck to its neighbors.

"Uh-oh," Stella said.

"This doesn't look good." I watched, praying we'd find something still legible about Naomi's death.

Although the woman had hesitated to come downstairs, now she seemed determined to find the right papers, and carefully separated the newspapers. They tore with each of her careful movements.

Stella sneezed. "Sorry. Mildew allergies."

"This one's from exactly one week before the obituary." She laid it on the table next to the box and flattened it open. The page in her left hand detached, and the rest of the pages had clearly melted together from the moisture, then dried solid that way. We weren't getting anything from them.

Stella sneezed again. "Sorry."

"I'm the one who's sorry. I knew we should have scanned these earlier, but it takes time we don't have. And now this," the woman said. She put her hands on her hips and looked at the basement as if she'd never been down here.

"There are no records of the old papers at all?" Stella asked. "Maybe at the library?"

"No. We always meant to send them off—first my dad, it used to be his paper, then me—but we never did."

"It takes time to get things together," I said. I tried to sound understanding, but I was bummed.

"It was the money, really. And it wasn't even ridiculously expensive. It's just that . . ."

She didn't need to finish her sentence. A small-town newspaper was about as far as you could get from the *National Bloodhound*. While Nicky Byrd was burning his paper's travel money digging up gossip about a reality TV star's death, papers like the *News Guard* were scraping by. And that's if they were lucky.

This time, I was the one who sneezed. "Thank you for trying to help us. Maybe we should go upstairs." I couldn't keep the disappointment out of my voice.

"Has the gentleman upstairs worked here awhile?" Stella asked. "Maybe he'd remember the death."

"Junior? Sure, he's worked here since the mid–nineteen sixties, but unless it's the score of a high school football game, I don't think you'll get much from him." We'd reached the main floor again. "Junior?"

"Eh?" Junior said, looking up from his computer monitor.

"These ladies would like to ask you something."

"You all are football fans, are you?" He swung his chair toward us.

"We have another question. About a death in Bedlow Bay about five years ago."

"Most of them kids go to Newport for high school. There was that tight end killed in a fireworks accident. Jonathan Bellows was his name. About the same time. Sad. His brother Jubal was a kicker, but didn't have Jonathan's talent." He shook his head slowly. "Now, for kickers, you wanted one like Denny Richard. Had dead-on aim and ran like a wild coyote. His father, Frankie, was a kicker, too, but—"

Stella interrupted. "This was a Bedlow Bay resident. Not a high school student."

"Naomi Salek," I said.

Junior watched us as we spoke. Probably a fair amount of his comprehension came from reading lips.

"Naomi Salek," he repeated. "Can't say I remember the name."

The hope that had stirred now vanished. We might never find out what happened to Marcus's wife, let alone Marcus himself.

"Unless," Junior said, "she was the one killed in that hit-and-run. Nasty business. They say she was pregnant, too. But this Naomi—"

"Salek," I finished.

"Yes. Well, I don't have much of a head for names. Sorry, girls."

"THAT WAS A BIG NOTHING," I SAID ONCE WE WERE BACK in the car. "Sorry I dragged you all the way down here."

"Maybe it was fruitful after all," Stella said. "Junior

seemed pretty sharp to me, if narrow in his interests. Maybe Marcus's wife was killed in the hit-and-run, like he thought."

"Like he kind of thought," I corrected. "If she were a high school football star, he would have remembered every detail."

"A hit-and-run is traumatic. It might explain why Marcus has been so closemouthed about it."

"There are lots of reasons he wouldn't want to talk about that." Especially if the car doing the hitting hadn't been found. Especially if he might have been driving that car.

As usual, Stella followed my train of thought. "You think he might have killed his own wife?"

Now that the words were out there, I couldn't commit to them. "It does seem far-fetched. I don't know what to think anymore."

Stella rolled down the window to let out the heat. "Well, what do you want to do next?" The Corvette's black leather interior was worthy of a James Bond movie, but the August warmth had turned my seat into a frying pan. "We could go on to Newport to see if we can find Naomi's death certificate."

Junior's story of the hit-and-run had got me thinking. "Why don't we find somewhere for lunch? Then, if you're game, we could drive to Bedlow Bay and ask around there. Maybe someone remembers Marcus and his wife. Then, if that fails, we can drive on to Newport."

Stella started the car. "I like that idea."

I had one more favor to ask. "While we're here, how would you feel about—"

"Visiting the kite shop, by chance?"

I laughed. Once again, she'd read my mind. "If it's not too much trouble. I don't get to many kite shops these days, and it would be great to see what others are doing."

Stella smiled. "I was going to suggest it if you didn't. Why don't we stop by there now, and get lunch in Bedlow Bay?"

The Pacific Winds kite shop was the largest shop on the Oregon coast. Not only did they have a huge selection of kites—many designed in-house and sent out to be built—they carried all sorts of beach equipment, from sun hats to towels. Getting through the winter was no problem for this shop. If you didn't want a kite, you could buy a windsock to hang in the garden or a "Merry Christmas" flag adorned with holly, or a "It's Happy Hour Somewhere" flag with a martini glass stitched on it. It wasn't the direction in which I wanted to take Strings Attached, but I admired their business savvy.

"Lincoln City makes Rock Point feel tiny," I said as Stella pulled the Corvette into a parking spot in front of Pacific Winds. The city's string of motels and fast-food restaurants was busy with RVs and tourist-jammed SUVs.

"I suppose this is what people like Marcus fear."

"Rock Point could go in the opposite direction, like Gearhart," I said, naming a town to the north loaded with the high-end beach homes of Portland's old timber families. "I mean, look at the Tidal Basin. It's even been in *Bon Appétit*."

A teenaged boy jumped off his skateboard at the sight of Stella's car. "Nice ride," he yelled.

"Thank you," Stella said.

The air-conditioning in Pacific Winds kept the store at a comfortable temperature I had to approximate at Strings Attached with fans and the clever cross-circulation I'd determined over weeks of experimentation. Thank goodness for the transoms in old houses.

"Good afternoon—Hey, you're Emmy Adler from Rock Point, aren't you?" the woman behind the counter said. She came around front to shake my hand. "Cheryl. Greg and I own this shop. I stopped by your store just after you opened. I love your handmade kites. We were talking about them at our kite festival. Why weren't you there?"

"I'd just opened the shop and couldn't leave it for the day." I felt like a celebrity. Is this how Jasmine had passed her time? I tried to tamp down my smile so I wouldn't look too much like an idiot. "Thank you so much."

"Of course, we couldn't make it if we sold that kind of fare. Folks don't want the artsy stuff here. How have you been getting by?"

Now my smile drooped without effort. "Not bad. Enough people seem to like the 'artsy' stuff for me to pay the rent." The rent at the store, that is. Avery cut me a good deal on living with her.

"Well, congratulations. And I don't mean to sound harsh. I've heard more than one real kite enthusiast in here talking about how much they loved your kites."

Much better. "I adore this." I waved toward a huge soft kite suspended from the ceiling. It was shaped like a pirate's galleon.

"The kite festivals help pay the bills. Rock Point has one coming up, doesn't it? Are you entering something?"

"It's this weekend, and yes, I'm putting together a new design. It's just about finished," I said, hoping Sunny had followed my instructions and kept her distance.

"I heard there was a little excitement up there, too."

My thoughts flashed to the *National Bloodhound*. Surely, Cheryl wasn't a subscriber. I was about to reply when Stella stepped in.

"So upsetting. Jasmine Normand died. Was killed, actually. I'm sure you saw it on the news."

Cheryl leaned forward. "Did you see her? I mean before, naturally."

So she hadn't read Nicky Byrd's column. I relaxed. "Only once, at a café in town. She seemed friendly." To Jack, at least, I added silently.

Cheryl leaned back and relaxed her voice. "It was probably a crazy celebrity stalker. If I were famous, I'd have a bodyguard watching over me night and day." When neither of us responded, she said, "Let me give you a tour of the store."

Half an hour later, I was overwhelmed by what a successful kite store could be. Strings Attached would never be the high-traffic business Pacific Winds was— not that I wanted it like that. Pacific Winds succeeded because it was a little bit of everything for everyone. I wanted more of a boutique shop, somewhere I could create my kites and connect with people who understood what I was doing. Was that a crazy dream? Would it ever be possible?

Stella and I waved good-bye.

"Wow," Stella said. "How many kites do you think they have in stock?"

"A couple hundred on the shelves alone." One thing I'd learned from my parents was that success was about more than sales volume or a fancy degree or a mansion. Still, seeing Pacific Winds had shaken me.

I waited for Stella to unlock the passenger-side door from the inside. As I looked over the Corvette's roof, I did a double take. There, walking into the kite shop, was the Tan Man.

I WAITED UNTIL I WAS SEATED AND STRAPPED IN BEFORE I said, "Did you see him?"

"Who?" Stella asked.

"That man. That man who looks like he should be advertising Panama hats. He was hanging around Rock Point a few days ago. Even came into Strings Attached."

Stella looked through the windshield to the store, but thanks to the store's curtain of windsocks and sport kites, we couldn't see anyone. "Are you talking about the guy with the tan the color of toasted filberts? I've seen him around town."

"That's him."

"Maybe he's on vacation. You know, driving down Highway 101 to California."

"All by himself? Dressed like he owns a plantation?"

We sat a moment and stared at the shop's window. Stella broke the silence. "Do you want to go back in and see what he's up to?"

I turned it over in my mind. "No. He's simply . . . strange. Let's go to Bedlow Bay."

As we drove a gorgeous nine miles down the coast, I understood why so many summer visitors to the area yearned to move here. The air was clear and warm, and the hills green and dotted with farms. And the ocean spoke for itself. Now, with afternoon sun slanting across it, the waves shattered into sparkles. What those coast-happy visitors didn't know, or refused to acknowledge, was that most of the year was rainy. By February there weren't enough sunlamps in the world to boost a new-comer's mood. Luckily for me, as a Portland native, rain was mother's milk. But that didn't mean I didn't appreciate a beautiful August afternoon.

Bedlow Bay was named after a square bay that was nipped from the coast as if a cosmic train conductor had validated it with his gigantic ticket puncher. Houses, mostly small and charming enough to grace calendars, rimmed the bay. The town was smaller than Rock Point, and a few times more charming.

Stella pulled the Corvette in front of a homey-looking fish restaurant. "How about a bowl of chowder?"

"Sounds perfect."

She shut off the engine but didn't get out of the car. "What's our plan?"

"Well," I said. "We'll eat lunch."

"And then?"

"And then we'll go to the post office." I turned to her. "What do you think?"

"Perfect. Let's cross our fingers we'll find another Jeanette."

Ridley's Chowder was in an old roadhouse, with a bar on the right and a diner on the left. I glanced into the dark bar as we entered. A few people hunched over the bar watching TV, and another couple sat at a table over a basket of fries. The diner, on the other hand, was full of light and bustle.

"Have a seat," a waitress yelled from the cash register.

We chose a booth by window. Outside, a grizzled man who appeared to be an ex-fisherman was working his gums with a toothpick while he examined Stella's car.

The waitress handed us plastic-sheathed menus. "Coffee?"

I flipped over my cup, the international "yes, please" sign. Stella did the same. The waitress filled our cups and then went to cash out another customer.

"I like this place," I said. The worn linoleum, the counter with a pie under glass, the coffee cups and saucers stacked behind the counter ready for action—it was picture-perfect. I knew from hard-won experience, though, that the chowder might come in a can from some restaurant supply company's central kitchen in the industrial park of a faraway city.

The waitress was back. She was about ten years older than I, and her hair had been dyed a gentle auburn. She'd taken the trouble to fill in her lips with cherry red. She looked as at home as if she'd sprung up whole in the diner, or the diner had been built around her.

"Ready to order?"

"Do you make the chowder here?" I asked.

"Sure do. You'll like it, I promise. One bowl of chowder coming up. And you?" She turned to Stella.

"Chowder for me, too."

When the waitress left, Stella turned toward the ocean beyond the seawall. "Just look at that. I can't get enough of it."

"It's beautiful." But my attention drifted back into the diner. Clearly, it had been here for years. Marcus Salek had likely eaten here—many times, maybe. He'd probably taken his wife here. I could almost imagine him settling at the counter and ordering a tuna melt. Another thought came. What if Marcus was in Bedlow Bay, right now? "Do you think the waitress would know Marcus?"

Stella's attention focused. "She just might, at that."

"Maybe we could visit his old house, see where he lived."

The waitress appeared, holding a coffeepot in one hand and with both bowls of chowder resting on plates on her other arm.

"Wait," I said. "Have you worked here long?"

"Hold on a sec. Crackers coming up." She left the dining room altogether.

Stella had already dipped her spoon into the chowder. The broth was thick, but not the gluey stuff from a can.

The potatoes still had bits of skin clinging to them, and the clams—lots of clams—were chopped in irregular bits, like a knife and not a machine would make.

I dug into my chowder. Delicious.

Just as I formed the thought, the waitress emerged from the bar and entered the dining room with a bowl.

"Hush," Stella whispered. "Let me handle this."

"Here you go." The waitress placed the bowl between Stella and me. It was full of buttered oyster crackers. "Does the chowder meet your expectations?"

"I love it," I said. And I did. I greedily spooned oyster crackers into it.

"It's wonderful," Stella added. "One of our friends in Rock Point, Marcus Salek, used to live here. He told us how much he loves it here."

"Here?" the waitress said. "Ridley's Chowder?"

"Is there a reason he wouldn't?" Stella asked.

"No, I just . . ." She looked perplexed. "No."

"Do you know Marcus?" I couldn't help asking. Stella glared at me. I concentrated on my chowder.

"Sure." The waitress managed to draw the word out into three syllables. "He said he loved it, huh?"

My pulse leapt. She knew Marcus.

"I assumed he meant here," Stella said. Obviously covering all her bases.

To my surprise, the waitress slid into the booth next to me. Someone who had been eating pie at the counter turned around and waved his wallet. "In a minute," she yelled to him.

We'd struck the jackpot.

Stella set down her spoon. "I'm just going to come right out and ask. What happened?"

The waitress swallowed. Her eyelashes lowered, and I wondered if she was going to leave and not come back except to give us the check. Stella continued to look at the waitress with her patented gaze of concern and firmness.

"Naomi," the waitress said.

I could barely breathe. Naomi, what? Stella caught my gaze. *Hush*, it seemed to say.

"His wife," Stella said.

"My little sister," the waitress countered.

Holy smokes. The diner seemed to turn silent, and the ocean outside froze. Even the chowder ceased to appeal. I bit my lip to keep from asking what had happened, if she'd seen Marcus lately.

"I'm sorry," Stella simply said.

She drew a long breath. "They never found who did it. Never. And the baby . . ."

Stella placed her hand over Naomi's sister's hand. "What happened?"

The waitress's gaze lost focus. "She was crossing the road, and she was hit." She looked first at Stella, then at me. "They say it happened instantly, she couldn't have felt it."

"And she died," Stella whispered.

Junior, the old sportswriter, had been right.

"Horrible. It was horrible. They never did find out who did it. Probably a tourist. There's so much traffic through town these days." She picked up a napkin and smoothed it on the table. Stella let her talk. "It was so hard on all of us. But worst on Marcus. He seemed to lose his mind."

"Marcus?" I said. Stella raised an eyebrow at me. I stared at my chowder bowl.

"Yes," the waitress said. "First, he shut himself in the house. Refused to come out. Wouldn't eat and barely slept." She pushed the napkin to the side. "I tried to sit with him, talk to him, but he wouldn't have it. We all tried."

"So awful," Stella said.

"He buried Naomi in his family's plot east of Rock Point. Then one day—one day he left." She fluffed her hair with both hands. I had the impression this gesture was pure habit. "Never saw him again."

"Never?" I couldn't help asking.

The waitress pulled a locket through the neck of her short-sleeved blouse. She unclipped the front, and Stella and I leaned in to look. The locket held two photos: one of a blond toddler sitting in a patch of daisies, and one trimmed from a wedding photo. The same wedding photo I'd seen at Marcus's house. This was Naomi Salek.

"She's lovely," Stella murmured.

The waitress snapped the locket shut and slipped it down her blouse. "I stopped by Rock Point once, on my way north, but he wouldn't see me."

"Why, I wonder?" Stella said. "Why would he cut off his past like that?"

The waitress opened her mouth to say more, but the man at the counter interrupted. "Ruth, you gonna cash me out, or what?"

The spell was broken. The waitress seemed to come back to the present. She rose, all business. "Tell Marcus I said hello. Haven't seen him since the funeral. I don't want his to be the next time we visit."

I couldn't tell if she was serious or not.

chapter seventeen

THE DRIVE BACK TO ROCK POINT WAS QUIET. BOTH STELLA and I were caught up in our own thoughts.

After nearly half an hour of silence but for the Corvette's hum, Stella said, "Do you really think he would have killed his own wife?"

"I can't see it. Not after what Ruth said. He was heartbroken. But what do I know?"

"He left town after her death and never went back. Like a guilty man would. Or a grief-stricken one."

"Why did he run this time?" I asked. "If he didn't kill Jasmine, then he's just plain foolish."

"He's certainly painted a target on his back." Stella popped in the cassette of the Lovepipers again, but it only took one of their sunshine pop songs before she ejected the tape.

"Assume Marcus is off the list. Who else is a suspect?" Stella asked.

"Besides me, you mean?"

"Sheriff Koppen knows better than that. Forget that *Bloodhound* reporter right now. Now. Who else?"

I thought back. "I suppose her husband should be at the top of the list. That's what they say, anyway. Plus, the man I saw in the kitchen window was tall, like him."

"Do you know where he was the night of the murder?" Stella slowed as we approached one of Highway 101's many blind corners.

"I heard he showed up in Rock Point the next day, and that he's driving a rental SUV. He's staying with Rose. I don't know where he was before he came to Rock Point."

"It might be worth finding out."

"True." I could ask Rose in a roundabout way. She'd probably know. "Caitlin was at the beach house the whole time. She should be a suspect."

Stella shook her head. "I bet the sheriff had a heck of time getting anything out of her."

"No kidding. The night of the reenactment, she seemed resentful to even have to go through it. The sheriff tried to pin her down about which bedroom she'd slept in, and even that information was tough to get."

"Seems strange, though, that she'd kill Jasmine, then stick around in Rock Point."

"She's the new kite festival judge," I pointed out.

"That's hardly a sufficient lure for someone like Caitlin."

We were driving through forest now. The trees

whooshed by, and the air that came through the cracked windows cooled. "As Caitlin's motive, what about Kyle, Jasmine's husband? Maybe Caitlin wants him. That would explain why she might have killed Jasmine and why she's sticking around town."

"Has anyone seen them together?" Stella asked.

Only in a small town like Rock Point could you ask that question. If Caitlin had been stepping out with Kyle, word would have been at the Brew House by the next morning. "I haven't heard anything."

"Me, neither."

"Who else would gain from Jasmine's death?" I asked. "Wait a minute. What about the *National Bloodhound* reporter? He popped up instantly, like he was waiting in a hole next to the road for the news."

"You think he would have killed Jasmine just to get the scoop?"

I pondered this. "No. He seems more like the type to be drafting his keynote speech for the chess club's monthly tournament."

Stella chuckled. "The boy does need to let out the hem on his pants. And that makeup only makes the acne scars stand out more. He's stuck around town a lot longer than the other reporters did, though, almost like he knew it would turn out to be a murder."

"There's one more possibility," I said. "Maybe it wasn't murder at all. Jasmine's overdose might have been an accident, like they thought at first."

"Or suicide. There's a lot about Jasmine we don't know."

Stella was right. Except for the bit I'd seen of *Bag That Babe* and our brief interaction at the Brew House,

Jasmine was a blank slate to me. "If it wasn't murder, why would she inject herself with a different brand of insulin?"

"Maybe she was using a leftover bottle. I imagine the sheriff is tracking down her insulin purchases."

"Okay, say it was an odd bottle she had around. Why would she throw it off the deck?"

"Good question." We were coming into Rock Point now, passing Lenny's filling station, where he'd almost certainly be taking note of Stella's Corvette, perhaps to pass on to Jeanette that we'd been out somewhere. In a couple of miles, we'd be through town and at Avery's house. "Could Jasmine have been on the deck when she injected herself? The bottle might simply have rolled away."

I closed my eyes and imagined the path. I'd only seen it in the dark, by flashlight. The bottle would have had to make some lucky bounces to get that far down the path. "It seems unlikely, but I can't say for sure. Don't know."

"I wish we could cross that possibility off the list."

"Just one more possibility," I said. There was so much we didn't know.

WHEN STELLA DROPPED ME OFF AT AVERY'S, DAVE WAS outside, carrying a ladder to the shed. From the new stretch of unpainted siding on the house, I could tell he had been helping Avery again with the nearly constant repairs the old Cook house seemed to demand.

I waved good-bye to Stella and turned to Avery, who was on the lawn in front of the porch.

"Did you have a good trip?" Avery asked.

"We found out that Marcus's wife was killed in a hit-and-run accident." Dave now joined us. "Are you staying for dinner?" I asked him.

He snuck a look at Avery, as was his habit. "No. I'd love to, but I'm leading an evening kayak trip."

"Maybe the day after tomorrow?" Avery said.

A smile lit Dave's face. "Sounds good." He waved as he backed his car out of the drive.

Sunny and Bear bounded down the porch. "Finally, you're home," Sunny said. "What did you find out?"

I told them about Naomi Salek, her unborn baby, and her sister's story about Marcus. "I understand now why Marcus is so anti-tourist."

"Is he anti-tourist enough to kill the kite festival's judge?"

"That's the question," I said, although in my heart of hearts, I couldn't see him doing it.

"Love, grief, and sacrifice," Sunny said. "Something for me to contemplate if you let me take your Prius to the cliffs."

"Here. And good riddance." I handed her my keys.

Bear jumped into the back. Sunny slipped into the driver's seat and rolled down the window. "Not much happened at the store. Between customers, I set up a ledger for you." She started the car. "Oh, and your kite is safe," she added quickly.

A few minutes later, both she and Dave were gone. I helped Avery clear away the tools and sweep the sawdust away from the house's foundation.

Avery and I had grown up together, spending summers

in Rock Point when my family visited, then been room-mates at art school. We'd talked about boys all the time. In my case, it was about boys I liked who wouldn't give me the time of day. With Avery's sweet nature and shy smile, she had more luck. Strangely, now that men and relationships were a real part of our lives, we didn't talk about them as much.

So it felt awkward for me to ask. Maybe it was Jasmine's death, or maybe it was the thought of Naomi Salek and Marcus's grief, but I couldn't hold it back any longer. "You know Dave has a thing for you, right?"

For a moment, I wasn't sure Avery had heard me. She picked up a scrap of wood and carried it to the firewood pile in the shed. I leaned on the broom as I waited for her to return.

"I know," she said.

"I think you like him, too." Avery didn't seem gaga, but she always found excuses to invite Dave over or stop by his store. Yet, as far as I knew, they'd never even held hands.

"I do. He's a good man. But . . ."

"But what?"

"What if it doesn't work out?"

"I know." This was not the response I'd give just anyone, but, over the winter, Avery had dated the Tidal Basin's charismatic chef, Miles. Although they had really cared for each other, they'd had a difficult relationship. Naturally, she'd hesitate to start something new.

"Dave is no Miles," I said softly. Definitely not. Dave was quiet, dependable, yet had a wicked sense of humor once you got to know him. "Has he said anything to you?"

She stripped off her work gloves. "No. I think he wants to, though."

He was being sensitive. Plus, Dave had patience. If he thought the prize was worth it, he'd wait it out. Jack, on the other hand, was more apt to act first and ask questions later.

"What do you want in a relationship?" I asked. In high school, it would have been a date to the prom and the social credibility of having a boyfriend, no matter who it was.

"I've been thinking about this a lot since Miles. Drama doesn't appeal to me anymore. I don't want to stay up late wondering if he really cares about me. I'm tired of trying to read cryptic signals." She started up the stairs to the front porch. "What about you?" she asked as we went inside.

"The same." I went to the refrigerator and found a beer. The day called for it. "I guess I want a co-conspirator, someone who has my back. Someone I trust and respect. Someone on my team."

"We sure sound like a couple of romantics," Avery said, "What about Jack? What's going on there?"

It was my turn to be evasive. "I'm not sure."

"Emmy, he asks you out, and you hem and haw." She nailed me with her gaze. "And eventually go. And then go the next time. And you can't tell me you aren't attracted to him."

"I know. I'm not ready yet, I guess. I just got to Rock Point and started Strings Attached. I'm not even sure the shop will make it through the winter." I remembered the compliments from Cheryl at Pacific Winds kite shop that afternoon and warmed. "I don't even have my own place." I touched Avery's arm. "Not that I don't love it here. But with Jack, well, I want to be more established first. More independent."

"I get it."

The sun was low now and cast long shadows through the firs surrounding the house. "I want to do it right. That means I need to be more stable first."

Avery looked at me as if she had a lot to say, but the only words that left her mouth were, "I see."

Later that night when Sunny was in bed, worn out from "getting in touch with the real me," and Avery was reading alone on the porch by a little yellow light, surrounded by the velvety dark, Jack called. We made a date for the next night.

chapter eighteen

AS SUNNY HAD PROMISED, MY KITE WAS SAFE, EXACTLY where I'd left it the morning before. I exhaled in pure relief and settled in to stitch the wispy lengths of tail that would portray the wind as they danced and rippled in the real wind above the ocean. Maybe I'd add a few ribbons of silver with the blue. I held a blue strip of Mylar up to the light next to a scrap of silver. Could work.

As I stitched, morning sun spilled through the kitchen window, creating a buttery puddle of light that moved across the floor as the hours went by. Sometimes I listened to music or audiobooks while I worked, but today I wanted to be alone with my thoughts. Every once in a while, the bell at the shop's door rang, and Sunny's perky voice greeted a customer. She was doing a good job. I even heard her recommend a particular kite "for its value." Maybe there was something to this finance thing after all. I'd rarely known her to be so excited about a subject. Even when she was really into cob structures, she only got halfway into building a bench before she'd abandoned it. Then there was her guerrilla mandala phase. She'd joined a group of people who showed up in the middle of the night and painted giant Buddhist geometric designs on the street. Come to think of it, she'd said they'd kicked her out when she'd criticized a mandala's symmetry. She always did have a mind for order.

The door opened a crack, and Sunny's head popped in. "Do we have any more high-test line?"

"Check the box under the soft kites."

"Thanks." The door closed, and I heard Sunny showing the customer options for length.

With my fingers busy, my mind found its meditative groove, and uneasiness set in. Someone had murdered Jasmine. Marcus was known for his bad temper, and now he'd vanished. I understood why the sheriff suspected him, but remembering Ruth's story, I had my doubts.

Stella and I had pretty well hashed out the possibilities for Jasmine's murderer, but they all felt thin. Rose had expressed frustration at her sister, but, thinking of Sunny, I got it. Frustration wasn't a strong enough motive for murder. The killer could be a crazed fan, but talk hadn't surfaced about anyone strange in town who might have done it. A shiver ran through me, and I set down the sewing needle. The Tan Man. He was handsome and slick and manicured. Jasmine would look good next to him. No one seemed to know what his business was in town. And he'd been in Lincoln City. Could he have followed us?

From the shop, the door's bell jangled. Sunny's sweet voice sounded strained. "You'll need to wait outside," she was saying. "My sister will get in touch with you when she has time."

"I think she'll be very interested in what I have to say." Nicky Byrd's clipped tones were unmistakable.

I tensed. Maybe Sunny would be able to run him off.

"Interested or not, she's not here. You'll have to go."

The floorboards creaked, undoubtedly from Nicky's bulk. "I took the liberty of peeking in the back windows just now, and she was in the kitchen, needle in hand, the very picture of Rockwellian home life."

I bit off an oath and set my kite aside. As I pushed out my chair, the workshop's door burst open, and Sunny, wild-eyed, entered. "Nicky Byrd the Third is here."

"Let me deal with him."

I threw back my shoulders and marched into the shop. "You," I said.

"Ah, the domestic angel arrives." Nicky Byrd appeared to be wearing the same high-water trousers and short-sleeved button-up shirt as before, and they were the worse for the wear.

"Is that supposed to be a compliment?" I took another step forward. "Look. I told you I'm not interested in talking about Jasmine's death. I have nothing to say. Period. You'll have to leave."

"Hmm. I'd hate to have to write that the suspect had no comment."

I bet Nicky Byrd got the stuffing beaten out of him in grade school. That greasy tone, that insinuation in every syllable he uttered, grated on my brain. "Suspect? The sheriff apparently doesn't think so. Why should you?"

"Who else threatened America's sweetheart in front of the whole town? Who else was standing on the beach the night she was murdered?"

I kept my outraged expression frozen in place, but now I was curious. Where'd he find that out? "Well, if you're so smart, why aren't you after Marcus Salek?"

Nicky swatted as if batting a fly. "Pshaw."

"What? He's the one who left town, not me."

"You have a blob of something on your chin," Sunny told him.

Nicky rubbed his palms on his face but only managed to displace some of his pancake makeup. "Got it?"

"No. Just below your lip. Looks like a piece of egg. There." She pointed, but wisely kept her distance.

He took a handkerchief from his pocket and wiped it away. "As I said, Marcus Salek is not my concern."

"Not even if you knew that his wife was killed in a hit-and-run accident, and no one was charged?"

If this was news to Nicky Byrd, he'd fooled me. "Naomi Salek? That's old news. It's you I want to talk to."

He knew about Marcus's wife. How? Tabloid reporters must have secret sources. What else did he know? "Like I said, forget it."

"I could make it worth your while." He pulled a wallet from his front pocket—a city move; no man in Rock Point would keep his wallet in front—and opened it to display a fat wad of green. "For only ten minutes of your time. All you have to do is tell me about your walk on the beach that night. What—or who—you saw."

I heard Sunny swallow at the sight of the cash. She was itching to give him investment advice, I knew it.

"No, thanks."

"You've already told the sheriff. It's not like you'd be revealing anything secret, or anything that could hurt anyone. Jasmine's death left hundreds of thousands of people in mourning. They yearn for closure. You can help."

Sunny's gaze met mine, then moved to Nicky Byrd's wallet, then back. I shook my head. The cash would be great, but I still had some dignity.

"Don't let the door hit you on the way out." I'd been dying to tell someone that for years.

WITH NICKY GONE, I TOOK OVER THE SHOP WHILE SUNNY had her informational interview with Rose. Business was steady, but not outrageous—yet. In a few more days, as the kite festival drew nearer, I expected things to pick up. A deliveryman had just dropped off a couple of crates of kite supplies, and with one eye on the clock— I had to get ready for my date with Jack—I unpacked and priced them.

The sound of someone singing "Money, Money, Money" reached my ears and I knew Sunny was coming before she skipped through the open door. I hadn't even had the chance to ask her how things went with Rose when she burst out, "It was the best! I love Rose."

"What happened?" I set the price gun aside and

leaned on the counter. "You've been gone almost two hours."

"Well, we talked—doesn't she have the most darling office? Plus, it's so smart of her to convert her garage like that. No extra rent, but a nice tax write-off."

"And she told you about what she does?"

Sunny raised her arms above her head and danced in a circle. "Not only that, but she offered me a job."

"That's fantastic!" We hugged. I pushed her away after a few seconds. "What job? What are you qualified for?"

"Well, I guess it's not really a job. More like an internship. She said that as long as I'm here, I can help her with data entry and getting her accounts ready."

"She's paying you?"

"A little. She said she'd write me a letter of recommendation for business school, too." She pumped her fists in the air. "I'm so happy."

"So, how long does this job last? Are you staying in Rock Point?"

Sunny looked mysterious as she helped me unpack the box. "I have a plan. That's all I'll say. But don't worry. I won't stay with you and Avery forever."

"A plan, huh?"

"Yes."

"That's terrific, Sun." I picked up the price gun again and started labeling some dual line packages. Maybe she'd work for Rose for a few days and give the whole thing up. It would be like Sunny to do something like that. Even Mom would approve of my letting her work for Rose, especially if it let her cross something off her list.

"I started today with some filing." She picked up the packages I'd priced and started placing them in the shop. When she returned for the next armload, she said, "Jasmine has a really fat file."

I halted. "Really?"

"I couldn't see what was in it, though. But it was packed."

As an actress, Jasmine probably had a lot of financial matters for Rose to deal with. Rose had said as much. Of course, Jeanette had implied that they might be more along the lines of letters from creditors rather than investment firms.

Two women, most likely window-shopping, wandered into the store.

"We're closing in a couple of minutes," I told them, and they glanced at each other.

"Not immediately, though," Sunny added. "Please, come in. Look around."

"Do you know a place we could get a margarita?" The one with the fringed handbag asked.

I gave them directions to the Tidal Basin. As was true with Caitlin, the Rock Point Tavern wasn't likely to meet their needs.

"What's with you?" Sunny asked. "Why not stay open a few more minutes if it means a sale?"

"Normally I would, but Jack wants to go to dinner tonight."

Sunny raised an eyebrow. "Too bad. You're going to

miss my pizza. Mom told me how to do a gluten-free crust, and—"

"At a nice restaurant. Jack wants to take me to the Tidal Basin."

"Oh. Fancy." Sunny got it. "Time to take things to the next level, huh?"

I played with a loose bit of kite line. "I don't know."

"Maybe you should try walking at Clatsop Cliffs. Some of my biggest insights have come there. Seriously."

I looked at my sister and wanted to make a smart remark, but felt suddenly self-conscious.

"You'd better get home and change. Don't worry. I'll close up here," she said.

Sunny had done a great job running Strings Attached that morning and, as a result, I'd made huge progress on my kite. All that remained was to attach the bridle and take it for a test flight. I could trust her to close the shop for the night. "Thanks, Sunny."

"One more thing. I ran some figures and talked it over with Rose. She agrees with me." Sunny pulled a sheet of paper from under the store's calculator. "Say you bought this building."

"I don't have—"

"Now, hear me out. You offer five percent below the selling price. We take that cost and amortize it over thirty years at four percent interest, add property taxes and insurance, and the payment is not much more than the average rent of a two-bedroom apartment in Rock Point."

I was only halfway paying attention. I had an hour

to get home and make myself presentable. For a date—a real date.

"Don't you see? You're paying only a little more, but you're getting the shop's rent for free. Overall, it's a big savings." She pushed the paper aside. "A no-brainer. The only trick would be coming up with the down payment."

"I don't even know how I'll make it through the winter, let alone buy a building."

"That's why they call it an investment. You find someone to help you, and they get a cut of the profit."

"And show this person what?"

Sunny took the price gun from me and continued labeling. "It's true that you need some guaranteed income until spring."

I glanced at the clock. "Well, when you figure that out, let me know. Meanwhile, I've got to get home."

"Fine," Sunny said. She added some smooching noises behind my back. "Have fun tonight."

chapter nineteen

A HUM OF CONVERSATION RIPPLED THROUGH THE TIDAL Basin. A jazz pianist had set up near the bar, and clinking silverware and occasional laughter punctuated a languid version of "All That I Am" played on the baby grand.

With a fluttering feeling, I scanned the room for Jack. He'd offered to pick me up, but I'd refused. It felt too— too intimate somehow. What I loved about spending time with Jack was how easy it was. He listened. He laughed. He seemed to like me the way that I was. In this environment, with all its unspoken romance, things were different.

Jack stood to catch my attention. He was at a table near the room's edge, and he'd apparently taken a moment to clean himself up, too. Normally, I would have joked at his pressed shirt and freshly shaven jaw. Tonight, the words couldn't make it past my throat.

"Emmy." Jack took in my crisply ironed sundress and attempt at makeup. "You look great." He pulled out my chair. This was new.

If words had been stuck in my windpipe a second ago, now they'd solidified into a solid clog. "Thank you," I croaked.

The piano now played "My Melancholy Baby." *Dad would love this place*, I thought. I'd grown up listening to his records of old standards. Mom used to play Bob Dylan and Joni Mitchell, but now she was more apt to reach for a Cleo Laine record, too. I wondered what Mom and Dad would think of Jack.

A waiter with a hipster beard—who knew that Abraham Lincoln's facial hair would become the rage 150 years after his death?—and a starched white apron tied around his waist, French style, handed us menus and recited a special. I caught "sea beans" and "Caspian Pink tomatoes," but my pulse throbbed too noisily to make out the rest. Is this what people did on real dates? And they thought it was fun? The tension was killing me.

When the waiter left, Jack set down his menu. "This is awkward. Do you want to get a burger and hang out on the dock?"

With those words, the lump in my throat dissolved. I smiled. Then laughed. "Thanks, Jack."

He laughed, too. "Seriously, though. I'm game if you are."

Sometimes I forgot about his silky gray eyes. I'd be caught up in conversation, then look up, and wham! There they were. And here they were again, soft and inviting. "Let's stay. It's a nice change. Did you catch what the special was?"

"Sea beans. I think it included sea beans. I don't remember the rest."

"Caspian Pink tomatoes. I remember that. Where do you think that name comes from? Is the Caspian Sea pink, or what?

Soon we had an open bottle of wine and plates of food between us, and I felt as loose and relaxed as I would have were we fighting over the last take-out French fry.

"How's your kite coming?" I asked. I pretended to be rounding up a leaf of arugula on my plate, but I shot a glance toward him.

"It's finished. And yours?"

"Sunny wrecked my last take on it, but it turned out to be a good thing. I went in an entirely different direction with this one. All I have to do is bridle it up." I set down my fork and looked him full-on. "It's a five-star, A-one, blue-ribbon kite. I'm afraid yours doesn't stand a chance."

He took the bait. "I admit you make a pretty kite, Emmy, but I've got you licked for performance. You get these wacky ideas—remember your comet kite?—that are more interesting than practical."

"That kite turned out great," I said. "Eventually."

"And despite sending spies to Sullivan's Kites—"

"Spies?" I said. "I did not."

"Your sister? Nice try."

"I didn't send Sunny anywhere." Well, well. Sunny was working for me on the sly. I'd have to order her a subscription to the *Financial Times*.

Jack set down his glass of pinot noir. "She came in

yesterday afternoon, playing dumb, but checking every-thing out. At first I had the strange impression that she wanted to see if I was a good prospect for you."

"Ha-ha-ha." I felt heat rise up my neck. "Why?"

"She asked if I owned the building, how I handled winter sales—that sort of thing."

I relaxed. "That's just Sunny. She's into business management these days. She had an informational in-terview with Rose Normand this afternoon."

"Rose," Jack said. "That's got to be tough."

I knew he was referring to Jasmine's death, not Sun-ny's visit. "No kidding. Her sister. She must look at everyone and wonder who did it."

"So does everyone else in Rock Point—and else-where. Did you see the tabloid reporter, the one with the rhyming name, again? They say he's still in town."

"Nicky Byrd the Third. He stopped by the store." I didn't want to talk about my own candidacy for mur-derer. "I'm not sure why."

Fortunately, Jack didn't press the point. "He came by my shop, too. Asked a lot of questions about the festival. About Jasmine, too."

"Why ask you about Jasmine?" Hopefully I didn't sound as peeved as I felt.

He glanced up, an eyebrow raised. "Somehow he'd heard about the scene at the Brew House the day Jasmine arrived. Maybe that's why he wanted to talk to you, too."

"That must be it," I said quickly.

The waiter returned to clear our plates and ask about dessert. We decided to finish the wine and forgo the marionberry mousse.

When he left, Jack cleared his throat. He fidgeted with the front of his shirt, then finally raised his head. "Emmy, I've really enjoyed spending time with you this summer."

There he was, across the table, funny and smart and, now, terrifying. The evening had been going so well, too. Anxiety fluttered in my gut. "And?"

He drew a breath. "There's something I think we should talk about."

"Don't say it." The words rushed out of my mouth unplanned.

Jack's nervousness vanished. "Why? How do you know what I'm going to say?"

"Whatever it is, I don't want to hear it."

"Why not? All I've told you so far is that I've enjoyed spending time with you."

"So far," I said. "That's what you've said so far. Next you might say that it's getting a little old."

"No. I wasn't going to—"

"Or"—and this was worse—"that you think we should talk about our expectations, or take things to the next level."

He stared at me, lips slightly parted. "And?"

"And I don't want to talk about it. I see no reason things should change. They're fine as they are." I tossed back a mouthful of pinot noir and choked a little.

"I didn't say they weren't fine. I said they were good. Remember?"

I reached for my water and choked again. I pounded on my chest and tried to say, "Sorry."

Jack grabbed the edge of the table. "Should I try the Heimlich maneuver?"

After a few more coughs, I sputtered, "No. I'm fine." One more cough. "There."

"I didn't think you'd take it this way," he said.

"It's just—"

"Just what?"

The piano had drifted into a dreamy rendition of "All That You Are." All around us, people were celebrating anniversaries and laughing and falling in love. I should be, too—who knew? Maybe I was. But the timing sucked. "I don't know what's going to happen with the shop, my sister showed up out of nowhere, and now Nicky Byrd the Third is on my tail and wants to take me and Strings Attached down."

"What are you talking about?"

"I can't do it."

The waiter discreetly slid the bill onto the table and backed away.

"That's okay, Emmy. It's not a big deal. We seemed to be getting along so well, that's all."

The emotion stirred up over the past ten days boiled over. I couldn't hold it in anymore. Wouldn't. With shock, I realized that tears were stinging my eyes. I pushed back my chair and stood up, tossing the napkin on the table. "No more change, Jack Sullivan. Do you hear me?"

Jack stood, too, and made a motion to come to my side of the table. I held up a hand. "No."

He froze. I stomped out of the restaurant. I didn't even turn around to see his expression. But he didn't stop me as I left.

chapter twenty

I MADE MY GRAND EXIT FROM THE TIDAL BASIN WITHOUT looking back, but apparently I wasn't paying much attention to where I was going, either, because not a dozen feet from the front door I slammed into a wall of muscle. Jasmine's husband, Kyle.

The wind was knocked right out of me, and I leaned against someone's Suburban to catch my breath.

"Are you all right?" he asked.

"Yes," I gasped. "Sorry. I wasn't paying attention." Good grief. I could see why football was his thing. He certainly wouldn't be easy to tackle.

"Say, you're one of Rose's clients, aren't you? The one with the sister who's helping her out now?"

"Yes. We met the other day." I extended a hand. "Emmy Adler."

His handshake, thankfully, was firm but not the

clamping I'd feared. My fingers tingled from contact charisma. "You really were hurtling out of that restaurant. The food's that bad?"

"The food's great." My breath was coming back now. "It's the company that was bothering me."

Kyle perked up at that. "Something you need me to do?"

"No. It's fine. I just—It's fine." I couldn't believe that I'd ever suspected Kyle of his wife's murder. He was a big guy, sure, but protective and sweet. "Are you going in for dinner?"

"Yeah. I'm here with Rose."

"Where is she?" The parking lot was dark, and except for the ocean's grumble, quiet.

"A few minutes behind me. I came ahead to look around first."

"The food's good, you don't need to worry about that. Unless—" Now I got it. "It's that tabloid reporter, isn't it?"

"Nicky Byrd?" Kyle said with a hint of sneer in his voice. "He wouldn't dare mess with me. No, it's—"

"Kyle. And Emmy," Rose said. She came from around the corner. I'd never seen her in heels. She'd even put on a dress and a touch of lipstick. The glamour that had made Jasmine a star was easy to see in Rose's face now, even with the practical set of Rose's mouth and her wash-and-wear hair.

"Hi, Rose," I said. "You look terrific."

Rose ignored me. "Is she here?"

"Who?" I asked.

"I haven't been inside yet," Kyle said.

"Is who here?" I repeated.

Kyle and Rose exchange glances. "I suppose it's all

right to tell her," Rose said. "Caitlin has been bother-ing us."

"She won't leave me alone," Kyle said. "I've tried to be polite, but I'm afraid she's taking things the wrong way." The shadows under Kyle's eyes deepened in the night's faint light, but they were genuine.

"I just finished dinner inside, and I didn't see her," I said. Jack would be out any minute now. I was a little peeved he hadn't followed me, even though I'd forbidden him to. "I never watched *Bag That Babe*, but they say that Caitlin was jealous of Jasmine. Maybe that extended to you, too."

Kyle started to speak, but Rose lifted a hand and interrupted. Kyle's mouth hardened. "It's a mess," Rose said.

"And now you have to clean it up," I said. Something was going on here. How much would they reveal? "The media, the bills, the movie contracts."

"What do you know about Jasmine's business?" Kyle asked.

A waft of fragrance drifted from Rose. If I wasn't mistaken, it had a kick of jasmine. "Nothing, really. I just figured it couldn't be easy." I kept my expression neutral.

"Oh, Kyle," Rose said. "We don't need to hide it. Not now. Not from Emmy." She glanced at her feet, then at me. "Jasmine was pretty much bankrupt when she died."

I gasped. Sure, Jeanette from the post office had said that she forwarded bills to Rose. But Jasmine had carried a designer bag and rented an expensive beach house.

"She's a celebrity. You'd think she'd have money to burn," I said.

"That's the trouble. She did burn it." Rose's hard tone softened. "Listen, I wouldn't want it to get out, but Jasmine had a gambling problem."

"What?" The thought of sleepy Jasmine sitting around a poker table with a bunch of card sharks flabbergasted me.

"It's true," Kyle said, looking into the distance.

"Gambling," I said, just to be sure I'd heard right.

"Mostly online, but she'd hit up a casino if she got the chance," Rose said. "I think that's why she didn't want to stay with me. She didn't want it to get in the way of her hobby."

I wondered if the sheriff had any idea. It certainly gave credence to the theory that Jasmine might have killed herself. "I'm sorry. For both of you. It must be awful."

"We're planning her funeral. Nothing elaborate or expensive," Rose said.

"Cremation and a private ceremony later this week," Kyle added. He straightened, and Rose followed his gaze. I turned at the sound of footsteps in the gravel behind me. It was Jack.

"Emmy," he said and grabbed my elbow, pulling me close. "Good. You haven't left yet."

The night was full of surprises. I closed my mouth and did my best to gather my wits. "You know Rose, of course," I said to Jack. "This is Kyle, Jasmine's husband."

Kyle raised an eyebrow at me. "Everything is all right here?"

Jack's hand was warm on my arm, and gentle. Yes, things were fine. I nodded.

"I guess we'd better be going," Rose said. Kyle and Rose rounded the corner to the Tidal Basin. And Jack kissed me.

JACK'S KISS ACTUALLY TOOK MORE BREATH OUT OF ME than slamming into Kyle had. When Jack and I separated, he said, "I think something went wrong back there. Let's try the conversation again."

Wow. I still couldn't speak. I leaned against the Suburban once again.

"I mean," he said, "if you want to."

"Yes. Sure." Whew. "I'm sorry I was so rude. Will you forgive me?"

He smiled. "Forgiven."

"Why don't we go down to the docks?"

Hand in hand, we walked the block to the old dock. I glanced toward Ace's boat. Its windows were dark. We were alone. We walked all the way down the dock, past the old fishing boats, past the family boats, and sat at the end, our legs dangling toward the sea.

"Just before you came to the parking lot, Rose and Kyle dropped a bomb," I said. It was easier to talk about this than about whatever was happening between us.

"Yeah? You were talking with them a few minutes." Jack's shoulder brushed against mine.

"Apparently, Jasmine had a gambling problem. Rose says she was completely broke."

"That day I bought her a latte at the Brew House, her

credit card had been declined. She seemed genuinely surprised."

"She's an actress, remember," I said. There was no doubt in my mind that she wanted to make time with Jack. Who wouldn't?

"The sheriff really thinks it's murder, huh?"

"An insulin overdose. Marcus is the sheriff's top suspect, especially now that he's skipped town."

"Hmm. Something doesn't seem right about that."

The ocean was relatively calm, sending rhythmic waves past the dock. The night smelled crisp and briny. Some people turned their noses up at the scent of seaweed and fish and salt water, but I loved it.

"What doesn't seem right?" I asked.

"Marcus, for one," Jack said. "He's a simple guy. If he were aiming to kill someone, he'd conk them over the head, not orchestrate an overdose. No, I don't see him doing it."

"The sheriff said that someone slashed Jasmine's tires and sent a threatening note."

"Now that sounds more like Marcus."

Jack's shoulder bumped me again. I was tempted to lean into it. "Then why didn't he stick around? Why run off?"

Jack took a moment to think it over. "Maybe he did threaten Jasmine but didn't kill her. He knew, though, he'd have a hard time proving his innocence, especially if he was at her beach house the night she died, slashing her tires."

Yes. "I've had the same thought. After all, why would you bother to slash someone's tires if you planned to murder her?"

"Kyle's the one I'd worry about."

This surprised me. "Because of the fact that most murders are committed by intimate partners?"

"No, I mean that he's a tough SOB who likes to take risks."

"What makes you say that?"

"His background in football. He was always the guy who'd try the Hail Mary, and a lot of times he got away with it. Maybe he didn't like the idea of having a bankrupt gambler for a wife, and he didn't want word to get around. It could have hurt his career."

I had seen a man Kyle's size in Jasmine's kitchen, I was almost sure. "Stella thinks we should track down where he was that night, too."

"What do you mean, 'we' should track down? This is the sheriff's business."

I might have said, *Sure, if the sheriff cared to look beyond Marcus, close this case for good, and get the* National Bloodhound *off my back*, but Jack was staring at me. He seemed to be examining the contours of my face. Which, by the warmth I felt, was flushing Caspian Pink.

"Uh—" My heart was kicking into overdrive. I forced my mouth to form the words. "Maybe we should talk about us. Straighten things out. I guess I wasn't very clear back there."

Jack drew away. I sure knew how to throw a bucket of cold water on a hot situation. He swallowed. "Okay."

I clasped my hands in my lap. "I like you a lot."

"Okay."

"I don't want to mess this up."

"Okay."

Was he ever going to say anything except "okay"?

"Things in my life are so unsettled now with the shop and my sister. Plus, I didn't want to say anything before, but that reporter from the *National Bloodhound* seems determined to make a public spectacle out of me."

"What? He can't prove anything."

"He's not the law. He doesn't have to."

"You could sue him for libel."

"Maybe. By then it would be too late. Strings Attached would be history."

Jack drew a hand from my lap and clasped it in his. "You're going through a rough patch."

"Right." He seemed to get it.

"And you want to slow things down until you feel sure of yourself."

"Right." His hand was so warm and comforting.

"So you want me to lay off for a while."

"Right." I was having trouble keeping my breathing even.

"Is that all you're going to say? 'Right'?"

The clouds layered the moon like Salome's seven veils. Here at the end of the dock, we were in our own quiet space, with the ocean lapping around us.

"Kiss me," I said.

chapter twenty-one

THE NEXT MORNING, HUMMING UNDER MY BREATH, I trotted up the sidewalk to Strings Attached and stopped short. Sitting on the porch steps was Nicky Byrd. I crossed my arms in front of my chest. "May I help you?"

He extended a hand. "How are you this fine morning?"

I stared at his hand until he pulled it back. "I don't have a lot of time to talk. This is high tourist season. I'll be selling kites."

"I'm quite interested in kites. Perhaps I'd like to purchase one."

I dropped my arms to my sides. "Really?"

"When in Rome, as they say. I'd enjoy taking purview of your wares."

"You're not just saying that to get my attention?"

"'Throw your dreams into space like a kite, and you do not know what it will bring back, a new life, a new friend, a new love, a new country,'" he quoted. "That's Anaïs Nin."

"Fine." Casting him a suspicious glance, I continued up the steps and unlocked Strings Attached. "Give me a minute while I open up."

Nicky Byrd followed me in. I flipped on the lights and hung a windsock with "Open" appliquéd down its side in spring green from the porch railing. It was another fine day. The morning sun lit the waves with brilliant sparkles, and the gulls were noisy on the beach. I propped the door open with a rock and returned inside.

"What kind of kite would you like?" I asked.

"Um. I'm not sure."

"Do you have much experience flying kites?" There was no use selling him something that required technical skill to keep afloat if he didn't know what he was doing.

"I spend a lot of time working. I don't have much of a chance to get outdoors." He was fingering a package that held a box kite.

I took the package from his hand and put it back on its hook. "Then you're going to want a diamond kite. They're the easiest to fly."

"A diamond kite?"

"Like this." I pulled down a blue diamond kite that I'd put together from a kit and hung with my art kites as a display model. "You know, the traditional kite shape." Maybe I should have tried to hook him on one of my handmade kites—it would have paid better—but if he was going to abandon it in his motel room, it might as well be something any kid could pick up and fly.

Nicky wasn't looking at the kite. "I imagine you have an especially nice kite for the contest."

What was he up to? "I do, in fact. Stick around and see." A photo of my competition kite in the *National Bloodhound* would be a real coup, although the tabloid would have preferred autopsy photos, I was sure, or at the very least a photo of Jasmine's cellulite. Assuming she had any.

"Now Jasmine Normand isn't judging it," he added.

What was he getting at? "No, I suppose she won't be judging the contest from beyond the grave."

"Certainly not. Her cremation is today," he said, keeping his gaze on me.

"How do you know?"

Now he was the one crossing his arms. His shirt puckered strangely at the shoulders. "That's my biz. I know all kinds of things. How was dinner last night at the Tidal Basin, by the way?"

"Fine." Lord, he was irritating. "I had a nice piece of salmon. What does the Byrd eat? Worms?" Good grief. Nicky Byrd brought out the worst in me. I was starting to sound like a five-year-old.

"Like I haven't heard that one before."

I silently counted to ten while Nicky Byrd watched me. "Look. Let's start over. You want a kite."

Still watching me, he withdrew a stack of bills half an inch thick from his wallet and began to flip through them as if he were counting. The few bills on the top were hundreds, but I couldn't see the others. "How much would a kite cost?"

Even if the stack were all hundreds, it wasn't enough

to get the shop through the winter, and I knew I'd never be able to live with myself if I took money from him anyway. I cleared my throat. "We've been there, and nothing has changed. I don't sell information. I sell kites."

"Fine." Without looking, he reached behind him and pulled a few packaged kites off the rack and plopped them on the counter. "Is this enough?"

"This"—I waved at the kite packages and his wallet—"is ridiculous. No. Worse. It's insulting. You'd better leave."

He didn't take the hint. He stared at me. Fine. Two could play this game. We'd see who would blink first.

"Jasmine Normand was a compulsive gambler," he said.

"Like that's news?"

"An addict. She was completely broke. Couldn't pass up a bet."

I feigned a yawn. "Blue kite or a red one?"

"Fine. Maybe money and gossip don't work for you. But I have something you can't get anywhere else. And you need it."

"What?"

He dropped the oily broadcaster tone. "Half a million subscribers and a circulation that leaves the *New York Times* in the dust."

"You mean—?"

"Yes. A feature, with ample photos of the kite festival and the unique creations of Emmy Adler of Strings Attached. Perhaps a few words about the kites Jasmine Normand particularly liked."

Nicky Byrd had to know that Jasmine had never been in the shop. I glanced toward my row of art kites. Had she, though, she would have loved the garden kite. I could add a row of faux jasmine vines to the tail in her honor. People all across the nation would see my work. And find my website. And get me financially through not just this winter, but longer.

Nicky Byrd watched me, a slight smile on his face. "We'd simply need a few words about how you saw her beach house that night, and—"

"No." He'd almost had me. "No, you're not going to put my story in some sleazy tabloid. Jasmine's death deserves more than that."

"The only other story I have is how you picked a fight with her the day she died. Readers will conclude what they must."

"Don't you blackmail me."

"It's extortion, actually. Not that I'm admitting anything. And what's this snobbery about tabloids, anyway? You sit around reading *War and Peace* all the time?"

"I just mean that Jasmine's death shouldn't be considered entertainment. To her family, it's not. All the *National Bloodhound* wants to do is sell papers, give people a thrill. It's not real news."

Nicky's body moved into a more aggressive position. He stood, legs slightly apart in their high-water trousers, and turned as if ready to deliver a karate chop. "So, you never watch TV?"

"Sure I do. Sometimes."

"And I suppose you never eat macaroni and cheese from a box."

He had me there. I loved the stuff. "What are you getting at?"

"Just that you don't have to be such a snob about reading. There are lots of people in this country who enjoy learning that a celebrity isn't perfect. Is there something wrong with that? Maybe they don't feel like slogging through the latest highbrow darling's work. Is there something wrong with them for reaching for a few words of entertainment after a grueling day at the factory? Huh?"

It took me a moment to gather my wits. "Don't distract me. You do what you do, and I do what I do. All I'm saying is, what I saw that night—if I saw anything— well, that's between Jasmine's family and me. It's not for the rest of the world to read about in your column."

We had reached a stalemate. Maybe he'd go ahead and slander me in the papers, but I didn't see any alternative that I'd be able to live with. When he didn't respond, I whispered, "Why aren't you going after Marcus Salek? He's the one the sheriff is after."

He shook his head. "Not a story. Nothing there for me."

"Why is this so important to you?" I asked. "Why can't you simply report the facts and move on?"

"I'm Nicky Byrd—"

The Third, I added silently.

"—And I have a reputation not only to uphold, but to build. You think it was an accident I was here so soon after Jasmine Normand's death? That was no accident. I have my connections."

"Surely you can build your reputation some other way. You could look at community issues, like"—I cast my gaze around the shop, as if "issues" would leap from the walls—"like how fast Rock Point is growing. That's a story."

Nicky seemed to gather himself together. "That's not a story for the *National Bloodhound*." He stepped closer. "Are you in, or not? You know your options."

We stood, face-to-face, close enough that I could make out every pockmark Nicky Byrd's makeup covered. "I know my options," I said. "And one of them is to file a restraining order. If you ever approach me again, I'll make sure you spend the night in jail."

He didn't bother to respond. He tossed a wadded-up twenty on the counter and, clutching a blue diamond kite to his chest, he left.

"STELLA! I'M SO GLAD YOU'RE HERE," I SAID LATER THAT afternoon.

As she entered, she brushed shoulders with a high school-aged couple holding their new kite between them.

Strings Attached had been busy, but after Nicky Byrd's visit I'd barely been able to keep my mind on business. I wrapped up a kite—one of my own designs—constructed from delicate tubes in shades of celadon, and handed it to a waiting customer, a collector of hand-made kites.

"Thank you," the customer said. "I can't wait to show it off at the club."

I waved her good-bye as Stella joined me at the back counter.

"I'm glad to see you, too," she said. Wisps of her silvery hair had loosened from her chignon and ruffled in the coastal breeze that was coming through the shop's propped-open door. She wore a man's shirt with the cuffs rolled up and a baggy pair of paint-stained jeans, yet looked more elegant than I ever could in my best dress. "I had to get out of the studio for a few minutes."

"How's the show coming?"

"I have two paintings left. They'll need time to dry before I can send them off, but then I'm finished." She leaned on the counter. "I think you'll like one of them, especially."

"It has kites in it, doesn't it?" Stella specialized in landscapes. I imagined a panoramic view of the beach, almost like a Courbet, but with the skyline dotted with kites.

"You'll have to wait and see."

"One of my kites, maybe? Oh, Stella, that would be gorgeous."

"Will you come with me to the opening? I'll show you then."

"Definitely." My smile faded. I looked around, but there were no customers in the store. "Nicky Byrd was in here this morning. He knows I was on the beach around the time Jasmine died."

"He's still in Rock Point?"

"I'm afraid so."

She let out a noise that was halfway between a "tsk" and a sigh. "I suppose he tried to buy your story."

"Worse. He threatened me. He said that if I didn't give him an exclusive, he'd play up the fact that I was there, plus what he'd already put in his column, that I had words with her at the Brew House." I looked around Strings Attached, at my beautiful kites swaying gently, suspended from the ceiling. "I said no, of course. Do you think I made a mistake?"

"No. Of course not, honey. But I can see how it would be tempting."

"He said if I did tell him the story, he'd mention Strings Attached in the article and include photos."

"The man knows his work. Wow." She picked up my pen and started doodling on the notepad I kept near the cash register. "How did he know about the reenactment, anyway?"

"I've wondered myself. I think it's my fault."

"How?" A remarkable likeness of Nicky Byrd was quickly shaping up on the notepad.

"I mentioned it to Jeanette when I was trying to get information about Jasmine. It would have been child's play for Nicky Byrd to squeeze it out of her." Jeanette might be a hard nut for me to crack, but any mention of Hollywood insider stuff—say, one movie star's weakness for tequila or the size of another's shoe collection—and Jeanette would fold like a leaky accordion.

"He's good. I see why the *Bloodhound* hangs on to him."

"The *Bloodhound*'s a weekly, right? That means the next one will be out in three days." I felt more than heard my voice tremble. Stella laid a hand on my arm for comfort. "I have another piece of information, but I'm not sure what to do with it."

"Tell me," she said.

Just then, a father and son came in the shop. "We'd like to see your sport kites."

I cast a glance at Stella, imploring her to stay. She

settled against the counter. "We have a few," I said. "Basic models. Here." I showed them the display, touching a standard red kite.

Sport kites were all about performance. They had two leads and were designed to swoop and dive. My stock tended to focus on kites that flew well, sure, but were beautiful to watch. For me, flying a kite is a form of meditation. With a kite in my hand, I feel like part of the sky, but with my feet on the ground. Jack loved sport kites, though, and the stock at Sullivan's Kites proved it.

"Is that all you have?" The man glanced around the shop, his gaze stopping a split second at the vase of roses by the cash register and the jewel-toned light splashing through the stained-glass window.

"You might try Sullivan's Kites," I said. "Jack specializes in sport kites." The man and his son were out the door before I finished my sentence. "Tell him I sent you," I called after them.

I had barely turned around when Stella said, "What? What extra information?"

"Well, I had dinner last night at the Tidal Basin"—to Stella's raised eyebrows, I added—"with Jack." Complicated, that, now that we had suspended our relationship. Sort of. I wanted to discuss it with Stella, too, but not right now. "And I ran into Rose and Jasmine's husband, Kyle, outside. You know Rose handles Jasmine's finances?"

"I'm glad she had someone responsible doing it," Stella said. She was finishing up Nicky's signature high-water pants on the notepad.

"Rose said Jasmine was addicted to gambling. She was on the verge of bankruptcy."

Stella dropped her pencil. "No. You're joking. Jasmine? You saw that episode of *Bag That Babe*. The whole season was like that. She barely had the gumption to get out of bed."

"I've been thinking about it, too. Maybe she needed the adrenaline rush from gambling to counteract her sleepy personality. Rose says she did it online, mostly."

Stella walked to the door and looked out. The caw of a seagull competed with the faraway voices of people on the beach. She returned to the counter. "I admit that I didn't know Jasmine personally, but after watching so many hours of her on TV, I feel like I did. I just don't see Jasmine hunched over a computer placing bets or playing poker or whatever it is they do."

"Addiction is a powerful compulsion. Plus, remember how she never seemed to have money? Both Rose and Jack mentioned it."

Stella let out a long breath. "I guess it must be true, then. Rose would know. So strange."

"What I wonder is if it figures into her death somehow. Could she have owed someone major money, but didn't pay up?"

"You think the Mafia bumped her off?"

When I thought of the Mafia, I thought of big cities, machine guns, and Italian restaurants with red-checkered tablecloths. I certainly didn't think of small fishing towns. Although we did have Martino's. But . . . the Tan Man. What was he doing here? Was he still in town?

"You're right. That's ridiculous. But remember the

tall man in linen trousers? Kind of looks like he should be lounging on a veranda somewhere in the Caribbean?"

"With the really good tan?" Stella said. "You think he might have killed Jasmine?"

The advantages of living in a small town included its speed-of-light grapevine. You couldn't choke on a peanut without news getting out. "I admit it's a long shot. I can't figure out what he's doing here, though."

"I saw him leaving Sullivan's Kites," Stella said. "Then again at the Brew House. He takes a double breve, by the way."

"Plus, we saw him in Lincoln City."

She shook her head. "No, I think Marcus is still the top suspect. I wish we knew what happened to him."

"I hate to think of him as a murderer."

"I know. Me, too. Especially after learning about his wife. Grief can do strange things to a person."

Stella had lost her husband a few years ago, then recently learned her son, whom she'd given up for adoption as a baby, had died, too. "You know grief," I said. "You're sane."

"I have my moments," she said and laughed. "Music has been a help."

I'd been so preoccupied with my own drama that I'd forgotten about Stella's concert. "The Lovepipers concert is tonight, right?"

Her face lit up. "It is. I'm going home to clean up in a minute and drive over to Spirit Mountain. Should be a great show."

"I can't wait to hear about it."

Stella patted my arm. "Things will work out one way

or another. They always do. Try not to worry about the *Bloodhound* too much."

"Thanks, Stella. You're a sweetheart. Enjoy the show tonight."

I watched Stella skip down the steps, bouncing her head to a song she undoubtedly expected to hear tonight. Despite her assurances that everything would be fine, I was still troubled. If Marcus was going to show up, I fervently wished he'd do it soon. For instance, before Nicky Byrd's new column hit the stands.

chapter twenty-two

RIDING MY BIKE HOME, I THOUGHT ABOUT THE DAY'S happenings. The events surrounding Jasmine's death were only becoming murkier. Where could Marcus be? He might have left the country by now, although the sheriff probably had law enforcement keeping an eye on airports and border crossings. I could understand Marcus's running away if he was guilty. But if he was innocent, he'd better come forward. Maybe he'd seen something that night.

Bear came bounding down the driveway to meet my bicycle. "Hi, you old thing." I ruffled my hands in his fur and kissed him on the head, then pushed my bike into the storage shed.

By the time I was around the front of the house, Sunny was on the porch, beaming. "We're having a special dinner tonight. To celebrate."

"Celebrate what?"

Sunny look mystified that I wouldn't know. "My internship with Rose. Plus, I officially dropped out of college today."

"Sunny! You dropped out? For sure?" Mom and Dad would have our scalps—Sunny's for doing it, and mine for not telling them of her plans.

"Well, not completely dropped out. But I'm taking the quarter off."

Thanks to the trees surrounding the house, the living room was cool. The aroma of coriander and garlic wafted through the house. I followed Sunny to the kitchen and set my bag on the counter. "You have to tell Mom. You've been here almost two weeks—"

"Not until this weekend—"

"—And she keeps calling, and you keep leading her on. What are going to do if she decides to make a surprise visit to deliver some tinctures or something?" I could imagine Mom unloading a basket from the VW Bus, reaching Sunny's group house, then wailing so loud that we'd hear it all the way in Rock Point. I shivered.

From the look on her face, Sunny felt the chill, too. "That could get grisly."

"You can't keep putting it off. It isn't going to get any easier. Tell Mom. She can give the news to Dad."

Sunny tilted her head to the side and softened her eyes into the sad puppy look she'd mastered so long ago. "I just wanted to have something concrete to tell them when we talked. To show them that I can figure things out on my own."

"By couch surfing with me and Avery and spending giant chunks of the day on walks through the woods?"

Sunny checked the rice cooker and added a handful of chopped cilantro to a pot simmering at the back of the stove. "No. Be fair. I'm making progress." Her voice trembled.

"I'm sorry. You are. You've figured out that you want to explore finance."

"Uh-huh." Her dreadlocks bobbed as she said it.

"And you even got yourself an internship. That's an accomplishment." I couldn't believe Sunny had me making excuses for her. "How's that going, by the way?"

Sunny turned to face me, any sign of hurt replaced by the smile that had earned her her name. "It's great. Rose was so surprised how good I am with her software." She waved a dish towel in her hands like a toreador. "I've been teaching myself online since last winter. You should consider getting the program yourself, Em. I could help you set it up."

I had to smile, too, at her sheer happiness. "Maybe I will."

Bear's collar jingled as he trotted into the kitchen. "Avery should be home in a few minutes. Dave's coming, too. And Jack." At this last name, she glanced up.

I kept my expression indifferent. "Oh, really? Great."

"Do you think Dave will ever ask Avery out? Not for hikes or kayak rides, but for real?"

"I hope so. I like him a lot."

"Yeah, some people are clueless about relationships." She snuck another glance at me.

"What?"

"You know what I mean," Sunny said. "Jack is a perfectly good guy, and he likes you. And you like him."

I turned my back to her and tossed a tennis ball down the hall for Bear. "Things are too busy now. Too uncertain. I have to get my business up and running."

"If you married Jack, you could merge your kite shops. It would be the smart thing, financially."

"Marry?" I started coughing. Somehow saliva had gone down the wrong pipe.

"His kites aren't your style, but they're not bad. Although I don't know why he went with a bright orange competition kite."

Bear nudged my leg with his mouth and dropped the tennis ball at my feet. I cleared my throat. "Orange?" Jack had mentioned that Sunny had come into the shop. "So, you're spying for me, huh?"

"It was the least I could do, since I wrecked your kite. I would have told you about it yesterday, but you were out so late. With Jack." She gave the stew another stir. "Two little lovebirds sitting in a tree, K-I-S-S-I-N-G. First comes—"

"Never mind that. Jack's kite. Did you happen to notice its shape?"

"He tossed something over it as soon as I came in, but from the quick glance I got, it didn't look like the other kites in his shop. In some ways, it looked like one of your kites, Em."

My kites? Jack's style was so different. A part of me was flattered that he might have taken some of my design sensibility to heart. "In what way?"

"Ask him yourself. He's coming up the drive."

* * *

JACK AND I GREETED EACH OTHER AWKWARDLY. NO PECK on the cheek, no hug like we might have a week ago. No passionate kiss like we'd shared last night. Fortunately, Avery and Dave didn't seem to notice anything different. Bear danced around our feet, cadging pets and scratches where he could.

"Dinner is just about ready," Sunny said.

"Should we eat on the front porch?" Avery asked. "The guys could move out the table."

My heart warmed. When we were kids and my family visited the Cooks every few weekends over the summer, Avery's mother had often set dinner on the porch. Those were some of my most cherished memories from childhood: Avery and I running on the beach, and Avery's dad coming down to fetch us since the surf's roar was too loud to hear over. We sat around the table until after dark, until the crickets chirped around us. After her parents died, Avery had quit suggesting porch suppers. I still took sandwiches to the porch sometimes, though, and thought about those summer evenings so many years ago. Now it seemed Avery was ready to try again.

"Give me a hand, Dave?" As always, Dave was ready to jump on Avery's command. Before he went to the dining room, he shared a smile with me. He got it.

Half an hour later, we were sitting around the table. A light breeze cooled the porch and ruffled the branches from a hanging pot of fuchsia.

Sunny emerged from the kitchen holding a Dutch oven between her oven-mitt-clad hands. "Dinner's on!"

We piled our plates with rice and waited as Sunny ladled brown, lumpy liquid over it. The table fell silent. Dave pushed at the stew with a spoon.

"Is that one of Mom's recipes?" I asked.

"You think I'd do that to you? No, this is from one of my old housemates, Sharma. You're going to love it." She set the pot on a side table and looked at us. "It's gluten-free." After another pause, she added, "What's wrong? Eat up."

Avery swallowed and lifted a fork of rice and goo to her mouth. We watched. Her uncertain expression melted into a smile. "It's good."

And it was. The stew was rich with layers of flavor. The next few minutes were silent as we dug in.

I was truly lucky. Even if Strings Attached couldn't make it through the winter, even if the *National Bloodhound* implied to the nation that I was a murderer, no one could take this away. I'd find something else to do with my life if the shop failed. I wasn't a killer, and the truth would come out eventually. It had to. But I had something vital: good friends and family, a wonderful home. I hadn't blown my livelihood by gambling. Paparazzi didn't make life tough for me. My friends wouldn't make eyes at my boyfriend. Under my lashes, I glanced toward Jack, on my left. Since I didn't have one. Sort of.

"Anyone know what's going on with the Jasmine's murder investigation?" Dave asked. His plate was clean. Avery raised an eyebrow, he nodded, and she spooned him some more.

"Marcus is still missing," I said.

"The sheriff is sure nothing happened to him?" Jack asked.

"He was spotted leaving town. Lenny saw him," Avery said, getting nods around the table.

"The sheriff doesn't seem to think we'll find his body anywhere." It was nice to sit next to Jack, with our shoulders nearly touching.

"I still wonder if Jasmine's death was suicide. Especially given her gambling," Jack said. "Maybe she couldn't deal with it anymore."

I told Dave and Avery about Rose's revelation in the Tidal Basin's parking lot.

"Jasmine was a gambler?" Sunny said, brow crinkled. "That's interesting, from watching *Bag That Babe*, I would have . . ." She let her words trail off.

"Addiction isn't predictable," Avery said. "You'd be surprised."

"The sheriff seems to have already ruled out suicide."

We appeared to have hit the end of our speculation. Crickets chirped from the trees surrounding the house. Avery asked Sunny, "Have you talked to your parents yet about being here?" Dave and Jack knew Sunny's story, so it was an okay topic of conversation.

"I will. Soon," Sunny said.

"They're coming out for the kite festival, aren't they?" Avery added.

"They are, and you don't want them to get the news by stumbling over you here," I told Sunny.

"I'm not ready yet. I need a little while longer for my plan," Sunny said. "I don't want to tell them I gave up on school without laying out exactly what I'm going to do next. I'm almost ready, though."

"It sounds like you have something in mind," Dave said.

"I can't talk about it yet," Sunny said.

"You haven't said anything about it to me," I said. "What kind of plan?"

"I told you, I'm not ready to talk about it yet."

I pressed my lips together and released them. "What are you going to do on Saturday, then? The beach and shop will be off-limits, and Mom and Dad might want to drop by the house, too, to say hi to Bear. You can't walk along the cliffs all day long."

Sunny toyed with a clump of rice on her plate. "I'll work at Rose's. I'm sure she'll let me do it. She already has clients dropping off their tax stuff. I can put together the schedules for her. It will save her tons of time, and I'll be out of the way. You can text me when Mom and Dad leave."

"Oh, Sunny—" I started.

From the living room, the phone sounded an old-fashioned, full-throated ring. Electricity was spotty up here during storms, and Avery's family had seen fit to keep a hardwired phone on the kitchen wall for emergencies.

"Let it ring," Avery said. "No one uses that line. It's probably a salesperson." The phone stopped ringing. "See?"

Sunny's plan left me uneasy, but I didn't see an alternative, except to rat Sunny out. "Okay. We'll do this your way. But—"

The phone began to ring again.

"I'll get it," Sunny said, clearly eager to get away from the table. "A telemarketer wouldn't call twice like this." She scrambled to the kitchen and returned after a moment. "It's for you, Emmy. Stella."

My napkin fell from my lap to the floor as I stood in surprise. Stella? She was at the concert. I picked up the phone's heavy handset off the kitchen counter. "Hello?"

"Sorry to interrupt you," Stella said. "I left a couple of messages on your cell phone."

"My phone's in my bag. I must not have heard it."

"I need to talk to you. It's urgent."

"Aren't you at the concert?" Stella was normally calm and logical. I wasn't sure I'd ever heard her so agitated.

"It's just about to start, but I'm coming home."

"Why? Stella, what is it?" I was clamping the handset hard enough to leave ridges in my palm. I switched it to the other hand. "You've been looking forward to this show for weeks."

"The sheriff is all wrong about Marcus. Remember what we were speculating about Caitlin and Jasmine?" She let out a frustrated breath. In the background I heard the jangling of slot machines. "Is it just you and Sunny there?"

"No. Dave and Jack are here for dinner."

"Good. Stay put. Don't leave for any reason. I have to talk to you."

"Why? What's this about Caitlin? If it's something urgent, maybe you should tell me now."

"I would, but . . . it's too complicated. Hold tight. I'll be there in an hour and a half." She hung up.

chapter twenty-three

TWO HOURS HAD PASSED, AND STELLA STILL HADN'T AR-
rived.

"How far is it again from Spirit Mountain?" I asked.

"An hour and a half tops," Dave said.

"Faster, the way Stella drives," Jack said.

"Like they've told you a hundred times," Sunny said.

The sun had completely set now, and a haze of clouds
obscured the moon. If not for the feel of the trees surrounding the house and swishing of the wind and roaring
of the tide, the rest of the world might not have existed.

I stood and looked over the porch's rail. "I can't help
it. She didn't even stay for the concert. You have no idea
how much she'd been looking forward to it."

"Maybe there's a lot of traffic right now," Avery
said. She rose, too, and began clearing the table. Dave
helped her.

"Shouldn't be much traffic now," I said. "Not at night."

"Or roadwork," Jack offered. "Let me check the traffic advisory." He pulled his phone from his pocket and swiped through screens. After a minute, he returned the phone to his pocket. "I don't see anything." I was grateful for the apology in his eyes.

"I'm going to try her again," I said. "She won't talk on the phone while she's driving, but maybe—if she stopped for something to eat, or something—she'll pick up."

"She didn't tell you anything? No hint?" Jack asked. Bear was leaning against his leg. That dog always did have a thing for Jack.

"No. She sounded glad we were all together, and she was adamant that we stay put. 'Stay put.' That's exactly what she said. And she mentioned Caitlin."

Headlights shone from Perkins Road, and we all turned toward them. They passed Avery's long driveway and continued on. It was only when I let out my breath that I realized I'd been holding it.

"She should be here by now," I insisted.

Jack and I looked at each other. "You're thinking what I'm thinking," he said.

"Night driving isn't safe," I said. "There are some dark stretches between here and the casino."

"I'll drive," he said.

Relief tapped the tension holding my body so tightly. *Yes*. Anything was better than waiting and worrying.

"Should I come, too?" Dave offered.

"No, you guys stay here and call me if Stella shows up. Give her some of Sunny's curry and tell her to wait."

Within five minutes, Jack and I were pulling out of

the driveway onto Perkins Road. Soon we were on the coastal highway. From there, we'd drive south, then head inland to the Warm Springs Reservation. Barring roadwork or avalanches, there was one route Stella would have taken to Spirit Mountain, and we were on it now.

Neither of us said anything, but the silence felt right. By unspoken agreement, we'd kept the radio off, too. Once we pulled off the main highway, traffic was thin. Jack was an easy driver, even in his old stick-shift vehicle, and while he didn't waste time, he didn't take any crazy risks, either.

I kept my sights on oncoming traffic, looking for Stella's sleek Corvette. The car had a distinctive shape, but it was black, and a few times I put my hand on Jack's arm, thinking I saw it in the distance. Both times it was another sports car. No Stella.

"Could she have changed her mind and decided to stay for the concert?" Jack asked.

"She would have told us." I was sure. "I just hope . . ." I didn't finish my thought. We both knew what I hoped— or desperately didn't hope—had happened.

Avery's parents had died in a head-on collision a few years ago. Marcus's wife had died in a hit-and-run accident. Even on an August night, visibility was awful through the coastal range.

"We're about half an hour from the casino," he said.

The road was an old highway, but narrow, with only one lane in each direction. The forest pressed in on both sides. Soon we'd be dipping into the valley, with its open fields and farms.

"What's that?" I bolted forward as much as the seat belt would let me.

Jack shifted down and slowed. "Looks like an accident."

No. My hands furled into fists. Couldn't be. It was something else, somebody else. Had to be.

Two police cars were parked along the shoulder with an ambulance, flanked by flares, blocking the lane. Jack pulled behind one of the police cars.

I could barely hear for the blood rushing through my head. A tall, thin policeman approached the car, and Jack rolled down the window.

"You'll have to go around," he said.

The ambulance's rear doors opened, and two men pulled out a gurney. "What happened?" I asked.

"A car went over into the ravine, hit a tree. Looks nasty." He stood, getting ready to wave us by.

"Wait," I said. *Please, no.* "Is it a Corvette?"

The officer didn't need to say yes. His surprise told me what I needed to know. I was out of the car before he could respond.

"Ma'am, come back!" the officer yelled.

The night was a blur of white headlights, flashing red emergency lights, and orange flares. I ran past the police cars and down the ravine. Stella's car had hit an ancient Douglas fir. The car's passenger side was smashed to the tree's trunk. The driver's side was still intact, but a car this old didn't have airbags. The impact of the car on two hundred years of tree would have been deadly.

My gaze shot to the stretcher, obscured by two men in uniforms. I moved toward them, but the police officer had caught up with me and grabbed my upper arm before I'd made it all the way down the hill.

"Stay back," he said.

"I know her," I said. I was panting the words. "Stella!"

One of the emergency techs glanced toward me, then returned his attention to the stretcher. I still couldn't see her face. Only the form of her body.

"You know her?"

"Stella Hart," I said. "Is she okay?"

The policeman opened his mouth, then seemed to change his mind. "Stay here. I'm serious. Don't move." His tone pinned me in place. Boots crunched on gravel before hitting the soft forest floor as he made his way to the stretcher, hitching sideways down the embankment. The exhaust from the ambulance mixed with the cool, piney scent of the forest. I felt Jack's hand on my shoulder. I hadn't heard him come over.

The policeman returned. Behind him, the men hoisted the stretcher up the embankment. "She's alive, but not conscious. They're taking her to Salem Hospital."

"Then it's serious."

The officer's expression was grim. "I'm afraid so."

Leaning on Jack's Jeep, I watched the ambulance pull away, its lights thrusting red and orange pulses into the black night. A cold shiver racked my body.

FOR A MOMENT, WE SAT IN THE DARKENED CAR ON THE highway's shoulder.

"Do you think it could have—?" Jack said, while I said, "I don't think this was—" at the same time.

"Stella likes to drive fast," I said, "But she's a good driver. She doesn't take stupid risks."

Ahead of us, the two police cars pulled away. They'd left the flares to burn out at the side of road. Down the ravine, the wreckage of Stella's Corvette disappeared into the night. At some point, probably tomorrow, a tow truck would haul off the car's remains.

"Maybe Stella saw something—or someone—at the show," I said. "Whatever it was she figured out was hot enough that she didn't want us to leave home."

"And that person messed with the car."

"Or ran her off the road. Or drugged her so she lost control."

We sat for another moment. A logging truck passed us, its bulk rattling Jack's Jeep. Whoever had threatened Stella was still out here somewhere.

He turned the key in the ignition. "It's not safe here. We'd better get on the road."

"What about Stella? If someone wanted to kill her, will she be all right at the hospital? Maybe we should follow the ambulance."

"For now she'll be safe," Jack said. We were back on the road again, pointed toward Rock Point. "If we're right, the killer is going to think he succeeded. Stella's car was destroyed. We won't be any help to her tonight."

"As soon as word gets out that she survived"—I prayed this would continue to be true—"she'll be a target again."

"If she remembers anything." Jack's voice was somber.

My mouth was dry. I swallowed. "Do you think they followed her? To check?" I whispered.

"Maybe."

"I'm calling the sheriff." I pulled my phone from my purse, along with Sheriff Koppen's business card. In my mind I pictured the phone ringing in the tiny office. No one would be there. It was past 10:00 p.m. I realized that I didn't even know where the sheriff lived. I imagined him in the yellow light of a kitchen somewhere, with his kids in bed and his wife calling for him to do the same.

After a voice mail message told me I should dial 9-1-1 if it was an emergency, it kicked me to the central office in Astoria. I explained to the man who answered the phone that there was an accident, and that it may have been intentional, and that it might be related to Jasmine Normand's murder. A flight of "maybes." He took the message and said he'd relay it to the sheriff and pass a message to the Warm Springs tribal force, as well.

I hung up. I'd done all I could do. For the moment.

chapter twenty-four

EVERYTHING HAD CHANGED. AFTER FRUITLESS CALLS TO
Salem Hospital—Stella was still unconscious—and as
much coffee as my stomach could bear, I went to see
Jeanette at the post office. I needed information, and I
needed it now. No more dillydallying. Whoever had hurt
Stella had to be found and made to pay. Now.

It was early, but Jeanette was in, sorting the mail. I
went around the back and crossed paths with the mail-
man. Most of his deliveries were by minivan so he didn't
have to leave the car to stuff the roadside mailboxes.
When his morning route was over, he'd walk through
town, dropping mail at counters and on porches. He'd
already started complaining about the size of his route.
Soon, Rock Point would need to double its team.

"Jeanette in?" I asked him.

"Yep." He held the door open for me.

The post office's back room was as small as its front room. Jeanette was lifting packets of mail from a rolling bin. When she saw me, she dropped the mail back into the bin.

"You can't be in here. Federal regulations," she said.

"I need to know where Nicky Byrd is staying."

"I don't know what you're talking about. You'll have to leave."

I shut the back door behind me. "I'm not leaving until you tell me where he's staying. Is it in town, or in Cannon Beach?"

As far as I knew, no one had ever succeeded in getting information from Jeanette through bullying, but lack of sleep and a surfeit of anger drove me to try.

She stuck out her lower jaw like a bulldog. "Leave, or I'm calling the sheriff."

"Great. I have something to tell him, too." I leaned against the wall and pretended to examine my fingernails. Jeanette was too small to take me down physically. And she was too nosy to let me go without finding out what I had to say.

"And what would that be?" she asked.

"That you've been blabbing to tabloid reporters about the reenactment of Jasmine Normand's death. I'm sure he'd like that a lot."

We locked gazes. It was a stare-down. I wasn't leaving until I got the information I came for, and Jeanette wasn't giving up her power so easily. I crossed my arms in front of my chest.

She buckled first. "Cozy Cabins, just south of town."

"Cabin number?" I said.

"What do you think I am, psychic?" She reached into the bin for mail. "Now, get out of here."

Lenny saluted from his perch outside the filling station as my Prius left Rock Point's main drag and merged onto the highway. Ace had the tow truck's front hood propped open in the gas station's parking lot.

The Cozy Cabins, a turquoise-painted 1960s motel, was less than a mile south of town. I pulled into a parking spot near the office. I'd have thought that the *National Bloodhound* would set up its reporters in tonier dwellings than this, but then again, Rock Point didn't have any five-star hotels.

It was barely eight in the morning and, Byrd or not, he likely was not of the early variety. I should be able to catch him in. Fortunately, there were only about a dozen units—none of them cabins—in the Cozy Cabins complex. Unfortunately, I didn't know which one was Nicky's.

I stood for a moment in front of the office. Cars whizzed behind me on the highway only ten yards away. Beyond the motel stretched the ocean, calm today, as languid and inviting as a belly-up kitten.

The office door opened with a chime. The yammering of the Portland morning news show drifted from a back room, and a coffee maker on the front counter gave off an acrid stench.

"Didn't you see the sign? No vacancy. There's a kite festival coming up," came a man's voice.

"I'm not looking for a room. I'm looking for one of your guests."

A short, elderly man with a bald head liberally appointed with liver spots stepped into the office. He was still wearing his bathrobe. "Which one?"

"Nicky Byrd." I held my breath.

He looked at me, glanced through the glass door behind me at the Prius, then returned his gaze to my face. "Never heard of him."

"Ha-ha. That's funny. Which room is he in? It's important."

"No can do," the man said.

"I guarantee he'll want to see me."

"How much exactly can you guarantee it?" He rubbed the fingers on one hand together in a recognizable gesture. "Then maybe I'd have something to say. If I knew who he was, of course."

So, that was it. Nicky Byrd had paid off the Cozy Corners owner so the complex served as his personal fortress. I had his business card. I could call him, but I wanted to see him right away.

"How's this?" I said. "I'll write a note. If for some reason Nicky Byrd shows up, maybe you'll give it to him. Who knows? He might be grateful enough to guarantee you a bonus."

I scrawled, "Nicky, please call me. Have reconsidered. Emmy Adler" and my phone number on the motel's scratch pad, folded it, and handed it to the manager. Without taking his eyes off me, he slipped it into the pocket of his robe. I expected he'd read it before I made it back to the car.

I took my time unlocking the Prius, and I looked up the row of rooms with cars parked at their doors. All the cars, except a run-down Chevy Nova, were new enough to be rentals. Probably most of them were. There was no clue as to which room could be Nicky's.

Fine. I'd call. As I pulled out of the parking lot, habit drew my attention to the view—and to the blue diamond kite bobbing above the beach. I knew that kite. I slowed down and returned to the parking lot, this time to its opposite side. I got out and scrambled down to the beach. There he was, glee written across his face. Nicky Byrd, flying a kite.

"NICKY!" I YELLED. "IT'S ME, EMMY ADLER. I NEED TO TALK to you."

Nicky cast one glance at me and took off down the beach.

"Wait!" Why was he running? He still held tight to the kite, which was climbing now. He must not know he was giving it line. I took off after him. Thanks to the kite and Nicky's paunch, I caught up with him after only a few moments of running.

"Stop!" I yelled.

He kept running, so I grabbed the back of his sweatpants, and—boom!—he hit the sand. Huffing and puffing, we both took a quick time-out to regroup. The kite dove for sea level and hit the sand almost exactly where he'd been standing when I first saw him.

"Stay away. I can't be within a hundred yards of you," Nicky said. "Remember? I don't want to go to jail."

In sweatpants, with a face rosy from exercise and bare of makeup, Nicky Byrd looked like a teenager.

"It's okay," I said, amazed the restraining order ploy

had worked so well. He must have experience with them. "The judge wouldn't give me a restraining order, anyway."

"You're sure?"

"I didn't even try."

Nicky brushed the sand from his knees. "So, what do you want?"

"I've reconsidered. I'm willing to tell you about the night Jasmine died."

Nicky shielded his eyes from the glare off the ocean and looked at me. "Why?"

"I need your help. I'm not stupid enough to think you'll give it without getting something in return."

"What kind of help?" I could almost hear the adding machine clicking in his brain. Little-boy-Nicky was morphing into oily-man-Nicky before my eyes.

I took the spool of line from his hand and started to reel it up. "Come on. Let's get this kite off the ground."

He followed me down the beach. Not surprisingly, his sweatpants hit a good inch above the recommended hem length.

"You know how adamant I was that I didn't want to talk to you about that night," I said.

"You had a few choice words about the *Bloodhound*, I remember." The slick voice was back.

"So you know how important this must be to me. I need to know what you can tell me about Caitlin Ruder."

"Fascinating. She tells me never to come near her, then the next day she's begging me for help. My, my."

Who was he talking to? His invisible friend? "This might be a matter of life and death. I'm not joking."

"And if I answer a few questions about Caitlin, you'll tell me about the reenactment?"

I cringed at the thought of the sheriff reading whatever purple prose spewed from "A Byrd Told Me." He hadn't told me to keep the reenactment to myself, but he probably didn't think he had to. He certainly couldn't have thought it would end up on breakfast tables and in supermarket checkout aisles. Now, not only would the sheriff never trust me again, I could kiss Strings Attached good-bye. Nicky would make me out to be suspicious no matter what I told him. It was the way of the *Bloodhound*. As painful as it was, it would be worth it to find whoever tried to kill Stella.

"That's what I'm saying." We'd come to the blue kite. I picked it up and dusted off the sand. Its spars weren't damaged, so I adjusted its bridle and handed it to Nicky. "Should be good to go."

"What do you want to know?"

"Let's start with Jasmine and Caitlin's friendship. How long did they know each other?"

"They met on *Bag That Babe*. Jasmine was either too kind or too clueless to see that Caitlin was using her for connections."

"Like what?"

"Getting her into the right parties so she'd meet the right people. Things like that." He narrowed his eyes. "Bet you didn't know that Caitlin got the movie role that Jasmine had been contracted for."

The package Jeanette had seen mailed. "What role?"

"The Kingmaker Spy's girlfriend."

Whoa. The Kingmaker Spy series had run through a number of stars playing Johnny Kane, the MI-5 spy, and at least three times as many of the spy's girlfriends, since he averaged a handful per movie. These movies were a big deal. Play Johnny Kane's girlfriend and you were guaranteed prime placement on posters in thousands of sophomore boys' bedrooms. Your career was golden.

"That's the kind of information on Caitlin you were looking for, wasn't it?"

Motive, check. Opportunity, check. Alibi, nonexistent. "Are you sure?"

"My sources in Hollywood are solid. No one can beat them. Ask at Fogarty Talent, if you don't believe me."

"Did Caitlin have a thing for Kyle, by chance?"

Greasy hanks of hair blew around Nicky's face. "Oh, wouldn't you like to know." He suddenly burst into laughter. "Naw. She doesn't play for that team."

"What do you mean?"

"She has a girlfriend in L.A."

I stood, stunned, a moment. "How come the *Bloodhound* hasn't reported that?"

"We have standards, you know. Her personal life is her personal life." He started toward the Cozy Cabins. "Come up to my room."

"You're joking," I said.

"You said you'd tell me your story, right? My notepad is in my room. I'll make you coffee." Dragging my feet, I followed. As we climbed the bluff, he asked, "Is that all you wanted to know?"

I'd learned enough to secure Caitlin's spot at the top of my list of suspects, but I wanted every nail I could pound into her coffin. "What do you know about her character?"

"Character?" he said, as if the idea that a person had character was new to him.

"You know what I mean. Is she capable of hurting someone to get what she wants?"

He stared at me. "You think she killed Jasmine, is that it?"

I raised my chin. "I just need to know."

He shrugged and continued up the bluff. "That's not the lead I'm following."

"Why not? What lead are you following, then?"

"Get a subscription and find out."

"Seriously, Nicky. Who else could it be? What am I missing?" He didn't suspect Marcus or Caitlin, apparently. He hadn't acted overly suspicious about me, although he'd play it up for the paper. Then it occurred to me. "You don't have any leads, do you?"

By his wince, I suspected I'd found the truth. "I won't say."

We'd reached the motel. Nicky Byrd's room was surprisingly tidy. He led me to a small table with two chairs and a view of the ocean. I watched him fire up the room's coffeepot and set out two Styrofoam cups.

"Cream?" He held up a packet of powder.

"No, thank you." I didn't plan to drink it, anyway.

"Would you like some breakfast? I haven't eaten yet."

"I'm fine, but please fix yourself something."

He rummaged in a suitcase that looked to be completely dedicated to food. I saw a box of cereal, some snack bars, and a six-pack of cola. "The life of the reporter, you know." He fixed himself a bowl of Cocoa Puffs, topped with milk from his room's dorm-sized refrigerator.

As he went about his morning routine, I thought about Stella. Had she seen Caitlin at Spirit Mountain and somehow learned about the movie role? People tell Stella things they wouldn't normally divulge. Caitlin might have let something slip. Then she'd realized she'd gone too far and had to stop Stella.

Nicky was scraping the last spoon of cereal from his bowl.

I had a sudden urge to get out of the room and find Caitlin. She'd gained a lot from Jasmine's death. To make the sheriff listen, I had to rule out suicide and confirm a couple of alibis. Then, I'd go to him with the full story. He'd have to listen then. If Caitlin had caused Stella's accident, I wanted her in jail. Now.

"Are you ready?" I said. I could tell my story in ten minutes and be out of there.

"Just a minute." He chugged a glass of orange juice, also from his mini fridge, and settled at the table. He held up his phone. "Mind if I record this?"

"Yes, I do mind."

"I thought you were going to tell me what I wanted to know."

"I am. I never said you could record me, though."

"Fine," he said and put his phone to the side.

I snatched it and flipped it over. It was recording. I tapped it off and kept it in on my side of the table. "That's playing dirty."

"Can't blame me for trying." He picked up a pen. "Now, tell me about that night."

Reluctantly, I ran through the night, starting with my walk on the beach, then seeing the lights on in the house and noticing a man's figure in what I now knew was the kitchen window.

"The sheriff thought it might be Marcus Salek, then Marcus disappeared." Nicky's phone buzzed, and he reached over to answer it, but I moved it out of reach. "Why aren't you interested in Marcus, anyway?"

Nicky seemed distracted by his buzzing phone. Thankfully, it stopped. "Marcus? I already know his story."

"His wife's death was never explained, you know."

"It was explained all right. Now give me my phone."

I didn't move. "Tell me about it." The sheriff was stuck on Marcus as a suspect. I needed to clear the slate of him.

Nicky fell back into his chair with a "why me?" wave of the arms. "His wife, Naomi, was run down while crossing the street in Bedlow Bay. She was pregnant. He was totally distraught."

"That's not news. He thinks it was tourists. That's why he hates them so much."

"No. That's not why."

I pushed back my chair an inch. "What? Marcus has been complaining about Rock Point's tourists all summer, and probably longer than that."

Nicky leaned back, clearly delighted to teach me something. "It's an interesting little story, actually. Bedlow Bay was getting a reputation as a cute beach town, and out-of-towners started buying houses there. The town was growing, so the city council decided to put in a stoplight."

"They're so small, though." I remembered maybe two four-way stops from Stella's and my trip.

"But a lot of traffic goes through there."

"A stoplight? That must have upset Marcus. I can see him railing away at a city council meeting that they didn't need a stupid stoplight just because of all those summer homes."

Nicky looked at me, at first confused, then with understanding. "Actually, he wanted a stoplight for that intersection. Desperately. He was the one who brought it to the city council's attention. It was voted down."

"But he hates that kind of thing. He's anti-growth."

"Could have fooled me."

"I don't get it," I said.

"Not a month later, his wife was killed at that intersection. With a traffic light, she would still be alive."

My jaw dropped. This wasn't what I had thought at all. Now it was clear. Marcus wasn't against Rock Point's growth, he just didn't want the town to grow without the proper infrastructure growing with it. "You knew this all along? How did you find out?"

"It's my job to find out. I'm not some hack. Jeez."

"But this is huge."

He cracked open a diet cola. An unconventional choice of beverage on top of coffee. "Huge in what way?"

"Marcus is suspected of murdering Jasmine Normand because he has a reputation for despising tourists and growth. But that's not true."

Nicky chugged some lukewarm cola. He tried—and failed—to swallow a belch. "So?"

Nicky was a solid journalist, just poorly directed. "Here's your story. It's not about some second-rate actress. It's about growth and what it means. Rock Point and Bedlow Bay aren't the only towns going through this. A town's growth isn't simply the struggle between people who want to keep things the same and people from the outside who want to change them. Look at Marcus. He knew Bedlow Bay had to change if it was going to grow. Ironically, in changing, it would no longer be what the newcomers wanted." I leaned forward. "There's your story. You could win prizes for this kind of journalism."

He stared at me as if I were speaking Mandarin. "I work for the *Bloodhound*."

"You do now," I said. "You don't have to forever."

Lips parted, he squeezed the cola can absently.

Nicky's phone began to buzz, and I jumped, rattling the table between us. I pushed it across the table. "Here. I've got to go."

chapter twenty-five

I DROVE STRAIGHT TO THE SHERIFF'S OFFICE. SHERIFF KOP-
pen was locking the front door. I leapt out of my car and
caught him before he was more than a few steps down
the street.

"Emmy," he said, catching my expression. "What's
wrong?"

"I have something to tell you, but, first, how's Stella?"

"Stable, but still not conscious." Something in the
way the sheriff fidgeted with his keys told me he was
troubled.

"You found something with her car."

"One of her rear brake lines had a clean slash in it.
It was the first thing the tech looked for, and he found it."

Neither of us had to say what this meant. Despite first
going after Jeanette, then Nicky, I must have somehow
hoped her accident really was that, an accident, because

for a moment, all I could do was stare at my car keys. "Is someone guarding her now?"

"The Salem police have an officer at her door. No one goes in or out but hospital staff."

Someone had tried to kill Stella. She saw something, she wanted to tell me, and she nearly died for it. "I just came from seeing Nicky Byrd, the *Bloodhound* reporter. I need to talk to you."

The sheriff unlocked the door and led me in. Instead of going all the way back to his office, we sat at Deputy Goff's desk. The shades were drawn, so the sheriff clicked on the small desk lamp.

"Tell me about it," he said.

"It's about Caitlin Ruder," I said. "Nicky told me that Jasmine was up for a big movie role. When she died, it went to Caitlin. It's the biggest thing that's happened in her career so far. Plus, she was feet away when Jasmine was killed. How could she have not heard anything?" Those were my two big facts. I knew better than to tell the sheriff she was a compulsive liar and never liked Jasmine anyway. He and I didn't give these phenomena equal weight.

"I see." Was that indifferent tone Koppen's natural way, or did they drill it into him at sheriff school? A few times, as I'd sewn kites, I'd tried to imagine him laughing at a barbecue, beer in hand, or smiling at something one of his kids said, but I'd come up dry.

"'I see,'" I repeated. "Is that all? Jasmine was murdered, and someone tried to kill Stella, and all you can say is 'I see'? Besides, Stella mentioned Caitlin when she called from the casino."

Sheriff Koppen sat up. "And said what?"

I hated to admit it. "Nothing. She cut off the call. But why else would Stella mention her? It has to be about the murder."

"Emmy, the DA's office isn't so sure it's murder."

"What?" The force of my voice shocked even me. "How can that be?" I asked more quietly. "The threats and slashed tires. The insulin bottle."

He shook his head. "They say that's not enough."

"But I—"

He held up a hand. "Stop. I agree with you. They're willing to let me question Marcus Salek, if I can find him, but that's it. And it's only because he ran."

"Marcus is a crank, I'll give you that. But do you really see him as a murderer?"

Again, the sheriff didn't reply. I thought I caught a hint of doubt.

"You know about his wife."

"It's been more than five years, and he's still not over it. Grief can grow and twist in a person's heart, Emmy. I've seen it. It can make a person do dangerous things."

"But kill?"

He leaned over the desk. "I didn't ignore Caitlin Ruder, you know. She has a clean arrest record. There's nothing in her past to suggest she'd do anything more than leave the beach house with an outsized cleaning bill."

"So you're not going to do anything about her."

"My hands are tied. Jasmine's death is no longer a homicide case."

I was so frustrated I couldn't speak. "How can you say this, with Stella in the hospital?"

"The tribal police are investigating her accident. But can you prove that it's linked to Jasmine's death?"

"Can you prove it's not?"

He rose. Our conversation was over. "That's not how it works. Right now my efforts are focused on finding Marcus. As for the rest, my hands are tied."

The sheriff had been clear. Caitlin was at the bottom of his list of suspects. Fine. I'd clear every other suspect off that list until she rose to the top.

I PATTED MY CARDIGAN POCKET. BOTH GLASS VIALS— once used to store pins for making kites—were there. North of town, I took the spur lane that ended in the beach house Jasmine had rented. I'd only seen the house from the beach, not from the street. From this side, with an asphalt driveway out front and crisply painted white trim, the house could have been lifted from a Los Angeles suburb. Only the hulking silhouette of the rocks in the ocean beyond, which gave Rock Point its name, told that the house was on Oregon's rugged coast and not the tamer beaches of Southern California.

A rental sedan was in the driveway next to the house. Caitlin was home. I hesitated, but thought of Stella, still unconscious in the critical care unit, and parked on the street. A quick glance behind me showed no one. I didn't need to be caught visiting the kite festival judge.

I rang the doorbell and waited a moment, but no one answered. In my experience, the chance that a doorbell functioned—even in a new house like this one—was fifty-fifty. So I knocked. That didn't bring anyone to the door, either.

I crept around the side, up the driveway, and up the stairs to the deck at the rear. There she was, Caitlin Ruder, stretched out on a chaise in a metallic bronze bikini. The architect had cleverly designed a waist-high parapet that opened to the ocean on the west, but shielded sunbathers from the wind down the beach. Caitlin's tan was already a shade more golden than her hair. Her take on the Kingmaker Spy's girlfriend would definitely play more dangerous than Jasmine's.

"Hello," I said loudly enough to be heard over the surf.

"Could you do something about the couch in the den? I spilled my drink."

I wasn't sure how to answer that. I opened my mouth to say something innocuous, and at the same time Caitlin reached for her glass. She sat up all at once, popping her sunglasses onto her hair. She squinted. "I thought you were the maid. What are you doing here?"

I decided to take that as an invitation and sat in the sculpted chair next to her. "I wanted to see how you are, if you need anything," I lied. "I know you've had a rough time with Jasmine's death."

She stared at me. "I'm fine." She held out her glass. "But if you care that much, you could make me another rum and coke." She pulled the sunglasses over her eyes again and lay back.

The living room was a mess of rumpled clothing and magazines. A jug of rum was on the counter. I opened the refrigerator. A bottle of diet cola and a to-go box were its only occupants, except for the row of insulin vials still inside the door. I hurried the door shut and reached into the freezer for ice.

It would have been so easy for Caitlin to kill Jasmine. She'd seen Jasmine inject herself with insulin, so she'd know where to put the needle. A few questions about dose, asked with feigned concern, would tell her how much insulin would be fatal. Then all she'd have to do is pocket a bottle and wait until the time was right. Jasmine was a heavy sleeper. Caitlin would have crept up the stairs, syringe in hand . . .

"What are you doing in there?" Caitlin shouted from the deck.

"Coming," I replied.

The drink I brought Caitlin was stronger than I'd make for myself, but I wanted her loose. I wanted her to betray herself. I wasn't sure what she'd say and how she'd give herself away, but she'd been here when Jasmine died. She surely held one of the pieces to the puzzle of her death. That is, if she didn't plan the whole thing herself.

I brought her the drink. She sipped, then relaxed again onto the lounge chair. "Perfect. Thank you. So, why are you really here?" If she felt threatened, she didn't show it. I couldn't tell under her sunglasses if her eyes were closed, but I guessed that they were.

"What do you mean?" I asked.

"I mean, it's not like we're best friends. You don't care if I'm fine—except that you need a healthy judge for the kite festival. What do you really want?"

"Okay, you're right. I was hoping you could help me out."

A short laugh escaped her, as if I'd asked something ludicrous. "You're kidding, right?"

I stood at the edge of the deck and looked down the path I'd taken that night. Up close to the house, the path cut between large rocks, meant to keep the bluff from eroding, and beach grass. About ten yards down, the bluff met the beach.

"No." I turned to her and leaned on the deck's railing. "It's about Nicky Byrd from the *National Bloodhound*. I thought you might be able to tell me how to deal with him."

She sat up. "He's not still in town, is he?"

"I just saw him this morning."

"Jesus." She slipped on a loose cover-up that rippled in the wind. "Let's go inside."

"I'd rather stay out here, if you don't mind. The sun feels good."

She looked at me as if she wasn't used to having her suggestions ignored. She picked up her drink and moved to a chair. Something she'd used to slick back her short hair shone in the light. "All right. Have it your way. What do you want to know?"

"What do I do? He won't leave me alone."

"What does he want to know?"

It bothered me that I couldn't see her eyes under her dark glasses, but her body was still. "He wants me to tell him about the night Jasmine died, what I saw from the beach, then the reenactment."

"Don't do it," she snapped.

"He offered me money and publicity for my store, and he even threatened to make up his own story that made me look like the murderer." I turned again toward the beach and felt for the bottles in my pocket. "I'm surprised he hasn't been after you, too."

"He knows he wouldn't get anywhere with me. Nicky Byrd is a pathetic fraud. His dream was to get on one of the TV entertainment shows, but they wouldn't have him. He doesn't have the looks, no matter how much makeup he wears."

"He's good at digging things up," I said. "You have to admit that." The bottle was hard in my hand. If Jasmine had taken her insulin on the deck, and the bottle fell and rolled, it couldn't possibly land as far as I'd found the bottle the night of the reenactment.

"Don't tell him anything. That's my advice. Once he sees that you'll give, you'll never get rid of him."

"Is he really that bad?"

"How do you think he gets the information he does? It's blackmail or bribery with him."

"Extortion," I said.

"What?"

"Blackmail is when you take money for not revealing something. With extortion, you get something you want through a threat."

She looked at me with faint disgust and jingled the ice in her now-empty glass. "Whatever. I'm going in for another drink. You want one?"

"No, thanks."

Her back would have to be to me to get in the freezer. As soon as she reached the kitchen, I dropped the bottle off the deck, as if I'd carelessly knocked it there. It rolled a few feet and stuck in a clump of beach grass.

No, the bottle I'd found had been thrown. If it was thrown, someone had wanted to get rid of it.

Caitlin was back on the deck, drink in hand, before I could throw the second bottle.

I took in the house with its designer angles. "Are you afraid of staying out here alone? I mean, I just walked up."

Her laughter startled me. "It's not you I'm worried about."

"Who are you worried about, then?"

"I've answered all the questions I need to with the sheriff."

Somehow, I'd rankled her. She settled uneasily into a chair.

"I did see someone lurking here that night, you know. No one seems to know who it was."

"I thought the sheriff suspected that local guy, the same one who slashed Jasmine's tires."

"He left town. They haven't found him yet."

Seagulls screamed nearby. To me, the beach was best when trees surrounded you, like at Avery's house. Up there we heard robins in the morning.

"I'm not afraid. Bored is more like it. If it weren't for that kite festival, I'd be home by now."

"You have a movie role, right? Nicky Byrd told me. The Kingmaker Spy movie. The role Jasmine was going to take." I'd called the agent Nicky Byrd had told me about that morning, and they confirmed that the role was now Caitlin's.

A hard look came into her eyes. "You're accusing me, aren't you?"

I didn't reply.

"Jasmine isn't the right type for that role. She was too passive."

"But they offered it to her."

Caitlin raised a meticulously plucked eyebrow. When I didn't respond, she said, "She needed it. She was stone broke."

"But she was a star. How could she not have money? Plus, what about Kyle?"

"Kyle." She shook her head. "He's worthless. Jasmine was his life raft. I suppose he'll hook up with Rose now."

"Rose? You're joking."

"You haven't noticed?" She took in a long sip of her drink. "She has a thing for him."

This was ridiculous. How could Caitlin say such a thing? "You've known Rose for a while, then."

"I don't need to." She moved to the lounge chair and rolled onto her back.

Caitlin's dismissive attitude was getting under my skin. "You know, some people might think you were the one with the designs on Kyle."

She was silent. I waited. "Nope. Not going to happen," she said finally.

"He's a nice-looking guy." I risked it. "Some people might think you'd even kill her yourself." I forced a laugh.

She laughed, too, but hers was genuine. "Go home, kite lady. Nothing's going to happen to me. I've got this all wrapped up."

All at once, I turned suddenly and threw the remaining bottle as far as I could. It hit a boulder and bounced just off the path, not as far as where I'd found the other bottle, but almost.

"What was that?" Caitlin stood abruptly, sunglasses in hand.

"Just something in my pocket I wanted to get rid of."

Caitlin glared at me. Her lips drew together. "You're counting on winning the kite festival, aren't you?"

I didn't tell her I'd already thrown the shop's future away with Nicky Byrd.

"Good luck with that," she said. "Good-bye."

chapter twenty-six

WITH THE KITE FESTIVAL ALMOST HERE, BUSINESS WAS brisk at Strings Attached. As I helped customers, I was curiously detached, as if I were watching a movie of the life I loved, but knowing all the while that it was on the verge of dissolving. When the *Bloodhound* came out tomorrow, it would all be over. It would be worth it, though, if I could put Caitlin in jail. Yes, Jasmine's death was awful. But no one was going to try to kill my friend and get away with it.

So, it was with a clear goal in mind that I closed up the shop for lunch and walked up to Rose's office.

The roses growing up the trellised side of her office hummed with bees and smelled narcotically sweet. Inside, Rose worked steadily, methodically. I was relieved to see that Sunny wasn't there.

I knocked at her windowed door. She lifted her head from the computer and motioned for me to come in.

"Hi, Emmy. This is a surprise."

I took the chair across from her. "I needed a walk and thought I'd check in to see how Sunny did. She said you offered her an internship."

Rose moved her mouse to do something to the document she was working on, then looked up from the computer screen. "She's a godsend. Business has been growing lately, and I've had a hard time keeping up with some of the basic chores. Sunny is so excited about finance that I couldn't resist. She's a perfect fit."

"She loves it. She came home with ideas to expand Strings Attached into an empire."

"Good ideas, too." Rose slipped on a pair of glasses and pulled an index card from a neat stack at her desk's corner. "I saved this one. It has to do with you buying your building again. She worked out some sound calculations."

"I don't have the cash right now." Not that it would matter, anyway, I thought. I took the index card from her, glanced at it, and returned it. "As you know."

"Well, don't worry about Sunny. She's doing great. Thank you for sending her my way."

I pressed on. "I'm glad she's thinning out your work, especially now with everything surrounding Jasmine." I couldn't bring myself to mention her death specifically. "I guess they still haven't found Marcus."

Rose's expression was hard to read. "No. The sheriff has had a lot of questions, though."

"I'm sure. Kyle has probably had to answer a few, too, about his whereabouts. A shame, especially given how awful he must feel, to have the police bothering him." I glanced up to catch her reaction.

She nodded. "It was a quick interview, and they let him go. I was in Portland for an estate-planning workshop. He flew in from L.A. that night. I picked him up at the airport and took him to get a rental car. He didn't leave for Rock Point until the next morning."

Kyle was in the clear, then. I could verify a morning flight from Los Angeles by looking online, although I wouldn't be able to tell if Kyle had been on the passenger list. The sheriff would have taken care of that. But I felt good about her explanation.

"I heard about Stella's accident," Rose said. "I hope she'll be okay."

My heart clenched. "I can't believe someone did this to her."

"What?" Rose's hand dropped to her desktop. "I thought she ran off the road. An accident."

"The sheriff told me yesterday. Someone messed with her brake lines at Spirit Mountain. She could have died." I swallowed. I'd get Caitlin if it was the last thing I did.

"Spirit Mountain, huh?" she asked quietly. "So strange." She fidgeted with a pencil.

"The sheriff says it was sabotage. Someone wanted her to run off the road."

"Oh, Emmy. What's happening around here?" Rose's expression held some of the queer mixture of anger and grief that I felt, too.

"I wish I knew." All these visitors were streaming into Rock Point for the kite festival, thinking it was just a charming fishing village with a good gastropub. Somewhere to spend a day, or maybe a weekend. In this case, ignorance truly was bliss.

I stood. So did Rose. "T'll let you get back to work. How was your dinner at the Tidal Basin?" I asked.

"Very good. Even Kyle was impressed."

"Great. You deserved a nice night out after everything you've been through."

"And you and Jack? Did you finish your business?"

I could tell from her eyes that "business" had multiple meanings in this case. "Uh, sure." Even if we were bosom friends, I'm not sure how else I could have responded. Jack had heard my plea to take things slowly, and he'd agreed. Then we'd made out on the dock.

"These things are complicated, aren't they?" Rose said.

I laughed. "It's embarrassing. The whole town is watching our—I don't know what to call it—"

"Maybe simply 'romance'?"

"—Unfold."

Rose slipped off her glasses. "I wouldn't worry about it. They've all been through the same thing themselves."

"Thanks for that." I had a hand on the doorknob but drew it away. I didn't want to, but I might as well think ahead. "Could we make an appointment to talk about what would happen if I have to give up Strings Attached?" I kept my eyes on my feet as I asked.

"What are you saying?"

"I mean, if I had to give it up, if I couldn't make ends meet."

"Emmy, you're not thinking of closing the shop, are you? From looking at your financials, you're doing really well." She gestured to the chair across from her. "Sit down. I hope I didn't give you the wrong message when I told you to plan for the winter."

"It's more complicated than that," I said, remaining on my feet.

"Now isn't the time to give up on Strings Attached. Look at your business again in the spring. Make a decision then."

"I wish it were that easy. You know the *National Bloodhound* reporter?"

"I've seen him around. He was bothering me, but Kyle scared him off."

"He's already printed a small piece implying that I had something to do with Jasmine's death. I'm afraid he's going to run something larger next time." I was too ashamed to give Rose the details. Worse, I was laying my troubles in front of her. She had enough to deal with already.

"Oh. I get it. Don't let it worry you. Jasmine had to put up with a lot of tabloid drama, and once she learned not to pay attention, it was fine. Who knows? Maybe it even helped her career."

I turned once again to the door. "Thanks, Rose. I should be the one comforting you, instead of the other way around."

"Don't even think of it."

On impulse, I hugged her. "You'll let me know if Sunny gets to be too much trouble, won't you?"

"Like I told you, she's great."

Rose's phone rang. She glanced at its screen, and her face tightened. "The funeral home."

STELLA'S HOME WAS ONLY A TEN-MINUTE WALK NORTH from Rose's. The quirky Victorian houses thinned, replaced by a handful of ranch-style structures that filled the old dairy pasture at the top of the hill. Stella's house was one of these. It was built into the side of the hill, so that her garage—no longer home to the Corvette, I remembered with a pang—and the face of her studio were set below the house, but had full western sun.

I climbed the stairs to her front door and felt under a planter of wild ginger for her spare key. There it was. I brushed the dirt from it and went inside. Madame Lucy sat next to her dish and let out a mournful howl.

"I'm sorry, baby," I told the cat as I looked through Stella's lower cupboards for cat food. "Your mama is away for a few days. But I'm going to take care of you. I'll come and visit every day until she's home."

In reply, Madame Lucy moved to the cupboard next to the refrigerator and pointed her nose toward it. Yes, there was her bag of food. "Thank you, Madame." I filled her dish and freshened her water before going in search of the litter box.

It felt strange to be here without Stella. The house was so still, so quiet. Stella had left her bed turned down and a gorgeous old cotton nightgown lying on it. Its collar was embroidered in white thread. From the impression in its center, it seemed Madame Lucy had made it a napping spot.

Stella had been intending to come home that night, like every night, even if this one would have been later than most, and go to bed. The turned-back blankets were too poignant a reminder for me. I pulled them up and straightened the quilt.

I found Madame Lucy's litter box in the corner of the bathroom. Stella had left the window open, and the afternoon air stirred the linen curtain. The cat, licking her whiskers, followed me downstairs as I checked to make sure the studio was secure. Upstairs again, I stacked Stella's mail on the dining room table and looked out the plate-glass window to the ocean, rushing in and out, strips of white frosting each wave.

A few more kites than usual bobbed in the wind. The kite festival was the day after tomorrow, and every vacation beach house and bed-and-breakfast in town was booked. Martino's Pizza would be doing a brisk business, and each of the Tidal Basin's tables would be filled by seven. Madame Lucy rubbed her head against my leg.

Among the tourists and the residents was a murderer. Rose and Kyle had been ruled out. Caitlin was at the top of my list, but Marcus was still out there.

I'll find whoever did this to you, Stella, I thought. *I will.*

I WAS AWFUL COMPANY FOR AVERY AND SUNNY AT DINNER that night. Sunny kept trying to tell me about the advantages of the accounting software she'd chosen for me.

"Wait until you see how easy it is. Even you could use it," she said.

"Uh-huh." I pushed a cherry tomato across my plate.

"And you should see the reports. Say you want to look at your utilities costs for the year. You know, see if it would pay to get a new furnace. You just push a button, and there it is."

Avery, bless her, actually seemed interested. "What did you say the name of this software is? I'm still keeping track of everything in a spreadsheet."

Sunny first looked horrified, then delighted. "Oh, Avery, let me set you up. You can email me the spreadsheet, and I'll enter everything for you. You're going to love it."

"I wouldn't do that to you—"

"Please." Sunny drew the word out into three syllables.

"If you're sure—"

"Ha-ha-ha," Sunny sang. "Tomorrow. After I get home from Rose's, I'll do it."

Avery rose and folded her napkin on the table. "And you really don't mind doing the dishes? I need to get ready to go out."

"Consider it my rent," Sunny said. She really was turning out to be an okay roommate, after all. Today alone, she'd swept the porch, vacuumed, and, of course, taken Bear for a long walk at Clatsop Cliffs. And she hadn't broken a thing.

"Go out?" I asked.

A hint of a smile crossed Avery's face. "Dave and I have plans. There's music down at the Tidal Basin. They're booked up, but Dave got us in."

My lips formed "Oh," and I smiled. "Wear that raspberry-pink dress. It looks great with your skin."

I had plans of my own that night. Once it was dark, I'd take my competition kite to the beach and give it a trial flight. I knew it was flight-worthy, I just wanted to be able to handle it with grace at the festival. Maybe Strings Attached's future was in peril, but I still wanted to show the world that I could make a champion kite. I'd take the kite to the stretch of beach just south of Avery's. After dark, it would be just me and the wind.

An hour or so later, I had the kite carefully rolled and tucked under my arm. I slipped on a fleece cover-up—even August nights could be chilly, especially right at the surf—and called Bear to come with me. He sprang up from his bed and trotted to my side. Sunny had her head deep into a book called *Richer than Croesus*.

The night was overcast, but the full moon illuminated the clouds with a pearl-gray glow that made it easy to find my way down the beach. The tide, tugged by that same moon, was on its way in, slowly creeping up the beach. I found an open spot with no washed-up tree trunks to stumble over. A few houses with lights still glowing dotted the bluff above the beach. I could just make out Jasmine's house—now Caitlin's—to the south. Superstition kept me from wandering that far down.

While Bear inspected a clump of seaweed a few yards away, I unrolled my kite and hooked the line to its bridle. Tomorrow I'd be able to see it in its full glory: Father Wind, his cheeks puffed, chiffon-like ribbons of wind unfurling into the breeze. Tonight, the kite would be a dim shape. Even so, I felt the shimmer of excitement that I always did when testing a new design.

I gave myself a few yards of line and lifted the kite. It was a large kite—better to wow the crowds with—and I braced myself to stay steady in the wind. Bear ran over, head up, to watch. Up, up, up went the kite, and I couldn't help gasping at its beauty—and power. Chills ran through my body. After a few minutes of giving it line, bit by bit, the kite was calm in the sky, its cheeks puffed and eyes firmly ahead, with those long, dancing furls of wind pouring from Father Wind's lips. I'd really outdone myself.

Giving a short yap, Bear ran down the beach. "Bear!" I yelled. I couldn't go after him, not with a kite of this size in the sky above me. I'd be pulled away. If I dropped the line, the kite could end up anywhere from dangling from a beach house's chimney to washed out to sea.

Squinting into the horizon, I saw a man's shape coming closer. For a split second, I remembered the man in Jasmine's window and the breath caught in my throat. Then I relaxed. It was Jack.

He had a kite with him, too. *Aha.* All I made out was its color—orange—and the fact that it looked as large as mine. The contest was in two days. I didn't want to give away my kite, but at this point, thanks to the upcoming article in the *National Bloodhound*, maybe it didn't matter.

Bear danced around Jack's feet as he came closer. "Emmy?"

I switched my attention to reeling in my kite, but I was very aware of his presence. "Fancy seeing you here."

"How's Stella? Is she conscious?"

"Not yet." I'd called every few hours through the day and gotten the same report over and over again. "They say she's stable, but not yet awake. The sheriff told me her car was definitely sabotaged." The wind chilled my arms. I wished I'd brought a jacket instead of just my fleece pullover.

"I don't believe it. Someone tried to kill her," Jack said. "It's sure now."

"I'm afraid so. She saw something or someone at the concert that clued her in on Jasmine's death. Had to be."

"Could it have been Marcus? As far as I know, he hasn't been found."

"Maybe." I still had a hard time seeing Marcus as a killer. A grieving, confused man, yes, but not a murderer. "She'll tell us. Although sometimes people lose their memory when they come out of a coma." I refused to admit the possibility that Stella wouldn't gain consciousness eventually.

Jack looked down the beach toward town. "I suppose we're safe here. He'll stay clear of Rock Point."

"You mean Marcus."

He took his time responding. "It seems crazy, but who else could it be?"

"Sheriff Koppen agrees with you."

"But you don't?" Jack said.

"I don't know what to think anymore." I'd eliminated every suspect from my list except Marcus and Caitlin. If only there were some way to get in touch with Marcus. I transferred my attention to my kite. Even at night, when I could barely make out its details, it was a showpiece. During the day, it would be stunning.

"Why not Marcus?" Jack asked.

I started to reel my kite in. "According to his sister-in-law, he was devastated when his wife died. They worried about him. It just seems like someone who could care that much couldn't be a murderer." Marcus's wife was buried in the cemetery east of town. An idea took root in my mind.

"Some people might say that's why he'd kill," Jack said.

Bear ran up from the surf and sniffed at the bundle Jack held.

"Is that your competition kite?" I asked. My kite was heavy with wind, so I was reeling it in slowly.

"Is that yours?" As the Father Wind kite came closer, ever so slowly, Jack made a low sound of appreciation. "Not bad at all."

The tone of voice he used told me he was bowled over, and I couldn't help but smile. "It was a last-minute choice. I'd spent hours—you have no idea how long—doing two appliqué kites of Rock Point, but Sunny wrecked them. Then I realized that I needed a block-buster, not some contemplative piece. This is the first chance I've had to take it out."

"That's clever." He pointed to the ribbons of fabric waving from Father Wind's mouth. "Instead of the tail following the kite, it almost looks like it leads the kite." He knelt and rolled his kite out onto the sand. "Too bad this one is going to take top prize."

Jack's kite was a strange collection of angles. I couldn't quite make it out. He unbundled some graphite spars and slid them into place, again, at angles. By the

time I had reeled my kite in, his was assembled. It was
a five-foot-wide multisided star, with no tail. Clean and
geometric, but not likely to be very fast.

"This isn't your usual style at all," I said. I let my kite
rest on the beach. It began to gently deflate. I wouldn't
say so to Jack, but I knew mine was the sure winner.

"I've had some artistic influences lately." He gave me
a side glance as he attached the kite's bridle.

"Really?" I flattened my kite and carefully rolled it
up, tucking its strands of wind into the body to protect
them. "And what would that be?"

"You hadn't guessed?"

Standing on the beach with the Pacific Ocean stretch-
ing thousands of miles toward China, we might have
been at the edge of the world. Where we stood, civiliza-
tion's lights dropped off, and the heavy ocean churned
and pulled with deceptive calm.

He looped an arm around my waist and kissed me.
When we separated, I murmured, "For a couple who
just put things on hold, we sure get along well."

"You have a problem with that?"

He pulled me close, and I rested my head on his chest.
Through his T-shirt, I felt his heart beat against my ear.
"No," I said. I sighed. "And yes."

Jack was one of the best things to happen to me this
summer. But there was too much going on now. What
if I went broke, lost Strings Attached, and moved away?
How would Jack feel about being with me then? I cringed
to imagine him reading my story in the *National Bloodhound* and knowing I'd sold myself out. Yes, Jack was
wonderful, but right now being with him was like pour-

ing chocolate syrup on the rotting remains of last week's dinner. I needed to straighten up my life first.

Regretfully, I pulled myself away. "It's not the right time. Not yet."

Jack's gaze was full of questions, but to his credit, he didn't argue. "Okay," he said. That was all. He turned his back to me and lifted his kite. It caught the wind and spun before slowly rising.

"I guess I should get back now. Come on, Bear." I didn't know when I'd ever said a more difficult good-bye. I didn't want to leave, but it would be wrong to stay. I picked up my kite. "I'll see you at the festival, Jack."

"Emmy . . ." He let one hand drop from his spindle of line long enough to touch my cheek. I felt each one of the next five seconds in every fiber of my being. "Never mind. Good-bye," he said softly. He returned his attention to the kite.

I walked up the beach toward home, Bear trotting ahead of me. My feelings were a tangle of desire and fear that clogged my throat. I turned around again. Jack's kite rose and rose, its features dimming in the night.

chapter twenty-seven

IT WAS A LONG SHOT. I KNEW THAT. BUT RIGHT NOW IT
was the only shot I had.

Just after the sun rose, I drove to Rock Point's only
cemetery, beyond the Methodist church. I hadn't had
the chance to wander there yet. The morning was quiet,
except for the sounds of birds. Conifers crowded the
gravestones and nearly threatened to swallow the cemetery whole. The sound of my car door shutting dis-
turbed a crow sharpening his beak on a cement obelisk
and he flew away, cawing.

The cemetery was old. The moss on the gravestones
told me that much. Someone had clearly come up here
from time to time to tend the ragged grass between the
graves, though. Naomi Salek was buried here somewhere, but there was no caretaker's office and no direc-
tory, so I'd have to search the cemetery row by row.

I trudged through the dew-heavy grass to the bottom of the graveyard and started walking a zigzag pattern. The graves weren't laid out regularly enough to sit in rows, so I had to double back sometimes to check names and dates.

Most of the plots were easy "no"s. They were crumbling or covered with moss old enough to have turned brown and become part of the stone. I passed scores of memorials for men lost at sea. Men had a lot of hubris, thinking that their flimsy wooden boats stood a chance against the ocean's massive power.

Naomi had died five years ago. She'd have a modern headstone, or, more likely, a plaque set into the ground. I kept searching.

Almost an hour later, I found the Salek family's plot. The cloud cover was beginning to break up, and I slipped off my pullover and tied it around my waist. Rock Point had been thick with Saleks, it seemed, and judging by the dolphins and compasses carved into their gravestones, many of them had been fishermen.

Here was Naomi Salek's grave. Its marble plaque read simply, "Naomi Whiting Salek, Loving Wife and Mother," and gave the dates of her birth and death. When she died, she'd been only a few years older than I was now. A bare plot lay beside her, almost certainly reserved for Marcus. Bundled at the foot of the grave was a handful of fresh daisies and black-eyed Susans that could have been pulled from anyone's garden.

It told me that the grave had had a recent visitor, maybe even a visitor who would return today. I could only hope.

"Rest in peace, Naomi," I said. I wiped her marble plaque dry and placed an envelope upon it.

DESPITE THE STEADY STREAM OF CUSTOMERS THROUGH Strings Attached, the day dragged. Every time I heard steps on the shop's porch, I raised my head, hoping to see Marcus. If Marcus was the man I thought he was, when he read my letter, he'd come. He hadn't come.

When the traffic of customers slowed for a moment, I called Salem Hospital. The nurse on duty recognized my voice from my many calls the day before, and she was almost as glad to report as I was to hear that Stella's vital signs were improving, and that she was responding to stimuli.

"Does that mean she's awake?" I asked, clutching the phone.

"She can't talk, if that's what you're asking, but if we apply pressure to her skin, she flinches, and she responds to sound. Good signs."

"So, she'll be back to normal soon."

"Can't say that. It's looking good that she'll regain consciousness, but there are no guarantees. If her brain was damaged, she might not recall anything. She might not be the person you remember, either."

Despite the nurse's warnings, I hung up with a huge feeling of relief. Stella was improving. That had to be good.

Besides waiting for Marcus—if he showed up—I had one more thing I was anticipating. The new *National Bloodhound* came out today. I'd seen Nicky yesterday morning, and I assumed that he'd had plenty of time to file his story. I was just waiting for someone to show up waving a copy and asking why I had blabbed, what I had gotten from it, and what role I'd played in Jasmine Normand's death. I didn't leave the shop for lunch like I usually did, in part because I still hoped Marcus would come by, but also because I couldn't face the crowd at the Brew House. Jeanette might have dropped a copy of the tabloid on the public reading pile, with the pages of particular articles folded down. I didn't want to be there. I didn't want to see it. I wanted to pretend, just for another day, that Strings Attached was happy and successful, and there was nothing to threaten its future. I didn't regret trading my story for information that would find Stella's attacker, but I didn't have to like it.

Morning turned to afternoon, then to evening, with no Marcus and no *Bloodhound*. My nerves were taut as a snare drum when it was time to close the shop. August days were long, and when I flipped the sign to "Closed" and brought in the windsocks, the sun still shone low over the ocean.

I didn't go home. I restocked the kites that had sold and moved to the front a few handmade kites I'd kept in my workshop in reserve. I swept the shop and cleaned the windows. I tallied the day's sales, thinking of the magical accounting system Sunny had promised. Then I called home.

"Avery? I'm staying late at the shop. I, um, have some sketches to do . . . Yes, super inspired. I'll see you later tonight."

The sun dropped lower. The beach was busier than

normal, even for a Friday night, which I chalked up to
the next day's kite festival. My stomach growled as if
jet engines were landing in my intestines, but I didn't
want to leave the shop, in case Marcus got my note.
Sunny had left some tofu pâté in the refrigerator, and I
finished it off with a spoon. A banana I'd rejected yesterday as over-the-hill became dinner's second course.

And I waited. And waited. Night fell, and I flipped
on the lights in the old house's kitchen, now my studio.
I listened to the radio and tidied my kite-making mate-
rials and did a competent sketch of the teakettle.

How long would I wait? Was ten o'clock late enough?
Or midnight? It was completely dark out now, and the
street's bustle had slowed to the occasional resident taking a constitutional on the beach. I yawned and stretched.
I hadn't slept much last night, not after saying good-bye
to Jack. Maybe that had been a mistake, too. A hot coal
burned right where my heart beat. Jack. I couldn't in
good faith have done anything else.

As Scarlett O'Hara said, tomorrow is another day.
Tomorrow was the kite festival. I'd fly Father Wind to a
crowd that appreciated it or possibly jeered at me, thanks
to the *Bloodhound*. Marcus would still be gone, or not.
Jasmine's murderer would still be on the loose, but maybe
the noose would be tightening around him—or, more
likely, in my opinion, her.

In my mind, Caitlin wore the bull's-eye. She had everything to gain from Jasmine's death, and she was only
feet away when Jasmine died. If only Marcus hadn't run.
He was the last suspect I needed to absolve in order to
clear the path to the person who had nearly killed Stella.

I couldn't keep my eyes open any longer. It was time to admit defeat and go home.

And then someone knocked on the back door.

THROUGH THE KITCHEN DOOR'S WINDOW, MARCUS WAS diminished. His eyes were bruised by not enough rest and too much worry. To me, he didn't look like a killer. He looked like a haunted man.

I opened the door, but he hesitated on the stoop. "Come in," I said.

Finally, he said, "All right." The funk of unwashed clothing followed him.

"Where have you been?"

"Around."

"Not at home, though," I said. "In Bedlow Bay?"

"In the woods." He seemed a little spacey.

"Are you all right?"

Instead of answering me, he said, "I remember when Mrs. Ratcliff had this house."

"Mrs. Ratcliff." I poured a glass of water and handed it to him. "Drink this."

He took the glass. "Second-grade teacher at Rock Point Elementary." He visibly relaxed. "Tough nut. She's in a home in Astoria now."

"No kidding. I always wondered who'd lived here." The house, although gloriously appointed with Victorian details, was modest. But it was in a fabulous location, just a block up from the beach. Many afternoons I'd imagined its original owners having horses stabled down the street, bringing in Dungeness crab for dinner, collecting salmon berries and morel mushrooms, walking up the hill in their Sunday best to church. Of course, that was long before Mrs. Ratcliff would have lived here. Marcus looked to be in his forties. Grade school was a good thirty-plus years behind him. In those days, President Reagan's speeches might have played on the television, and a station wagon with faux-wood paneling might have been parked in the alley behind the house.

Marcus's dreamy expression sharpened. He drew my letter from his pocket. "You left this for me."

Poor Marcus, wandering the graveyard, afraid to come home. "Are you hungry? I don't have any food," I said, sorry I'd licked the tofu pâté container clean, "but I can make you some tea."

"Nothing stronger?"

"Afraid not."

He sighed and took one of the kitchen chairs before downing the glass of water. "They really tried to kill Stella?"

That had been my ace in the hole. When I'd written it in the letter, I knew that if Marcus was innocent, when he heard about Stella, he'd be shocked. He'd come. "Yes. She's in Salem Hospital. She's looking better, but still not conscious."

"What happened?"

"Someone cut her brake line, and her Corvette ran off the road between here and Spirit Mountain. Before she left the casino, she called and said she knew something about Jasmine's death. She was on her way to my house when she had the accident."

He dropped his face into his hands.

"Marcus?"

He didn't respond. But he was here. I decided to make tea, anyway. I put water on to boil and set out the teapot with a few spoonfuls of Darjeeling.

"I didn't think it would come to this," he said. "When I—left, I had no idea."

I took the chair across from him. "Marcus, I know about your wife. You tried to get that stoplight in Bedlow Bay, but you were blocked. It wasn't your fault."

He hid his face, but from his heaving back, I knew he was sobbing. After all that time on the run, grieving and fear had taken their toll.

"And I know you didn't kill Jasmine Normand. I'm certain."

We sat silent for a few moments until the kettle whistled, and I filled the teapot. When I returned to the table, he had calmed and looked at me straight on.

"What's happened since I've been gone?" he asked.

I told him about what I'd seen from the beach, the reenactment, and Nicky Byrd. I told him about Kyle coming to town, and Caitlin staying on at the house. I told him that the sheriff was looking for him, but that wasn't news to Marcus. "That's what I know," I said. "Will you tell me what you know?"

I poured us tea in the bone china cups that had belonged to my grandmother. The cups' filigree and roses looked especially delicate in Marcus's awkward hands.

"All right. I'll tell you." He set down the cup. "I was at Jasmine Normand's house. You know, Naomi died almost five years ago to the day."

I nodded. "Go on."

"I was crazy with grief. She was hit by a car, you know."

I nodded again.

"People don't know how to grow a town. They think they can come in and make your home a cartoon of what it really is. That's what they tried to do with Bedlow Bay. They liked the atmosphere. They wanted to keep it cute." He spat out the last word. "But we were growing. Just like Rock Point is growing. It couldn't stay the same."

"But they wanted to keep it the same."

"And it killed Naomi." He wasn't going to drink his tea.

I wouldn't drink mine, either. I pushed away the cup. "What did you do?"

"I've been thinking about it ever since. When I moved to Rock Point, I saw the same thing happening. Tourists started coming, folks started buying vacation homes here, but the town didn't keep up." He stared at teacup, as if the few leaves settled in its bowl could tell him something.

"And then?" I nudged.

"I thought if Rock Point could go back the way it used to be, things would be all right. The kite festival was fine as long as it was mostly locals. But Jasmine Normand would draw crowds. I kept thinking of my wife, and . . ." He swallowed. "It was all too much. I wrote Jasmine Normand a note, told her to leave town."

I gave him a moment, then asked, "What else?"

"I went to the beach house that night, and I slashed the front tires of the SUV. I guess someone saw me nearby, because the sheriff came knocking around. I heard about her death, and I lit out. I knew that if there was any chance to pin it on me, they'd do it." He looked at me, pleading. "It was crazy. I know that now. If I could take it all back, I would."

So far, nothing he'd said had surprised me, but I was gratified to hear it all the same. "I'm sorry," I said quietly. After a moment, I added, "When you were at the beach house, what did you see?"

He tilted his head to the side, as if he were calling forth a picture. "I didn't get too close to the house, you know. I didn't want to wake them up."

"But you saw something inside?"

He looked straight at me for the first time that night. "The light was on in the south side of the house."

"The kitchen," I said.

"I saw the other one, the other TV star. It looked like she was talking to someone."

"Caitlin? You saw Caitlin?"

He waved his hand. "I don't know her name. You saw her. The one who was with Jasmine at the Brew House the day you cussed out Jack Sullivan."

He'd seen Caitlin, awake and talking, probably to Jasmine. Caitlin had sworn she was asleep all night. It had to be Caitlin who killed Jasmine. "Marcus, I know you're innocent. You slashed her tires, but that's minor. If the murderer goes free, more people like Stella could be hurt—or killed."

He toyed with the cup's delicate rim but said nothing.

I leaned forward. "Are you willing to talk to the sheriff about this?"

He dropped his head to the table.

"I'll stand behind you, I will. You have important information."

"He'll just want to throw me in jail," came Marcus's muffled voice.

"He wants to find the real murderer. You can help."

chapter twenty-eight

MARCUS WASN'T EASILY CONVINCED, AND IT TOOK A DE-
tailed reminder of Stella's crash scene to get him to
consider talking to Sheriff Koppen.

"I'm not going to his office," Marcus said. "I'm not
leaving here. I don't want to see anyone."

I didn't blame him. Even though it was late, there
was the chance that a resident would spot him and call
the police, or worse. "Once they know you've helped
put the real murderer in jail, your reputation will turn
around," I said. "You'll see."

He made a mumbling noise I couldn't interpret.

With an eye on Marcus, fearing he'd change his mind
and run off, I called the sheriff. As expected, the phone
was forwarded to the county seat in Astoria. "This is
urgent," I said. "I have to talk to the sheriff." I didn't
want to freak Marcus out by saying "I found a fugitive,"

so I bent the truth a bit. "He told me to call him if I found myself in this situation."

"Then why don't you have his cell phone number?" the dispatcher said.

Why not, indeed? "It's someone he's been eager to talk to. About the Jasmine Normand case." This got the dispatcher's attention. "Tell him to meet me at Strings Attached. He knows where it is." I suppressed the urge to ask that the sheriff bring food. No use pushing my luck.

Marcus sat, undisturbed. Apparently, once he'd made up his mind to talk to the sheriff, he'd stick to it. I was grateful.

"Tell me about your family, about growing up in Rock Point," I said. We had to fill the time until the sheriff arrived. I didn't want Marcus to have second thoughts.

For a moment, I thought Marcus hadn't heard me. Then he said, "Rock Point's still a small town, but it's grown a lot since then."

"You don't like that very much."

"Actually, I don't mind. It brings opportunities for everyone. What I don't like is thoughtless growth. People come here, make Rock Point bigger, then resent that fact and refuse to do anything to help it grow sensibly." His expression shifted to a sneer. "So charming," he said, mimicking a woman's voice. "They think they can have their cake and eat it, too. They think it's fine if they build a fancy beach house and run a store selling French cheese, but they want the rest of the town to stay exactly like it is."

He was warming to his subject. "Like just now. You

called the sheriff, and the call probably bounced up to Astoria. At what point do we get big enough to have law enforcement available twenty-four-seven? With tourists, with more people, we're going to have incidents all night. But some summer-home owner will get mad that we have to move the sheriff out of that hole next to Martino's and build a new office, maybe even with a holding cell."

This was so not the Marcus I thought I knew from a mere two weeks ago. But I supposed it had been the real him all along. I'd just never bothered to find out. "You make a lot of sense. Have you thought about joining the city council?"

"In the nineteen-thirties, Farmington Salek was mayor of Rock Point. My great-grandfather."

Marcus didn't look particularly mayoral right now with his feral blond beard laced with gray and his less-than-fresh wardrobe, but he was articulate. He cared. He was also wanted by the sheriff for murder. At least we could try to do something about that.

As if on cue, Sheriff Koppen's head and shoulders appeared in the back door's window. I opened the door. The sheriff's hand was on his gun, his elbow away from his body, ready to draw.

"It's okay," I said. "There's nothing to worry about here. Marcus wants to talk, that's all."

The sheriff fixed his gaze on Marcus, still sitting at the dining room table. I stood between the two men and wouldn't move until the sheriff relaxed his arms. I realized that I'd never seen the sheriff not in uniform, even on weekends, even at the grocery store. Now, he wore blue jeans and a T-shirt with the high school's mascot on it, plus a long-sleeved plaid wool jacket. With a gun in its pocket.

"All right, Emmy. You can let me in now."

I stepped aside and pulled out the chair I'd sat in just a minute ago. "For you. I'll sit here." With Father Wind suspended behind me, I moved to the stool at my drafting table.

"It's been a while, Marcus." The sheriff put his hands on the table, palms down. "You knew I needed to talk to you."

"Of course I knew. You wanted to put me in jail for killing that TV star. I didn't do it." Marcus slouched, his arms firmly crossed in front of his chest.

"He saw Caitlin," I said.

The sheriff shot me a warning look. "Should we go over to the office?"

"No," Marcus said quickly. "I want to stay at Mrs. Ratcliff's."

Sheriff Koppen apparently got the reference, because he nodded. "Why don't you tell me your story first, then we'll get into specific questions?"

Marcus's gaze dropped to the sheriff's jacket. We both saw the bulge of handcuffs. Of course, the gun was a quick reach away, too.

"I don't have proof that I didn't do it, but I heard about Stella," Marcus said. "I suppose I'd better tell my story."

"Listen to what he says," I urged. "Then question Caitlin again. That's all I ask."

At the squeal of brakes in the street, I leapt from the stool. Someone was pounding on the shop's front door.

Marcus bolted for the back door, but I placed myself in front of it, both arms out to stop him.

The sheriff stood, but remained calm. "Calm down. It's backup. I didn't know what I'd find here," he told us. "Just a moment." He went through the shop and unlatched the front door. As far as I could tell, two men in uniforms stood on the porch. I watched from the workshop's door, but I couldn't make out their conversation.

"The police?" Marcus asked.

"Yeah, I think so. They're leaving."

The sheriff bolted the front door and returned to the kitchen. "Sorry for the interruption. By the way, I asked them to bring back a pizza. That okay with you?"

Marcus raised his eyebrows, and I smiled.

It was all going to be all right.

chapter twenty-nine

BEFORE I GOT OUT OF BED THE NEXT MORNING, I CALLED Salem Memorial to check on Stella. My phone was on my nightstand, and calling the hospital's phone number was the simple matter of hitting "redial."

Stella was conscious, the nurse on duty said. I made her repeat the news twice. Conscious! The relief I felt was so strong that I realized just how much I'd feared the worst.

I sat up. All at once the day was sunnier, happier. Stella was awake. And now that Marcus had told his story, the sheriff would be knocking on Caitlin's door. Soon Stella would be able to corroborate what I knew had happened the night Jasmine died.

Last night, once a few slices of pizza had been de-voured, Marcus had told the sheriff everything he had told me, and more. Sheriff Koppen had him walk through his movements that night, minute by minute. Marcus must have arrived at Jasmine's shortly after I'd left my spot on the beach. He'd seen Caitlin, awake, downstairs, despite what she'd told the sheriff earlier. The only thing that bothered me was that Marcus hadn't seen a man, as I had. It was possible, though, that Caitlin had a "guest" that night, and he'd left by the beach.

Sunny's voice interrupted my thoughts. "Can I come in?" She didn't wait before pushing open the door. Bear followed her and jumped up on the bed.

"Stella's conscious," I told her. "Want to come to the hospital with me?"

"You won't have time to visit her until after the kite festival," Sunny said.

The kite festival. With all the excitement about Marcus and Stella, I'd nearly forgotten. I jumped out of bed and grabbed my robe. "What time is it?"

"Take it easy. It's still early." She dropped to the bed and ran a hand over Bear. "Why were you out so late last night? I thought you were 'on hold' with Jack. Whatever that means."

"I found Marcus Salek." While I dressed, I told her about leaving the note at the cemetery, hearing Marcus's story, then convincing him to talk with Sheriff Koppen. "The deck is cleared of all the suspects except for Caitlin. And now that Stella is conscious, the case should be wrapped up soon."

"She might not remember anything, you know." Sunny stood and pulled a pair of kite earrings from my jewelry box. "Wear these. You're amazing, you know? I can't believe you got Marcus to confess to the sheriff."

"I won't lie, I'm feeling pretty smug right now."

"Well, Your Royal Smugness, I'm going into Rock Point after breakfast. Rose said I could play with the accounting software once I get the data entry finished."

"Today?"

Sunny fastened me with her "duh" look. "Mom and Dad are coming, remember?" She followed me down the stairs, Bear trotting behind us. "I wish I could see you fly your kite, though."

I turned to her. "That's so sweet. I wish you could, too. When the festival's over, let's you and I go down to the beach together and fly it."

"Thanks." She smiled. "That would be great."

I poured myself a cup of coffee from the thermos Avery thoughtfully left us when she went into the Brew House that morning. With all the visitors for the kite festival, it would be a busy day for her.

"Maybe today would be a good time for you to talk to Mom and Dad," I said.

"Like I told you. I'm not ready. Yet. I almost have a plan. Don't you see?"

What I could see was a snowballing disaster if Sunny didn't come clean soon. "You know Mom loves her surprise visits. It would be a lot better for you to tell her before she finds out by accident."

"I know, I know. But not yet."

She would tell them eventually. I knew she would. I'd never seen anything engross her the way finance had.

In some ways, dropping out of college had been one of the most mature things Sunny had ever done. I sipped Avery's satisfyingly strong coffee and gazed through the kitchen window.

Stella was awake, and the sheriff was onto Caitlin. The kite competition was a few hours off, and my Father Wind kite was a doozy. At last, things were coming together. Not that everything was perfect. Sunny, for instance. And I still hadn't see the latest issue of the *National Bloodhound*. But, all in all, it was shaping up to be a good day.

On the way to Strings Attached, I stopped at a minimart, braced myself, and bought a copy of the *Bloodhound*. I couldn't bear to look at it right away, so I set it in the Prius's passenger seat.

Once I was at the shop, I tucked the paper under my arm and stood on Strings Attached's porch, looking down to the beach. Already, kite enthusiasts were flying a regular Thanksgiving Day parade of kites. A giant octopus hovered near the Tidal Basin, and a dragon with a long, winding tail flew a bit farther up the beach. All at once, a set of six red sport kites leapt one after another into the air for a synchronized routine. My heart caught in my throat. I knew the kites' handlers would be working like athletes, a spindle in each hand, twisting, jerking, letting out line so that the kites danced and dove in patterns as eloquent as those performed by the Blue Angels.

Just above the new docks, a wide portion of the beach would be cordoned off with orange traffic cones. That's where I'd be soon, showing Father Wind to the world.

Reluctantly, I pulled myself away from the spectacle

and unlocked the store. My plan had been to open the shop early for the hordes of festivalgoers who might want to give kite flying a try themselves. Sunny couldn't work, since she was afraid of running into our parents, but Stella had said she'd gladly step in. Now that wasn't a possibility. Using a large sheet of sketch paper, I posted a sign in the front window saying the shop wouldn't open until after the contest at noon.

Now for the moment I'd dreaded. I flattened the *National Bloodhound* on the workshop counter and took a deep breath. The cover displayed a selection of starlets in bikinis, with circles drawn around their hind ends to point out their cellulite. Irritating. How come they never featured men's balding heads or potbellies?

I flipped through the tabloid page by page, but I couldn't find "A Byrd Told Me." Starting again at the beginning, I ran my finger over each page, but didn't see Nicky's byline at all. I closed the tabloid. Strange. Was he saving the story for a big reveal next week? If so, he was damned lucky. The news about Caitlin would likely come out later today. Hopefully, he'd focus on that, and my lurid recounting of that night would fade into the background—or maybe even be dropped completely. Plus, with Caitlin in jail, there was no way he could insinuate I had anything to do with her death.

The day was getting better and better.

I unhooked Father Wind from his station and was fastening the kite's bridle when I heard a knock at the door. I turned to see Mom and Dad's faces pressing against the glass. Mom waved her hand above Dad's head. With a huge smile, I opened the door.

"Hi, honey!" Mom's tsunami-like presence washed through the store. She hugged me, then pushed me away to examine me. "Let me see your tongue." Obediently, I stuck it out, and she turned my head toward the window. "Your chi looks vigorous. Good."

"Emmy." Dad hugged me, too. He was more subdued, but I knew his affection ran deep. His jacket smelled just a touch of mulch.

"How are things in the composting club?" I asked him.

"Great. The Eisenbergs are having a devil of a time keeping their number one pile moist in this heat, but we're rigging up a drip irrigation system."

While Mom spent her days sprouting grains and making tinctures with her croning circle, Dad had the entire neighborhood composting. Every two weeks, he and a few friends met for their Watergate reenactment group, which Mom didn't partake in due to the foul language and absence of female roles.

"Did you have a good drive over?" I asked.

"It took forever to get the bus over the hill—" Mom started.

"The VW engine is durable, but not made for speed," Dad told her.

"Honestly, honey. We were passed by an RV towing a boat. Can't we think about a little car? Maybe an electric vehicle?"

I'd heard this discussion before. They'd even bought a Prius at one time, but ended up passing it along to me when Dad just couldn't stay away from the bus. "Will you be in town for dinner?" I asked this question thinking of Sunny. It would be the perfect chance for her to talk to them—or she'd need to know so she could avoid them.

"Surprise!" Mom said. "We'll be here for dinner and breakfast. We're staying at the Morning Glory. I told your father we could camp in the bus, but he's so thoughtful." She slipped an arm around his waist and squeezed. "He said we should have a treat."

"Great," I said, but I was thinking I'd better call Sunny ASAP. Rose's office was three houses down from the Morning Glory Inn. She'd need to be stealthy about her comings and goings.

Mom released Dad and circled the shop, touching kites here and there and running her hand along the old fireplace's mantel. She poked her head into the workshop and stopped at my competition kite. "This is it, isn't it? The kite you're entering today."

I warmed with pride. I could tell from Mom's breathless tone that she loved it as much as I did. "Yep. At first I was going to do an appliqué rendering of Rock Point, but when Su—when I saw how much trouble it was, I changed direction." I tried to play it cool. They didn't seem to notice my slip of the tongue.

"It's lovely, Em," Dad said with the awe he normally saved for neighbors who achieved a high worm-to-compost ratio.

My pride doubled. Take that, Jack. This contest was in the bag.

"I'm glad you're doing so well, hon. We don't need to worry about you. You'll do fine."

Implied was that she worried about Sunny. I pasted on a smile. "Have you heard from Sunny?"

In two strides, Mom was at my side. "I have a feeling something funny's going on with her. Every time I call, she acts evasive."

"I'm sure she's okay. She's just doing that college thing. You know." How was that for nonsense? "Why don't you get a good spot on the beach? I'll be down in a few minutes."

I watched them walk down the steps. On the beach beyond, the crowd thickened, some setting out chairs and blankets, others snapping group photos. From where I stood, the judge's dais was hidden behind a building, but I knew entrants would be starting to gather, kites in hand.

I'd be there soon, too. But first I had to get in touch with Sunny.

chapter thirty

SUNNY DIDN'T ANSWER MY TEXT. I GLANCED AT THE TIME.
Fifteen minutes until the contest. I called.

"What?" Sunny answered.

"Mom and Dad are in town."

"I know."

She wasn't listening. "I know you know. I just wanted
to tell you that they're staying up the street at the Morning Glory Inn. Maybe you'd better simply face them.
It'll be better all around."

"Sure," she said.

Sure? "Sunny, what's wrong?" Despite myself, my
breath quickened.

"Rose asked me to tabulate some expenses, and when
I was in the software, well, I saw this other file, and—"

My shoulders relaxed. She was simply distracted by
some financial thing.

"I think it's a lie."

"What?" I took the phone to the window. In the distance I heard the loudspeaker from the judge's dais.

"It doesn't add up. If Jasmine were a gambler, this would . . ."

"Would what?" I had ten minutes, tops, before I had to leave the shop, and I still wanted to smooth my hair and get my wits together.

"Stella was coming back from Spirit Mountain casino when she had the accident, right?"

What did this have to do with anything? "Uh-huh."

"We need to find the sheriff right away. It's not Caitlin at all who murdered Jasmine. I think that's what Stella was trying to say."

"What? Tell me." Chills prickled at my neck. Her words were too similar to Stella's when she'd called from Spirit Mountain.

"Hi, Kyle." Sunny's voice sounded uncertain. In a quieter voice, she said, "I have to go now." The line went dead.

"Sunny!" No response. She'd hung up. I called again, but she didn't answer. Something was very wrong. I glanced out the window at the thickening crowd, then grabbed my purse and ran for the Prius.

Cursing the split-second delay from the stop sign at Main Street, I sped up the hill to Old Town and halted the car in front of Rose's house. I caught my breath. My bicycle, which Sunny had borrowed that morning, still leaned against the garage wall.

But I couldn't see movement in the office. I ran up the driveway and yanked at the door. It was locked. All the lights were off. If not for the bicycle, Sunny might never have been here at all.

I whirled around and ran for the house. Maybe Rose was home. Her practical Kia was still in front of the house. I pounded on the door and rang the doorbell, but no one answered.

Then I saw it. There on the sidewalk at the foot of the driveway was Sunny's macramé keychain. Sunny had been here and had left, fast. Or—I could barely breathe at the thought—had been taken away.

What had she told me? She said the numbers didn't add up, that someone had lied. She said Kyle's name. That night on the beach, a man's silhouette filled the kitchen window at Jasmine's. A tall man. Like Kyle. Kyle had my sister. I clenched my fists, driving my fingernails into my palms, and released them.

Think, think. Where would Kyle take Sunny?

The cliff walk, that's where. Sunny made no secret of her daily walks along the cliffs. It would be the perfect cover-up for a death. A simple slip, and the Devil's Playpen would swallow her up for good. There was no time to call the sheriff. I had to find Sunny. Now.

THE HIGHWAY WOULD BE CLOGGED WITH CARS FROM the city, full of tourists coming to Rock Point for the kite festival, so I took the back roads. Every time I had to put on the brakes for traffic, I comforted myself with the thought that Kyle would have had to slow, too. If I was right about Sunny, that is, and that he took her to the cliffs instead of somewhere else. Oh, how I hoped I was right.

I pulled into the trailhead's narrow parking area and saw Kyle's SUV with its rental car sticker right away. *Relief.* Both Kyle and Rose were standing just outside the vehicle. The rest of the parking area was empty.

Kyle and Rose. Both of them. I took a second to process this.

Could Rose be in on it, too? Maybe I'd been mistaken. Maybe they simply wanted to take a walk, and when I'd arrived at Rose's office, Sunny had ducked out to get a sandwich.

Then Rose nodded toward me and mouthed something to Kyle. Their body language was complicit. That's when I knew. Rose had covered for Kyle when I asked about him, telling me he was in Portland the night of Jasmine's death. I felt dizzy. How could I have been so wrong? Worse, there were two of them and one of me, and I didn't have a weapon. But they had my sister.

I idled the Prius behind their SUV and flew out of the door. "Kyle! Rose!" I yelled.

"Emmy," Rose said. "Aren't you supposed to be at the kite festival?" From her tone of voice, no one would have suspected that they'd killed one person, attempted to kill a second person, and kidnapped a third.

I ignored her question. "Have you seen Sunny?" Surprisingly, my voice didn't shake.

"No. Why do you ask?" Rose said.

I had to think fast. Sunny was in the back of that SUV. I knew it. The tinted windows were too dark to see through, but I'd bet anything she was bound and only feet away in the car's rear. "Sunny said she needed her, um, inhaler." I'd been the one with childhood asthma, not Sunny, but they didn't know that. "When she needs it, she can't wait."

"She never said anything about asthma."

"She wouldn't. She's shy about it." Then I had another thought. "I went to your office and saw her bicycle, but she wasn't there."

"So you came here?" Kyle asked.

"You know how she likes to walk along the cliffs. I thought maybe she'd caught a ride or something." That was lame. First I say she's having an asthma attack, then I say she's decided to go for a hike. "But her bike was there. Plus, she left me a note at Strings Attached."

"A note?" Kyle said.

"Sure. Said she'd be at Rose's and to please bring her inhaler. The note's still taped to the door. But why are you guys here? I'd have thought you'd be at the kite festival, too." Would they bite?

Rose took a step forward. I braced myself, but she said, "We're taking some of Jasmine's ashes to the cliffs for a ceremony." She touched a metal canister the size of a loaf of bread. She glanced at Kyle. "We thought it would be best to sprinkle some of her ashes when there wouldn't be a lot of people. The cliffs meant a lot to Jasmine. We'll have a real ceremony later."

Rose's voice was soft and mournful, but a muscle in her jaw twitched.

"You might have Sunny to contend with—if she came out here for a walk," I added quickly.

"I'm worried about her bike," Kyle said at last. "Clearly, from the note"—he traded glances with Rose—"she needs her inhaler."

I nearly fainted with relief. He'd swallowed my story. At least Kyle would be out of the way. "She can be so scatterbrained sometimes. If her asthma is troubling her, she shouldn't be walking back into town. I'd go get it for her—and take down that confusing note—but I need to bring her an inhaler."

"Her note." Rose echoed.

"I bet—" I turned to Kyle. "I bet you anything it's still there."

Kyle's eyes flicked to Rose. "Time slipped away from us, Rose. I had no idea how late it was getting. Why don't I pick up Sunny's bike and come back with it?"

He took the bait. But he wasn't going to take Sunny with him. I held out my keys. "Take my car. It's blocking you in, and there's a bike rack, see?" I silently thanked Dave for setting up my car with the rack.

Rose met his eyes, and I thought she communicated a hint of a nod. She turned toward the trailhead. "Come on, Emmy. Let's look for your sister. Kyle, I'll see you soon."

Kyle slid his bulk into my tiny Prius and started the engine. In a moment, he was on the main road. Rose stood, holding her sister's ashes. "Come on, Emmy."

There was no way I was following her into those woods.

chapter thirty-one

I HELD MY GROUND. THE TRAIL STARTED IN THE WOODS, then thinned to the clearing where Jack and I had sat a quarter of a mile or so in. The old lighthouse was farther up the hill. I doubted Rose would try anything until we reached the clearing. Even then, she might wait for Kyle. It would be easy enough for them to explain that they'd come up to cliffs to sprinkle some of the ashes, but it was too late. Sunny and I had had a tragic accident.

"You know," I said, heading to the SUV I suspected held my sister, "maybe I'll just wait here for Kyle to get back."

Rose grabbed my arm before I'd made it a few feet. "Why? You want to find Sunny, right?"

I looked at her arm, and she dropped it. It was time to be direct. "I do want to find her. And I think she's in your car."

Rose pulled a handgun from her handbag. "Too bad. Walk." She grabbed my arm again, and this time pushed me in front of her. I felt the gun's muzzle jab into my back. I hadn't expected she'd be armed.

"Sunny!" I yelled.

"She can't hear you. Walk."

I should have been terrified, but somehow the cold metal through my cotton sundress focused me. I became alert. The bird song was crisper, and every fiber of my skin felt the breeze. Rose planned to march me to the cliffs and let the Devil's Playpen take care of the rest. When Kyle returned, Sunny would meet the same fate. If she was still alive, that is.

Rose jabbed again with the muzzle, setting me in motion. I started slowly down the trail and reviewed my options. My best hope was that someone else would be on the trail, too. Two—or more—people would stand the best chance of overpowering her. But there were no other cars parked at the trailhead. Everyone was at the festival.

We marched on. I could try to trip her. I slowed, and the gun's muzzle urged me forward. Any stumbling, and I'd get a gunshot through my gut.

We were now halfway to the cliffs.

Then I caught an off-key rendition of "Send in the Clowns." Rose heard it, too. The muzzle slid down my back a few inches before righting itself. The singer was getting closer. My calm dissolved in a frenzy of hope. The singer emerged from around the corner.

Never had I been so happy to see someone as I was

to see Nicky Byrd. "Nicky!" I said. Rose pulled me just off the trail.

Nicky's eyes narrowed as he looked from me to Rose and back to me again. "What?"

"I'm so glad to see you." I fastened my gaze on his and willed him to—to anything. We could rush Rose, call the police, grab the gun, scream, anything.

He backed up a step. "Why aren't you at the festival?"

Rose found her voice. "We're going to one of my sister's favorite places to bid her farewell." With her free hand, she showed Nicky the canister.

Clarity replaced Nicky's suspicion. "You're Rose, Jasmine Normand's sister."

"Yes. I'm sorry. If you'll excuse us, we're not feeling very sociable right now."

"Why is Emmy with you?" he asked.

You're on the right track, Nicky, I thought. *Keep it up.*

"She's been such a good friend," Rose said. "She doesn't want me to be alone."

The gun twisted in my back. "Yes," I croaked. "Come with us."

Nicky, clearly already drafting his first-person account of Jasmine's sister's tearful good-bye, opened his mouth to say yes.

"No," Rose said. "We must do this alone." I couldn't see her expression since she was behind me and to the side, but her voice softened. "I'd love to talk to you later, though. Maybe this evening? I have so much to share about my sister."

"I'm onto a bigger story now. I'm through with this

celebrity nonsense." He lowered his voice. "Sorry. Your sister was a fine woman."

"Tell me about your story," I said, hoping against hope that he'd figure out that there was a pretty damned big story happening right this very minute. He wasn't stupid. I was supposed to be at the kite festival, not walking in the woods with a can of ashes.

"Actually, I have you to thank, Emmy," he said. "I started thinking about how Rock Point's growing, what happened with Marcus Salek in Bedlow Bay, and I thought, this could win me a Pulitzer. So I got in touch with a friend at the *Washington Post*."

He did look happy. He hadn't even bothered with the face makeup.

Rose turned, pivoting me in front of her so that Nicky wouldn't see the gun if he turned.

"Good-bye." He waved and broke into "Happy Days Are Here Again."

With him went my hope. I could have yelled, but I knew Rose would kill me just as surely as she'd somehow played a role in killing Jasmine. If I were dead, there would be no way for me to help Sunny.

When Nicky had rounded the corner, Rose pushed me forward. "Hurry up."

"How did you do it?" I finally managed to say. I didn't have to specify what "it" was.

Rose was silent a moment. "I suppose it doesn't matter if I tell you. Not anymore."

I didn't like the finality of those words. We were now only a few minutes from the cliffs. I walked just the tiniest bit more slowly. Maybe Sunny would escape and save me. Maybe Rose would suddenly change her mind and pocket her gun and go home. Maybe the ocean below would vanish in a puff of steam.

"You probably heard that Jasmine died of an insulin overdose." She didn't wait for my reply. "Kyle did it, but it was my idea." She said it almost with pride. "He's a good boy." The gun's muzzle dug into my back. "How did you find out?"

"It was a different brand," I said. "The insulin he used. I found the bottle on the beach."

I couldn't see her, but I imagined her rolling her eyes. "Figures Jasmine would buy a different brand. I bet she forgot her insulin and had to get more here. I should have predicted it."

"But why did you do it?" I thought I knew the answer to this one, but I wanted her to say it.

She shifted the gun to her other hand, and it happened too fast for me to take advantage of it. "Kyle isn't perfect. He's a gambler. I figured it out almost right away once I started handling Jasmine's finances." The exertion of our climb hurried her breath. "She drove him to it. I'm sure."

"How did Jasmine's finances tell you anything about Kyle?" Here and there along the trail, hand-sized rocks protruded from the dirt. Could I snatch one? I could pretend to fall. But I didn't want to be on the ground with Rose, armed, above me. The tree branches were too far above us to grab.

"Someone was stealing from her. Taking big draws of cash from her bank account and using her credit card. If it had been just one or the other, I might have thought a stranger was stealing from her. But both? It was Kyle. Luckily, he had me."

"What could you do about impending bankruptcy?"

"You can't bankrupt a dead woman. And a dead woman can't ruin her husband's career because he gambles sometimes."

Despite the afternoon's warmth, my skin prickled. Kyle stole from Jasmine, and when she was dead broke— she may not have even known it—they killed her. Their cold-blooded planning filled me with disgust. And horror.

"Someone will find out about Kyle's gambling. They'll put it together." Like Stella. Stella saw Kyle gambling at Spirit Mountain, I was sure now, and she nearly paid for it with her life.

"No." The word came out with force. "I'm helping Kyle overcome that. Once we're married, I'll take care of our finances. He knows I can save him."

And he'll bankrupt you, too, I thought. But Rose would always have this over him. She'd sacrificed her sister for him. She could incriminate him for murder. He'd live in an emotional prison.

"Caitlin was there the whole time. She must have heard something," I said.

Rose laughed, and I stumbled at the strange reaction. "She heard it, all right," Rose said. "She won't talk. Kyle buddied up to the Kingmaker Spy's producer. He fixed it so Caitlin would get Jasmine's role in the movie if she kept her mouth shut."

We'd reached the clearing on top of the cliffs. Nothing but a cement bench and low wooden parapet stood between us and the rocky ocean below.

"And Sunny?" I said. I could barely summon the breath to talk. My words got lost in the rush of the wind.

Rose understood me, though. "She has a keen eye for fraud. Could be a forensic accountant if she put her mind to it." Rose set down the canister and pushed me forward. I swung around to face her. She now held the handgun with both hands at chest height. "Walk. To the cliff."

"No." If she was going to kill me, she could damn well drag my body to the edge. If she was going to kill me anyway . . . I took a step closer to her.

Her finger curled around the trigger. The rushing wind and surf and the roar of my heartbeat deafened me. Down the beach behind Rose, kites as brightly colored as dancing jelly beans trailed their tails above the ocean. I wondered if anyone missed mine.

Rose, her back to the trail, turned slightly to see what I stared at. She was too far away for me to tackle, but I lunged forward and grabbed the canister of Jasmine's ashes.

"Catch!" I yelled and tossed the ashes toward her chest. Miraculously, she fell for it. She dropped the handgun and lunged for the canister. Closer to the cliff. She stumbled sideways. "Watch out!" I said by pure reflex as I reached for the gun.

The canister seemed to pull her forward. It pulled her toward the bench, and she tripped, falling to the ground. The canister rolled to the parapet.

Now I had the gun, but it dangled at my side as I watched in horror.

Rose, on her hands and knees, reached for the canister, only inches from the cliff's edge. She grabbed it with one hand while the other clutched a tuft of wild geranium. "Got it." She rolled to standing, still clutching the canister, and the satisfaction in her face flashed to blind fear. She pulled the canister to her chest and reached forward but couldn't right her balance.

Rose was falling. She knew it. Shock, anger, and, finally, resignation passed her face in less than a second. She closed her eyes and disappeared from view.

chapter thirty-two

I RAN THE FEW STEPS TO THE CLIFF'S EDGE AND PEERED over. Rose was caught on a narrow ledge at least ten feet down, the hungry teeth of the Devil's Playpen roiling in white-capped waves below her.

"Rose!" I yelled. "Are you all right?"

"I can't move. My foot." She clutched her ankle. The ledge she was on was just wide enough to hold her if she didn't move, but there was no way I could save her on my own. We needed ropes and at least two experienced rock climbers. "I lost Jasmine." Rose began crying. The sound of the surf nearly swallowed her words. "She's gone."

"Don't move. I'm going to get help."

I backed far away from the cliff. Sunny was still in the SUV. I ran back to the parking lot, holding the gun out to my side as if it would burn me. I hurried, stumbling over tree roots and whispering, "Please, please, please," as I ran. I burst out from the trailhead. Only the SUV was there, thank God. Kyle hadn't yet returned. I pounded on the SUV's windows. Oh, please, please let Sunny be alive.

"Sunny! Are you in there?" I glanced up at the entrance to the trailhead to make sure Kyle wasn't coming, then shoved the gun in my bag and picked up a rock from the row separating the parking area from the forest. I threw the rock at the passenger-side window up front. If Sunny was inside, she'd be in the back.

The glass formed a web of tiny glass particles into a bowl-shaped indentation, but they stuck together. Almost crying with anger and fear, I hurled the rock at the window again. This time it went through.

I reached inside, unlocked the door, and threw it open.

Sunny looked up. I nearly cried with relief. She was bound and gagged, and her cheekbone and jaw were puffy and red, but she was alive. Without speaking, I crawled over the seat and pulled down her gag. "Are you all right?"

"Where's Rose and Kyle?" she said, her voice strangely groggy.

"Kyle will be here any second. Rose is trapped on a ledge below the cliff."

"In my pocket," she said. "Front pocket."

I reached into her jeans pocket and pulled out a black fob and key with the rental car agency's tag hanging from it. "This?"

"I got it from Rose while she was tying me up."

By God, she was amazing, my sister was. Looking over my shoulder, I struggled with the rope tying Sunny's hands. She could untie her feet herself. We didn't have the seconds to spare.

"Emmy?" Sunny said from the rear as I backed into the trailhead and spun the car around.

"What?"

"I think I'm ready to tell Mom and Dad about college now."

"Great. After we talk to the sheriff."

Gravel flew as I made for the main road. Just as I reached the entrance, my Prius zoomed in from the opposite direction. Kyle looked ridiculously large behind its wheel. He saw me, and his expression morphed from intensity to shock. I didn't stick around to see where it went from there.

"Hold on!" I yelled and slammed on the gas.

In the back, Sunny swayed, but she had a firm grip on the back of the passenger seat. "What happened to Rose?"

"She fell off the cliff." In my rearview mirror, I saw the Prius. It was still a good distance back, but making progress. Who knew that car had that kind of pep? I pressed harder on the accelerator. The SUV's transmission whined as it kicked up a gear.

Then a bullet hit our rear with a *thunk* that pulled the car to the right. I clenched the steering wheel.

"He has a gun!" Sunny said.

"Quick. In my bag."

Sunny reached over the seat and pulled Rose's handgun from my purse. "This?"

A bullet ripped through my side mirror. I only had a mile to go, and we had the advantage of horsepower. "Can you try and shoot out his tires without exposing yourself?" I yelled.

"I don't know how to work a gun."

This time Kyle's bullet shattered the rear window. "Are you all right?" The road's noise roared around us.

"Fine." Sunny yelled. She pointed the handgun through the SUV's rear. Nothing happened.

"Just pull the trigger!" I yelled

Oh no. We were closing in on a car towing a camping trailer that had slowed thanks to the reduced-speed signs posted outside Rock Point. We had no choice.

"Hang on!" I yelled again and yanked the SUV to the left. Coming at us was a Ford Fiesta. I jammed the gas pedal again and narrowly shot the gap back to the right lane as the Fiesta's driver wailed on his horn.

We were practically on Rock Point's Main Street now. Kyle couldn't shoot at us here, could he? I slowed the SUV just enough not to mow down pedestrians and aimed for the sheriff's office. There was no parking today, but I didn't give a damn. I'd go straight to the sheriff's own spot, reserved twenty-four hours a day for him.

The camper abruptly pulled off to the right, and now the Prius was again directly behind us. The outrage in Kyle's eyes sent spikes of fear through me. He couldn't shoot us here, not with all these people around. He couldn't.

There was the sheriff's office. I slammed on the

brakes just as a shot rang out. People on the street screamed and scattered out of the way as I screeched to a stop.

The Prius, a tire shot out, plowed straight through Martino's front window.

"Got him," Sunny said.

chapter thirty-three

THE NEXT DAY, DAD TOOK ME TO SALEM HOSPITAL TO see Stella. I wasn't up to driving yet. The emergency technicians said I had whiplash, and the spots on my face and torso that had been puffy and tender were now purpling into real bruises. Sunny was in similar shape. Somewhere else in the hospital, Rose lay under custody. The sheriff said she'd broken a leg and an arm, but she'd be fine to stand trial.

"Only a few minutes with Ms. Hart," the nurse, a Russian man, said.

"Stella." I took the chair by her bed and laid my hands on the sheets next to her.

She had an IV hooked to one arm, and a multitude of machines gathered at the head of her bed. She looked good, though. Possibly better than I did. Even in a hospital gown, she was elegant. If anything, her bloodless skin heightened the effect.

"You look awful," she nearly whispered.

"Don't talk. The nurse said you broke a few ribs, so it probably hurts even to breathe. I just wanted to see you."

I saw the gratitude in her eyes. And the concern.

"Kyle's in jail, and Rose is injured. She fell into Devil's Playpen. Plus, Martino's needs a new front window. When you're feeling better, I'll tell you all about it."

She frowned. Her lips formed the word "kite."

The kite festival. "I missed the festival, but that's okay." It wasn't okay, but the alternative was worse. When Caitlin hadn't shown up to judge the kite contest because the sheriff was questioning her, Darlene grabbed the closest thing Rock Point now had to celebrity, Annie Gluck, a resident whose uncle had once been on *Mister Ed*. Annie had been enraptured by a kite shaped like a teddy bear with strings of hearts trailing from his eyes. So Jack didn't win, after all.

At least the *Bloodhound* hadn't taken down Strings Attached. Maybe I'd still be able to make it through the winter. Or not.

Stella lifted a hand and patted the sheet under it. I slipped my hand in hers.

"You're getting stronger." I kissed a papery cheek. "I'll be back."

"I need a new car," Stella whispered. "What do you think about an old Mustang?"

I laughed. "I need one, too. Maybe we'll get matching Mustangs."

*   *   *

"ARE YOU SURE YOU WANT TO DO THIS?" I ASKED SUNNY.

"Yes." Sunny, with a shiner the color of patent leather under her eye, sat in the workshop of Strings Attached with a dish towel pinned around her neck. Mom and Dad hovered near the stove.

"We could get a professional," I said.

"Oh, honey." Mom sank into a chair.

"Do it," Sunny commanded.

I raised the scissors and clipped a dreadlock at chin length. Sunny swallowed. "Are you sure?" I said.

"Keep going."

The dreadlocks were thick, but the razor-sharp scissors I used for the appliqués sliced through them easily. In five minutes, Sunny's dreadlocks were piled around the chair, Bear sniffing at them.

I handed her a mirror. "What do you think?" I was sad to see the dreadlocks go. For me, they'd held some part of her spirit. I hated to think of her getting too corporate.

Sunny turned her head one way, then the other, and smiled. "I love it. It will show the tattoo I'm planning to get right here." She pointed to her shoulder. "Of the formula for calculating interest earned."

My concern for Sunny lifted.

"How do you think the admissions officers at Portland State's business school will like it?" Sunny added.

"Oh, honey," Mom repeated.

"PSU? That's what you've been waiting on, haven't you?" I said.

"Wherever you want to go," Dad said. "We'll make it work, Sunny. Or do you want to go by Belinda now?"

"Sunny is fine." My sister worked at her hair with her fingers. It looked good. The shorter length brought out her jaw.

Once she'd opened up to Mom and Dad, she'd done it all the way, telling them everything from quitting Evergreen to seeing signs on the cliffs to applying to PSU's business school. She'd been so passionate that Mom fell to the couch at Avery's, and Dad's mouth stayed open for the better part of a minute. They couldn't possibly refuse her, especially once she'd whipped out the spreadsheet with the projected costs of her education compared to potential future earnings.

The shop's front doorbell rang, and I went out, intending to tell the customer we were closing early so I could have a family lunch before Mom and Dad headed back to Portland. To my surprise, the Tan Man was at the door. I looked at Sunny and mouthed "Tan Man." She slipped off the chair and followed me into the shop.

"Hello, madam," he said to me.

He was as crisp and debonair as ever, and he didn't flinch at my bruises or my sister's hacked-at hairdo. Instead, he went straight to my competition kite, which I had hung across the shop's ceiling. I'd pinned up the strands of "wind" so it would look like Father Wind was blowing, although the effect wasn't as satisfying as it was on the beach.

"Beautiful," he said.

"Thank you."

"I looked for you at the kite festival."

"I wanted to be there, but, um, other things got in the way." Who was this man, anyway? He'd been showing up here and there for two weeks, but no one, not even Jeanette the Postmistress, had any idea who he was. Emboldened by the last day's happenings, I planned to find out. "I've seen you around town, and if you'll pardon my saying, you don't seem like the usual tourist."

A smile softened his sharp features. He pulled a business card from his wallet. "Carlos Negrete, Marketing, Ile Fantastique Caribbean Resorts," it read.

"Oregon is a long way from the Caribbean," I said. Sounds of shuffling told me my family had come out of the workshop and were lined up behind the counter. Mr. Negrete examined my competition kite while I made a "what are you doing?" face at them.

"You create these kites yourself?"

"Yes, I designed and made that one, along with these." I pointed to the row of kites fluttering behind me.

"How many can you make in a week?"

"What?" I said.

Sunny stepped from behind the counter and peeled the business card from my hand. "Sunny Adler, Emmy's business manager," she said. "What a terrific idea to sell handmade kites at your resorts. They're a high-end product, that's for sure, but uniquely beautiful. You'd be looking for stock during the winter months, when you're at your busiest, am I correct?"

"Yes." An amused smile played on the man's lips, but I thought he had respect in his eyes. "I believe we could sell all the kites Ms. Adler could make."

"It's a labor-intensive process," I said. I already had

patterns for two dozen kites or so. "I might be able to sew ten kites a week for some of the styles." I pulled forward a kite shaped like a stingray. "Others," I said, thinking of the late Rock Point kite, "take much longer because of the detail."

"Let's talk terms later this afternoon," Sunny said. She and Mr. Negrete made plans to meet at the Brew House after lunch. Sunny shook his hand and waved as his elegant figure descended the porch steps.

When the door closed, Mom stared, slack-jawed, at Sunny. "Honey."

Dad patted her on the back. "I'm proud of you, Sunny."

"Oh, I'm not done yet," she said. "We need to look into financing for buying this building. Right, Emmy?"

What was that line from Anaïs Nin that Nicky Byrd had quoted? "Throw your dreams into space like a kite."

Ready to find
your next great read?

Let us help.

Visit prh.com/nextread

Penguin
Random
House